OLD BONES
A Gideon Oliver Mystery

Aaron Elkins

When Guillaume du Rocher drowns, few are surprised. Even his family accepts the verdict of death by accidental drowning, without hesitation. Then a human skeleton is found beneath the floor of the ancient du Rocher chateau.

Dr. Gideon Oliver, a forensic anthropologist, is asked to examine the bones. All the information leads the police to conclude that the skeleton belongs to a Nazi officer known to have been murdered in the area in 1942. But Oliver has his doubts – and when a second du Rochers is poisoned, he's convinced that someone wants old secrets to remain buried.

OLD BONES
A Gideon
Oliver Mystery

AARON ELKINS

John Curley & Associates, Inc.
South Yarmouth, Ma.

Library of Congress Cataloging-in-Publication Data

Elkins, Aaron J.
    Old bones : a Gideon Oliver mystery / Aaron Elkins.
        p.   cm.
    1. Large type books.   I. Title.
[PS3555.L48O43 1989]   813′.54—dc19   88–8478
ISBN 1–55504–828–5 (lg. print).   CIP
ISBN 1–55504–804–8 (pbk. : lg. print)

Published in Large Print by arrangement with Mysterious Press in the United States and Canada along with the Abnor Stein Agency in the U.K. and British Commonwealth.

Distributed in Great Britain, Ireland and the Commonwealth by CHIVERS BOOK SALES LIMITED, Bath BA1 3HB, England.

Printed in Great Britain

1

So still and silent was the fog-wreathed form that it might have been an angular, black boulder. But there are no boulders, angular or otherwise, to mar the immense, flat tidal plain that is Mont St. Michel Bay. When the tide is out there is only sand, more than a hundred square miles of it. And when the tide is in, the plain becomes a vast, rolling ocean from which the great abbey-citadel of Mont St. Michel itself – St. Michael's Mount – rears like some stupendous, God-made thing of dark and gloomy granite, all narrow Gothic arches and stark, medieval perpendiculars.

The mist eddied, then shifted, and the figure was revealed to be a lean, elderly man in a fur hat and a heavy, well-tailored black overcoat, kneeling in the sand and hunched over a limpet shell in his leather-gloved left hand. But though his head was appropriately inclined, the old man was not looking at the shell.

He stared without seeing, his thoughts far away. His right hand was thrust deeply into

1

the pocket of the overcoat. For many minutes he remained so, unmoving, lost in reflection, and then he tensed suddenly. His head jerked up, then cocked to one side, the better to listen. The wide, aristocratic forehead was inquisitively wrinkled, the thick, white eyebrows arched. A terrible, white scar that began at the left corner of his mouth and disappeared under a black satin eyepatch seemed to tghten, so that his thin mouth was jerked out of line. His right eye, gray and clear, held a look of strained disbelief.

The old man, who never spoke to himself, spoke to himself.

"The tide?" he whispered, and again: "The *tide!*"

He dropped the mollusk and rose stiffly to his feet. He bent again to fumble with one hand for the woven-straw mat on which he'd been kneeling to protect the knees of his dark-gray trousers, but then he flung that away too, turned, and made grimly for the Mont, more than a kilometer away, which was visible only dimly and intermittently through the mist. The man moved quickly but jerkily, his crippled leg throwing his balance off, his left hand energetically swinging, his right immobile in its pocket.

The tide! How could he have lost track of time so completely? It hardly seemed

2

possible, but there was no mistaking the sound of it, nor the rush of cool, salt-laden air that streamed before it. "With the roar of thunder," went the old Breton nursery song, "and the speed of a galloping horse, comes the tide to Mont St. Michel."

He did not require the aid of metaphor to understand his predicament. The speed of the incoming tide was not quite that of a galloping horse, but it was fast enough – a gleaming skin of water rolling smoothly into the bay at nearly twenty-five kilometers an hour, its face endlessly collapsing and tumbling in on itself. It was no towering tidal wave of death, he knew that; but a seeping, stealthy flood that was not there one moment, sloshed at one's ankles the next, then at one's hips . . .

The wind had brought with it an icy squall of sleet, and already the man's wool coat was wet, the rims of his ears burning. The thin fog shredded before the wind, wrapping the spires and turrets of the Mont with otherwordly filaments of silver, tinged pink by the pale and dying sun. On the rampart of the north tower he could see a few people, tourists, waving him earnestly on; shouting too, he thought. Simpletons. Couldn't they see that he was moving as quickly as he could? That he was an old man and lame?

3

Why didn't they come down and help him instead of jumping uselessly about?

Even as he asked it, he knew it was a foolish question. Although the *tour du nord* was at the base of the walls surrounding the abbey buildings themselves, it hung high up on the rock, over fifty meters above the tidal plain, and the path down was rocky and uneven. They could never reach him in time. And why should they risk their lives in the treacherous sands to help him?

He didn't let himself think about whether he could outrun the water, but limped on, his warmly booted feet dragging through the sand. The water was not yet visible behind him; there was only the thrumming. That and the rush of moist air. His chest heaved, and inside it hot needles twisted in his scarred lungs. The old wounds in his leg and foot burned. Still, he was advancing on the Mont. He was close enough to hear an occasional shout now. Perhaps, after all, there was a chance –

He stopped abruptly. There was water in front of him. He stared, blinking, at the shallow, mauve-tinged rivulet that ran from left to right across his path twenty or thirty steps ahead. He understood perfectly what it was and what it meant. The tide did not advance with a solid front, but threw out

4

long tendrils – how beautiful they looked from up on the Mont – in sweeping, almost circular curves that first isolated, then encroached upon, and finally engulfed great bays of the yellow sand.

While he looked at it, the long finger of water became an arm of the sea, spreading and deepening before him. He spun about, expecting to see the main body of water close behind, but except for a few tentative feelers, it was still far away, perhaps a hundred meters. He had a chance yet, by the good Lord!

He plunged ahead into the ankle-deep water, knowing he ran the risk of stepping into a submerged stream or a patch of quicksand, but knowing too that he had no choice. His calf-high boots kept the wetness and cold from his feet, but they seemed to pull him down, as if they were lined with lead and not with wool, and each step was an exhausting effort that puffed out his lean cheeks. The furrowed scar pulled at the satin-covered socket of his empty eye now, so that his entire face felt awry.

"*Vite!*" they shouted from the north tower. "*Vite!*" As if they thought he was taking his time!

With dismay the old man watched the arm of water through which he plodded swell and

5

send out tendrils of its own. It was almost up to his calves now, and the leading edge rolled onward, pulling maddeningly away from him as he dragged himself towards it. His heart pounded with each lurching step through the sucking sand, and he was hot and fearfully cold at the same time. Icy water began slopping onto the tops of his boots, weighing him down still more and setting his limbs to convulsive shivering.

The boots, he thought. If he could get them off . . . But he knew he couldn't afford to stop in the rising water, and he knew he didn't have the strength to do it; not with only one good hand. In growing confusion he tore off his fur hat instead and threw it away. The chilling blast of sleet on the back of his neck made him cry out and tremble so convulsively that he could barely see. Still, with the water sloshing in his boots and his breath like knives in his throat, he managed three more blind steps before he finally stumbled into the quicksand.

The infamous *sable mouvant* of Mont St. Michel Bay is not quicksand, strictly speaking, not a slippery, shifting mass of smooth-grained sand and upward-percolating water; it is a phenomenon unique to this colossal tidal flat: deep pockets filled with water and covered with a layer of sand that somehow floats on top of them. From the battlements of the north tower they are invisible, and to the small, avid crowd gathered there it seemed as if the legs of the staggering man on the darkening plain below suddenly disappeared. A woman screamed and locked her fingers over her mouth. The others watched in rapt, shocked silence. Below, the tiny figure struggled, flailing at the still-shallow water with one arm and sinking all the more rapidly for it.

Until the very instant it closed smoothly over his head he was wriggling so desperately it seemed he must come up again, but the surface remained unbroken except for an innocuous dimple that marked the place he had been. And within a few seconds it was as if he had never been there at all.

2

Lucien Anatole Joly, *inspecteur principal* of the Police Nationale's Provincial Department of Criminal Investigation, Côtes-du-Nord, tapped his long and graceful fingers noiselessly on the lined tablet that lay on the flat writing arm of his chair, which was in the center of the second row. He was not the sort of man who skulked to the back of the room when he attended a lecture; he came to listen and to learn.

So far, however, the Eighth Annual Conference on Science and Detection, held for the first time in St. Malo, had failed in its promise of useful edification. After a full morning the lined tablet held only a quarter of a page of Inspector Joly's neat, symmetrical script. Moreover, he was bored.

Inspector Joly was easily bored and not inclined to bear it magnanimously. There were many things he did not bear magnanimously. His subordinates referred to him as "Monsieur Giscard" because – Sergeant Denis had confided to him one day – of a resemblance to the former president of France; they were both tall, both bald and long-faced, both lean. So Denis had said. But Joly knew better. He knew very well that he looked nothing like the old conservative, whom he in fact admired greatly. No, the nickname had caught on because of a certain regal stiffness the two had in common, an awkwardness and impatience with trivia, and sometimes with social intercourse in general, that often projected itself as arrogance. Well, that was fine with him. As reputations

8

went, it wasn't a bad one for a policeman.

The morning session had been a lecture
and slide presentation by a dour Finnish
entomologist who mumbled away in such a
bizarre combination of French and English
that he would have done as well to deliver it
in Finnish. No doubt a part of the problem
was the subject: "Sarcosaprophagous Insects
as Forensic Criteria" – less than inviting in
any language. Even with the language
barrier, however, Joly now knew far more
about the actions of blowfly larvae on
decomposing corpses than he liked.

He was hoping – without much confidence – for a little more from the afternoon's
topic, "Forensic Anthropology." At least he
knew what it meant. Well, perhaps not
precisely, but he could pronounce it, and that
was an improvement. He settled back in his
chair, his lunch of *omelette aux champignons*
and coffee sitting well inside him, and
studied the speaker, who was arranging a few
index cards at the head table while the
conference chairman droned on with his
remarks. Joly glanced again at the program
notes:

Dr. Gideon P. Oliver, Professor of
Anthropology, University of Washington

9

– Port Angeles. Dr. Oliver has an outstanding reputation in the fields of biological anthropology and human evolution, having authored the distinguished text *A Structuro-Functional Approach to Pleistocene Hominid Phylogeny,* now in its third edition. He is almost equally well known to the inter-national police community as "The Skeleton Detective" for his remarkable achievements in the forensic analysis of human skeletal remains.

Well, he certainly didn't look like Joly's idea of a scientist-*cum*-skeleton detective. Gideon Oliver was no gaunt and dessicated elderly man steeped in the dank aura of the morgue – or more appropriately the shallow grave in the open field. (Professor Wuorinen of the blowflies would have done perfectly.) He was, surprisingly, a big, wide-shouldered man with a broken nose and an easy smile, who looked more like a good-natured prizefighter than a professor. Joly had noticed him during the milling-about of the registration period, talking familiarly with the equally large Hawaiian FBI man – who didn't look much like the inspector's idea of an FBI special agent, for that matter. Ah, well, the world was changing.

10

"...And I know we've all enjoyed and will much benefit from this morning's fascinating presentation." The conference chairman, Pierre Chagny, Deputy Director of the Central Directorate of Criminal Investigation of the Police Nationale, paused with a smile on his round face and mimed the clapping of his hands, encouraging a spiritless spatter of applause for Professor Wuorinen, who acknowledged it from a seat at the back of the room with a gloomy frown and a curt nod.

"And now it will be my pleasure to introduce a speaker already known to many of you as the Skeleton Detective of America..."

Gideon winced. Obviously, this skeleton detective business, hung on him by a fanciful crime reporter years before, was not going to go away, and in fact he had begun to resign himself to living with it. But "the Skeleton Detective of America"? That was another rung up the ladder of absurdity. With luck, it might never get back to his academic colleagues, but he doubted it. They were maliciously efficient at ferreting out such tidbits, and it wouldn't be long before he arrived at some committee meeting to find a meticulously printed place card labeled

11

"Dr. G. P. Oliver, the Skeleton Detective of America." That or worse.

He sighed, laid down his note cards, and looked around the room. Ninety people, sitting on stackable plastic chairs and regarding him with the sleepy and unhopeful gaze of an after-lunch audience that believes it is in for a long, dry lecture. Since France was the host country this year, most of the attendees were French, but everyone was supposed to have a command of English, the organization's official language. This Gideon doubted (certainly Professor Wuorinen's command was dubious), and he had considered speaking in French, but his courage had failed him. They would have to settle for English, along with printed translations of his charts and tables.

Off to the side in the second row, John Lau slumped on the small of his back, comfortably askew, one ankle up on the empty chair in front of him, and already two-thirds asleep. Old friends, they had come to St. Malo together, John to attend lectures and Gideon to give them. If that was as much enthusiasm as he could expect from his one and only crony in the place, Gideon thought, he was in big trouble.

"... my privilege to put you into the capable hands of the renowned Dr. Oliver

12

for the first of his four presentations on forensic anthropology. I know you will find him thoroughly fascinating. Dr. Oliver."

Gideon rose to transparently doubtful applause, shook hands with Monsieur Chagny, and waited for the room to settle down.

"What I hope to do over the next few days," he began, "is to acquaint you with what bones can tell us, and how they tell it. I'm afraid we'll have to work with medical school specimens; there haven't been any murder cases involving skeletons in Brittany for some time, unfortunately. Or perhaps fortunately, depending on how you look at it. . . ."

Without looking at the dark, solemn servant who proffered the tray of apéritifs, Mathilde du Rocher waved him away with an impatient flick of a beringed and impeccably manicured hand.

"I, for one," she had been saying, and now said again for the benefit of her amiably smiling husband, "I, for one, find the entire business intolerably overbearing on Guillaume's part, and inexcusably rude as well. We've been waiting here for nearly an hour. *An hour!*" She compressed her firm mouth eloquently. "Collecting seashells!"

"Well," said René du Rocher, accepting a champagne cocktail, "I'm sure there are reasons."

Mathilde did not dignify this feeble response with one of her own. She merely glared at his newly furry upper lip with a look that said: Your moustache is utterly ridiculous. René smiled pleasantly and sipped his cocktail.

Mathilde turned to her son. "That's your second martini. Where did you learn to drink martinis?"

Neither were these comments acknowledged. Jules du Rocher's plump arm swept the long-stemmed glass from the tray directly to his lips, which he smacked loudly after downing half the drink.

"What are *they* doing here, is what I'd like to know," he grumbled, openly staring across the room at another threesome, who sat stiffly in their high-backed wing chairs, as removed and alienated as if they'd been walled off.

"If I'd known they were really going to be here, I assure you we would still be in Frankfurt," said Mathilde, grimly watching her son drain his glass with a second swallow and then go grubbing with a pudgy thumb and forefinger after the anchovy-stuffed olive at the bottom.

"Don't do that, Jules," she said disgustedly.

"Well, why don't they put a toothpick in it, then?" he asked, not unreasonably. He capitulated, however, bringing the glass to his lips, upending it, and helping the olive into his mouth with a pinky that followed it in rather more deeply than Mathilde thought strictly necessary.

That, said Mathilde's look, is repulsive. Unconcerned, Jules concentrated on liberating the anchovy with his tongue, then munching with deep satisfaction, first the anchovy, then the olive.

"Now, Mathilde," René said reasonably, "if Guillaume invited the Fougerays, he must have had a very good reason. And you know he's not being late on purpose. He's probably forgotten about the time; you know how absentminded the old fellow's been getting."

You, his wife's eloquent look said, are not the person to talk about absentmindedness.

René took no offense; indeed, he seemed to take no notice. "So why upset yourself?" he continued. "There's no point, is there?"

Indeed, there wasn't. The patriarchal Guillaume du Rocher convened these "family councils" – formal meetings of the dwindling and farflung du Rocher clan –

whenever it pleased him, and he ran them however he wished. If it was increasingly in his nature to be high-handed and eccentric, well, that was to be borne with good humor. What choice was there?

"Best to simply be thankful these things occur so infrequently," René concluded with a radiant smile, his logic triumphant and irrefutable.

René du Rocher was a soft, placid, somewhat dandified man of sixty-two, a year younger than his wife – with shiny, thinning, plastered-down hair, a cherubic pink-and-white complexion, and small, delicate hands that he frequently rubbed together with a dry, rustly sound. He was clean in his habits, used cologne liberally, and took pride in the masculine vigor of his three-week-old moustache.

In all, he looked like an affable and self-contented bank manager, which in fact he was. Or close enough; Monsieur du Rocher was a corporate-lending officer in the international division of the Crédit Lyonnais in Frankfurt, to which city he had moved three years earlier with his family, after three decades of unexceptional advancement in Paris, Geneva, and London. The advancing years had enhanced his naturally sweet temper and, less fortunately, his pre-

16

disposition towards a slight vacancy of mind. At the urging of his superiors, he was now contemplating retirement.

"I've always liked this room," he said mildly. "Did you know that Henri IV and his party were once feated here? In 1595. The manoir was already a hundred years old."

"Oh, be quiet," Mathilde said absently, picking an invisible shred of lint from the dark, broad, woolen field of her bosom.

Jules had consumed the olive. His eyes roved to the hors d'oeuvres tray on the coffee table. "The point *is,*" he said querulously to his father, "that Cousin Guillaume hasn't asked the Fougerays to a family council in *decades,* or haven't you noticed?" Emulating his mother, he had adopted this petulant, deprecatory tone toward his father at fourteen, had found it satisfactory, and had not modified it in the ensuring sixteen years. "And with good reason. Look at the man; the quintessential peasant. Aside from a certain repulsive fascination, it's awkward to be in the same room with him. Is he *really* related to us?"

"You shut up too," Mathilde muttered, now brushing a thread from her ample skirt. "What a prig you are, Jules."

If her son felt injury at this inconsistency,

17

he did not show it. He concentrated instead on loading a triangle of buttered toast with all the beluga caviar it would bear and conveying it slowly and carefully to his mouth. As cautious as he was, a few oily, shining beads fell into his lap. Mathilde lowered her lids and looked the other way.

Across the room, Claude Fougeray smiled stonily at his wife and daughter, not easy for a man whose hyperthyroid condition afflicted him with a pop-eyed stare of permanent, outraged surprise. "Let them look down their long noses at us, these damned du Rochers," he said. The tight smile faded to a sneer. "Look at them. I could buy all of them put together, if I wanted to. I have –"

Leona Fougeray, tiny, vivid, raven-haired despite her fifty-three years, interrupted her husband. "Yes? I'd like to see you buy Guillaume du Rocher." Her mobile lips turned downward. "And you're drinking too much. As usual."

"Goddamn it," Claude whispered throatily, bald head lowered like an angry bull's, so that his neck, thick and stubby at the best of times, all but vanished. "I didn't say Guillaume, did I? I said anyone in this room. Do you see Guillaume in this room?"

Leona, on the verge of replying with heat,

18

thought better of it and settled for glaring reproachfully with her intense, jet-black Italian eyes. This was lost on Claude, who glowered at the ancient Aubusson carpet, an artery throbbing sluggishly at each temple.

"*I'm* not leaving," he said suddenly. "They can kiss my ass. Who the hell are they supposed to be? They don't even live in Brittany. They don't even live in *France*." He took an angry gulp of his third Pernod. "And what are *you* looking so glum about?"

The question was directed at their daughter, who sat staring mutely at her untouched glass of *blanc-cassis*. Of necessity she had long ago grown used to being snubbed by her distant relatives, but she had never felt it so keenly.

"I asked you a question, my girl."

She started and looked up. "Father," she murmured, "no one is talking to us. Nobody wants us here. Please, mayn't we go?"

Her lips trembled slightly, emphasizing the tiny, radiating lines that had recently begun to appear around her mouth so prematurely. Not yet thirty and never beautiful, with fine, pale hair, she already had a wan, faded look that her birdlike mother would not have at eighty. Only her eyes, a lucid gray-green, shone with warmth,

19

but there were often cast down, as they were now.

"Why should *we* go?" Her father's voice was harsh. "Didn't we get invited?" He finished the Pernod and hissed at the solemn servant for another. When he got it he took a long pull, then nodded to himself and smiled. "Well, I know a few things they don't know. Oh, yes, they have a surprise coming, a big –"

"*What* do you know?" Leona said impatiently, tossing her head, her Italian accent broadening, her eyes flashing more dramatically still. "You're living in a dream world. Claire is right. They'll make us look like fools."

A second interruption was more than Claude Fougeray could tolerate. His hand clenched, his eyes bulged a little more. "Shut up, you Italian bitch!" he said in a voice that carried plainly throughout the room.

The effect on Madame Fougeray was immediate and colorful. Bright disks of crimson leaped out on her cheeks, as round and red as a pair of checkers. Her mouth, caught closed while forming a word, sprang open with an audible pop. She stood abruptly.

"The master speaks," she hissed. "Master of the sausages!"

20

She spun about, the full, Turkish-style trousers of her red-and-black Paco Rabanne outfit swirling dramatically around her, and stalked out, her blazing eyes focused straight ahead of her. A few moments later her heels could be heard clacking forcefully up the stone stairs leading to the bedrooms.

On the other side of the room Jules du Rocher had watched this domestic scene with amused, piggy eyes. "Did you hear that?" he asked through a mouthful of *pâté de foie gras* and bread. "Wait until she gets him alone. She'll eat him alive." He snickered at this witticism and glanced at his mother, who busily aligned her rings.

Jules' words, coming as they did in a moment of silence, carried further than he had intended. Claude Fougeray jumped out of his chair, brushed away his daughter's hesitantly restraining hand, and marched quickly to the du Rochers.

"Do you want to repeat that?" he said flatly, staring down at Jules, his thick fists held at his sides.

Superficially they were somewhat alike, short and stubby-limbed, with torsos like beach balls, but Claude, older by thirty-five years than his distant cousin, was tense and compact while Jules was soft, flaccid, and spreading.

21

"Apologize," Claude said.

Jules coughed and blinked. Uneven streaks of red mottled his round cheeks.

"I apologize."

"Louder."

Jules glanced dartingly at the others in the room: at his parents; at Claire Fougeray, who looked utterly miserable; at the dark, grave servant who stood against the wall watching impassively; at another threesome that sat looking on silently from a grouping of carved wooden chairs on the other side of the Louis XIV billiard table.

"I apologize," he repeated, his eyes on Claude's belt buckle.

"Louder," Claude said again.

"Really," Mathilde said, pulling at her pearl choker.

René du Rocher echoed his wife weakly, reflecting her gesture with a tug at his little moustache. "Really...really, my dear man, this is really –"

"No one's talking to you," Claude said savagely.

"Well...well, I was only –"

"Don't encourage him," Mathilde said under her breath in German, her face stiff. "Ignore him. He doesn't know any better, the –"

"Speak French!" Claude shouted sud-

22

denly enough to make the three of them jump. You're in France. Don't give me any of that damned Boche! Ik-bik-blik-bluk!"

"Who in hell are you to say that to anyone, you collaborationist bastard?" The speaker was one of the three people on the other side of the table, a square, big-boned woman of fifty in a functional tweed suit. She had observed quietly until that moment, then leaped to her feet and shouted, her husky voice strained with emotion.

Claude turned on her. "Don't you ever say that to me!"

The woman was on the edge of tears, but her voice held steady. "I just said it." She lifted a trembling chin. "Do you want to hear it again? Collaborationist bastard!"

"And – and what do you know about it, Sophie?" Claude shouted. "You were a baby; you don't know anything. Why don't you go back to America where you belong, where everything is so wonderful? You and your – your cowboy husband."

He was losing his momentum. Jules, who had been sitting rigidly, sank inconspicuously back, flowing into the crevices of his soft chair like melting butter, as if he thought he might escape Claude's notice altogether.

Claude stared menacingly around the

room, as if to ward off attack, and leveled a stubby finger at the woman. "You know how much worse it would have been around here if I hadn't gone along with the Boches? Sure, all the heroes were running around the hills singing songs with the *Maquis,* but I was the one kissing Nazi asses and saving lives. If not for me –"

"If not for you," the woman said, "Alain would still be alive."

An electric silence gripped the room. Mathilde jerked sharply and gasped.

Claude stared at Sophie, paralyzed with rage or shock; it was impossible to say which.

Sophie began to speak again, then closed her mouth as her eyes filmed over with tears. "Oh, the hell with it," she said in English, and then turned away from him and strode out of the room.

Her two companions, still seated, looked uncomfortably at each other. After a moment, the older man stood up, gray-haired, and rawboned like his wife, and went quietly out after her. The younger man continued to sit, embarrassed by the intensity of a scene he had imperfectly comprehended. Then he too stood up, and the eyes of the others swung to him. Uneasy at being the sudden focus of attention, he cleared his

24

throat softly, nodded to the room at large, and self-consciously followed the other man out, his eyes on the floor.

Once he'd pulled the heavy door shut behind him to stand outside in the graveled courtyard, he released the breath that had stopped up his chest. His bland, freckled, good-natured face was set, his pale-blue eyes tense.

What had he gotten himself into? Why wasn't he back in his cozy, cluttered office at Northern California State University getting ready for his spring-quarter seminar on comic dramatists of the Restoration? There was plenty of prep time needed, God knows, and when was he going to find it?

Although the March air was chilly, he patted beads of perspiration from his forehead with a clean, folded handkerchief. Emotional explosions and disorder were as unsuited to the nature of Raymond Alphonse Schaefer as – well, as propriety and order were to the early comedies of Congreve. He smiled at the thought, feeling a little better. Perhaps he could work it into the seminar. Omitting the personal reference, of course.

He stood in the clear, gray Breton light, his reddish eyebrows knit; a man of thirty-four whose stooped shoulders and air of dusty, bookish abstraction made him seem ten years older than he was, and wondered what he was doing in this place, with these strange, fervid people. Well, he knew, of course, in a literal sense. In January, a few days after his mother's death, one of Guillaume du Rocher's lordly summons to a family council had arrived for her. The letter had been characteristically terse.

"I have reached a decision on a matter of singular family importance," it had said in his blunt yet oblique style. "We will discuss it at Rochebonne on 16 March." That was all.

Ray, who had visited Guillaume at Rochebonne but had never been to a family council, had written to his elderly relative, informing him of his mother's death and saying he would be pleased to attend in her place. Guillaume had scrawled the briefest of replies, curtly expressing condolence and telling him that he could come if he wished; it was up to him. And so he had. Rather impulsively, it now seemed.

He folded the handkerchief into a neat square and placed it in his pocket, peering around in search of his Aunt Sophie, the only du Rocher he had known as a child, aside from his mother. Living in Texas as she did with her husband, he had seen her no more than once every two or three years, but from the earliest times he had looked forward to their visits as welcome lulls in the unending war of bickering and veiled provocation his parents waged. As a youngster he had fantasized about how it would have been if the gentle, humorous Ben Butts had been his father and the comfortably starchy, rocklike Sophie his mother; Sophie, unprovokable and serenely equal to any emergency.

That's what was worrying him now. He had never seen her shout before, never seen her cry, or curse, or lose control. And here, in the space of a few seconds she'd done them all.

He walked across the courtyard to the tall stone gateposts and looked both ways down the tree-lined country lane, right towards Ploujean, left towards Guissand and the road to Dinan. No sign of Ben and Sophie. They might be walking along one of the nearby forest paths, in which case he'd be unlikely to find them. Or perhaps they were behind the house; there was a pond back there with swans in it and benches beside it.

3

They were there, on a white-painted wrought-iron bench facing the pond. Ray rounded a clump of smoothly sculptured bushes and came upon them from behind, deep in conversation.

"That rat!" Sophie Butts was saying. "That turd!" (He was most certainly going to have to revise his assessment of her if this kept up.) "That little toad! Can you believe that Guillaume actually asked him here? Someone ought to shoot him! Claude, I mean."

"Now, honey," her husband said soothingly, "you don't mean all that. You know what my daddy used to say about revenge?"

She smiled weakly. "What?"

Behind them, Ray smiled too. One could always trust Ben to pull a rustic aphorism out of his pocket when things needed smoothing over.

"My daddy," said Ben, his Texas accent thickening, as it did whenever a homily was in process, "he said ain't nothin' costs more nor pays less'n revenge."

28

REE-venge was what he said, and Sophie smiled a little more bravely. He reached for her hand and squeezed it. "It was a long way back, Sophie. Time to forget."

"Forget Alain? Oh, Ben, if you'd known him . . . Do you know," she said, her voice trembling, "I haven't seen Claude Fougeray in over forty years, not since I was ten years old. But I'd gladly shoot him myself, today, right now –"

"I know, I know." Ben held her hand in his and slowly stroked the back of it.

Ray's instinctive tendency was to quietly go away, but something in him also wanted to go to Sophie. While he dithered, Ben looked up and saw him.

"Come on over, Ray."

"Sophie?" Ray said hesitantly. "Are you all right?"

"Yes, of course." She sniffed, pulled herself together, and patted the arm of a garden chair next to the bench. "Sit," she said, her throaty, pleasant voice more controlled.

Obediently he sat. His thin legs, not overly long, seemed nonetheless to wrap themselves around each other three times, with his left ankle ending up behind his right foot.

Sophie appraised him with her lips pursed. "Poor man, you must think we're all crazy."

29

"No," he said quickly, "not at all." He smiled tentatively. "Perhaps a bit, er, histrionic?"

She fixed him with a candid eye. "Raymond, just how much do you know about what went on here during the war?"

"Here at the *domaine?* Almost nothing. I know Guillaume was a hero in the Resistance, but that's about all. You know the way he is, and Mom never had much to say about it either."

"Yes, she was in Paris then with Aunt Louise, but I think it's time you learned. Wouldn't you agree, Ben?"

"I would, hon. Looks like we're choosing up sides in there, and we may as well have Ray on our side. Better to have him inside the tent pissin' out than outside the tent pissin' in. So my Uncle Floyd used to say."

Having made his contribution, he leaned back and away, against an arm of the bench, giving center stage to Sophie. He held out one hand, trying to attract the attention of a swan that had glided over.

"All right, then," Sophie said. "Raymond, do you know who Alain was?" There was a tremor at her mention of the name.

"My uncle?" Ray asked uncertainly. "That is, your brother?"

"Yes, or rather my half-brother. René and

30

I are full brother and sister. Which means," she added out of the side of her mouth, "that the unmentionable Jules is my nephew. And your cousin. In any case, my brother Alain was a product of my father's first marriage; he was quite a bit older than René and me, almost as old as Guillaume."

"Ah," Ray said, already lost. He swallowed and sat up straighter, knitting his sandy eyebrows to improve his concentration.

"Early in the war, our parents were killed and our home was destroyed. All of us – Alain, René, and I – came here, to the *domaine*, to live with Guillaume. That was in the days when there were three hundred acres, before it got sold off piece by piece, as if Guillaume weren't rich enough already. René and I were children, of course, but Alain was grown."

She dug in her purse and came up with an old locket, its filigreed pattern tarnished and sad. She clicked it open and handed it to Ray. "My brother Alain," she said simply. Ray noted with a surge of sympathy that she avoided looking inside it.

On one side was a flattened, dun-colored lock of hair, possibly once chestnut. On the other a sepia photograph from the 1930's of two elegant, athletic-looking men in their twenties, wearing white duck trousers and open-throated shirts with the cuffs folded casually back on their forearms. One sat on a simple wooden bench looking up at the other, who stood beside him, one foot on the bench, smiling directly into the camera. Both held old-fashioned wooden tennis rackets with long handles and small, round heads.

"He's the one standing up," Sophie said. "He had a moustache, but you can hardly see it."

Ray was reminded of old photographs taken in Palm Springs of Gary Cooper, or Gilbert Roland, or Robert Taylor in much the same sort of pose, with similar rackets and identical clothing, except perhaps for the addition of tennis sweaters draped over their shoulders, the sleeves knotted casually around their necks. No, on second look, the sweaters were here too, tossed in a jumble onto the bench.

"He's very handsome," Ray said, not sure what was expected of him. "And he looks nice."

Sophie smiled at him gratefully. "Oh, I wish you'd known him. I wish," she said, looking at her husband, "you'd both known him. He was so – so very – I thought he was the most wonderful man in the world. René adored him too. Everyone did. And he –

he thought I was a princess, a little queen."

"Who's that with him?" Ray asked, a little embarrassed. This was another new side of Sophie. "René?"

"René!" Sophie laughed. "No, René always looked like a little butterball, even when he was a boy. Besides, René's only two years older than I am. He wouldn't have been more than seven when this was taken. You haven't been paying attention. No, that's Guillaume."

"Guillaume?" Ray echoed with surprise. There wasn't the faintest intimation of this dashing, good-looking youth in the bleak, coldly meticulous old man he knew, with his single grim eye and crippled limbs.

"Indeed. Guillaume was quite attractive in his day, and a marvelous athlete. He had problems with his legs even then, you know – some sort of mineral deficiency or some such thing as a child, but you'd never know it on the tennis court. I remember a time when he and Alain went at it for seven hours...Ah, well." She smiled to herself. "They look a great deal alike, don't they? The du Rocher look; you have it too – the long nose and the skinny legs."

"Thank you," he said dryly, examining the two lithe, aristocratic figures again, "but

33

I'm afraid there must be more to it than that. I seem to be missing something."

"Well, it's nothing but your terrible posture," Sophie said from force of old habit. "How many times must I tell you? Look at you, scrunched up in your chair like an accordian."

"Come on, Sophie, let him be," Ben said. "He's grown up now."

"I suppose that's true," she said, eyeing Ray doubtfully.

Ray wiggled uncomfortably and unknotted his legs a little. He handed the locket back to her. "They were close, then?"

"Tremendously close. They lived for each other. But as unlike as can be. Guillaume was very much the way he is now. Domineering, aloof, cold . . . but Alain – Alain was like the sunshine, like . . . This is ridiculous," she said with some surprise. "I'm becoming positively maudlin."

She snapped the locket shut with a no-nonsense click and arranged her stocky body more squarely on the bench. "Now let me get on with it. I want to tell you what happened." She put the locket in her purse and zipped it up, then took a deep breath with her eyes closed.

Ben had been sitting motionless, his fingertips out to the reluctant swan. He let

34

his hand drift back to Sophie's shoulder and squeezed it. "Honey, I know the story pretty near as well as you do, even if I wasn't there. I can tell him if you want."

She shook her head. "No, I want to; I'm fine." She breathed deeply and opened her eyes. She didn't look fine. "Raymond, I think you know that in 1942 the Germans occupied this part of France."

"Yes. I've always been interested, of course, and I enjoy history anyway, so I've read just about everything I could find about the occupation of Brittany."

"Yes –" She dropped her chin, raised her eyebrows and studied him quizzically. "*History?* Do you consider the Second World War *history?*"

"Well, yes. It was ten years before I was born."

"*Ten years?* Good gracious, young man, when were you born?"

"Nineteen-fifty-three." He spread his hands. "I'm sorry."

"Nineteen-fifty-three," she repeated. "Do you mean to say we have college professors who were born in 1953? God help us."

From her other side Ben smiled across at Ray and nodded. Thank you, he was saying, for shifting her into a more Sophie-like gear. Ray smiled back, pleased with himself.

35

"Now then," Sophie said, quite business-like. "You should know that Alain was also active in the *Maquis* –the Resistance – even before Guillaume was. He was a sector leader in the area around Ploujean."

A highly successful leader, she went on to explain; so successful that in January 1942 the SS descended on Ploujean to take control from the regular German army and stamp out local Resistance efforts. With their usual methods they found out about Alain, arrested him, and executed him in the basement of the town hall in Ploujean.

"I'm sorry," Ray mumbled.

Sophie made a small shrugging move-ment, staring over his shoulder and up the hill towards the back of the manoir. "They executed five others at the same time. There's a plaque in the town square."

There was more to tell. The grieving, raging Guillaume somehow managed to get to the SS *Obersturmbannführer* who had been responsible and assassinate him. The very next day.

"My God," Ray breathed, "they must have massacred the whole town in re-taliation."

"No, somehow that didn't happen, but of course Guillaume had to flee. He ran off to join the Resistance in the caves near Dol and

36

he was quite a hero, they say. That's how he got those scars, as I'm sure I don't have to tell you. A bombed building collapsed on him, as I understand it. He certainly looked it."

Guillaume's having been a Resistance hero came as no surprise to Ray. There was a rocklike, Olympian quality about his formidable relative that would have made anything credible. To have heard that he had wound up by Montgomery's side at the very invasion of Normandy – or by Charlemagne's at Roncesvalles – wouldn't have amazed him.

Sophie returned her eyes to his. "Now you know."

"But I don't understand. What was that you said to Claude Fougeray? How could he have been responsible for Alain's death?"

"Claude," she said, and made a growling sound. "That worm. How he has the nerve to sit there in that house –!"

"Honey," Ben said, "I think I'll tell this part of it." He went on before she could respond. "Claude worked at the *mairie* in St. Malo during the Occupation. He was a clerk for the mayor – which meant, of course, for the German military administration. Now, a lot of people had jobs like that, and it doesn't necessarily mean –"

37

"Oh, yes it does," Sophie said with a snort. "Do you know how he got that job? He informed on a family that was hiding two Jews. That's how he proved his heart was in the right place. The Germans shipped them all off together and then rewarded Claude with his precious job."

"Now, honey, that's all hearsay; Nobody knows –"

"*Everyone* knows. It's common knowledge."

"Well, anyway," Ben said to Ray with a sigh, "it wasn't that Claude was responsible in any direct way for Alain's death . . . Now, he wasn't, Sophie; you know that." He waited for his wife to subside. "What happened, Ray, was that Claude was privy to some inside information. He knew there were going to be some SS arrests two days before they happened. Apparently he even knew Alain's name was on the list, and he . . . well, he never warned anyone."

"He never . . ." Ray was shocked. "You mean to say he – he just . . . His own cousin . . .?"

"I know, but the Nazis told him if word got out they'd shoot everybody in Ploujean instead, and him too."

"So he said," Sophie put in bitterly.

Ben made a tck-ing sound, tongue against

his teeth. "I don't know; I can feel for the poor bugger. Things were hard."

"That's not an excuse," Sophie said stolidly to her hands. "He could have done *something*. But he didn't. And so there he is, sitting in the manoir, grosser, and fatter, and more disgusting than ever . . . And Alain and five other good, brave men have been dead for forty-five years." Her eyes shimmered with held-back tears. "Forty-five years, and nobody knows where they're buried. If the damned Nazis even buried them."

In the quiet that followed, Ray reached out to pat her hands, which lay loosely clasped on the purse in her lap.

"Afterwards, Claude holed up behind the walls in St. Malo with his Nazi pals," Ben went on, "where the *Maquis* couldn't get to him. When the Germans pulled out he ran too. Turned up in Avranches, near Mont St. Michel, where nobody knew him, and started a butcher shop. Now he owns a meat-processing plant in Rennes; the sausage king of Brittany, so they say." He smiled crookedly. "He started out to be a surgeon, if you can believe it."

"You're not serious," Ray said.

"No, it's true," Sophie said. "He studied medicine for a year or two, but the war put an end to it. It's a family joke."

39

"A joke?"

"They say one profession was as good as another to Claude," Ben said. "He just likes the feel of raw meat. That's always good for a laugh from Jules."

Sophie stood up and shivered. "The sun's gone in. Maybe we ought to go inside. Guillaume's probably back by now."

They began to walk up the patch towards the house. "There's still something I don't understand," Ray said.

Ben lifted an eyebrow in his direction.

"What's he doing here? I mean, why would Guillaume invite him to a family council?"

"Well, I think that's what we're all wondering. But he's actually Guillaume's closest relative, a lot closer than Sophie or René. You're even further off, and there isn't anyone else in the family. So if there's some sort of important business, I guess he's got a right to be here."

"I don't see why," Sophie said. "He's only related because his father married Guillaume's aunt."

"Only!" Ben laughed. "That just makes him Guillaume's first cousin, that's all! Way back when, he was next in line for the *domaine*, but when Guillaume got back after the war he cut Claude out of his will. Naturally enough."

After a few more steps Ben spoke to Sophie. "Did you see the way Mathilde jumped when you mentioned Alain's name? I wonder if she's still carrying a torch for him. Poor old René."

"For Alain?" Ray said. "Mathilde?"

Sophie nodded. "They were engaged. I suppose they were having an affair, although I was too young to know about it."

"But – but she –"

"Don't look so censorious, dear. She and René weren't a thing yet. And she was very beautiful, in a monumental sort of way."

"Yes, but she was only ... How old could she have been?"

"Oh, about seventeen, I suppose. And Alain was in his early thirties."

Ray blinked, not with mere prudish disapproval – not entirely – but with astonishment. His straitlaced, comically stuffy Aunt Mathilde a teenaged beauty carrying on an illicit affair with the dashing Alain?

Sophie laughed softly at his expression. "As a matter of fact, that's what I like most about her; that she loved Alain."

When they got to the top of the path, Ray said he thought he wouldn't go in yet, but

41

would stroll down the quiet lane toward Ploujean. Maybe he'd look at the plaque. They'd given him a lot to think about. He turned from them, walked a step, and came impulsively back to put his arms around Sophie in an awkward hug.

"Aahh," she said, "dear Raymond," and laughed, and patted him lightly on the shoulders, and kissed the air by the side of his freckled cheek.

"What a nice boy he's turned out to be," she said to Ben as Ray headed down the alley between the rows of bare plane trees, "but I do worry about him."

"What's there to worry about? He seems fine to me."

"But he's so – well, he's like an old maid, and he's not even thirty-five. I don't suppose he'll ever get married now. I don't know if he even likes women. I'm not sure he *knows* about women."

"Maybe not, but hell, he's happier with those dusty old books than most men ever are with wives, and that's what counts, isn't it?"

"Yes, of course," she said, unconvinced. "Still –"

"Sophie, don't worry about him." He pulled open the door for her. "You know, ol' Ray reminds me of what my

Uncle Bobby Will used to say about perfessers..."

When Ray joined them almost an hour later there had still been no word from their host, and Sophie was beginning to worry. "It's not like Guillaume – No, thank you, Marcel."

Ray and Ben also turned down the coffee being wheeled around on a tray by the quiet, dark servant. As he had moved on to the Fougerays, whom Leona had icily rejoined but not yet favored with speech, the telephone on a side table near the door chirred softly. The servant stopped, bowed gravely to Claude, who was ignoring him, and went into the study to pick up an extension telephone.

In a few moments he emerged, his demeanour for once shaken, his olive face gray. Something in the air made everyone stop talking and look at him. Marcel licked his lips and glanced uneasily around the room.

"Well, what is it, for heaven's sake?" Mathilde demanded.

Marcel seemed grateful for the prompt. "It's the police, madame. There seems to have been an accident at Mont St. Michel. Monsieur du Rocher has been, ah, drowned."

43

4

Ray steeled himself for a violent outburst of emotion at this news, but the reaction around the room was one of quiet disbelief. It was as if word had come of the death of a distant, godlike figure whose mortality was not heretofore assured. And so, he supposed, it had.

Claude, as the nearest living relative, was asked by the police to go that afternoon to the mortuary at Pontorson, the little town separated by a mile-long causeway from Mont St. Michel, to identify the body. When it came out, however, that he had not seen Guillaume in over forty years, he and René went together, driven by a mournfully respectful *gardien de la paix* who called for them at the manoir.

Everyone would stay on for a few days to attend the funeral. This caused some more-than-customary grumbling on the part of Beatrice Lupis, Marcel's wife, a large woman with swollen ankles, who wore tentlike, dun-brown housedresses and was easily aggrieved. Her dissatisfaction over cooking and

44

cleaning for the nine family members for several additional days contributed to an unpleasant scene with Claude Fougeray, whose muttered demand for *un pichet* of wine was met with a muttered response to the effect that he would just have to wait until she was good and ready, and that he had already had more wine than was good for him.

Unfortunately for her, Madame Lupis' penchant for instant irritation, impressive though it was, was no match for Claude's, and his sudden explosion rattled the leaded windows of the salon. An imminent physical confrontation was headed off by Ben Butts, whose retelling of what his Uncle Willie Joe used to say about drinking wine ("Makes you feel fit as a fiddle when you're tight as a drum"), while rendered senseless by translation, managed to muddle the situation long enough for Marcel to appear with the requested carafe.

"I will see to it, monsieur," he said, his face as usual expressionless, "that there is a full *pichet* on the sideboard at all times for your pleasure."

"And a glass," Claude said sullenly.

"Of course. Monsieur enjoys red wine?"

"Monsieur enjoys Château Haut-Brion," muttered Claude.

45

"I'm sorry, monsieur –"

"I know, Guillaume was too cheap to stock anything but crap." He snatched the carafe and retreated to his room, talking to himself as he climbed the stone steps.

At dinner the same day, Claude was involved in another unpleasant scene, this one having unexpected consequences for Ray. As usual the Buttses and du Rochers – and Ray – were at one end of the long dining room table, the Fougerays clustered at a smaller table as far away as possible. Claude and Leona were quarreling again, their sharp whispers increasing in volume through *crûdités, potage au cresson,* and *loup de mer* until, just after the meat course had been set down, Leona leaped up, her eyes blazing. She leaned forward and slapped her husband's face with a resounding smack.

"Pig!" she spat.

Claude's eyes bulged wildly. "Sit –!"

With a grand and graceful swoop of her slender, Hanae Morae-clad arm she flung her napkin into his face, then spun dramatically about and clicked out of the room on wobbly spike heels. Ray began to wonder if they did this every day.

"Ah," murmured Jules du Rocher drolly, "the evening's entertainment begins." But he was careful this time to keep his voice

46

within the hearing of his table companions only.

Claude tore the napkin from his purpling face and began to shout something after her, but Claire laid her hand on his.

"Father..." she murmured.

He brushed her away and stood up, looking after Leona, his head lowered menacingly. Claire rose anxiously with him.

"Oh, leave me alone, for Christ's sake!" Claude snapped. "Stay where you are!" He glared at her until she sank miserably back into her chair, then clumped off after his wife, staring pugnaciously at the assembled Buttses and du Rochers in passing.

Jules waited until he was in the stairwell, safely out of hearing, then patted the corners of his plump mouth with the folded edge of his napkin and looked slyly around the table to indicate that a witticism was on the way.

"I must remember to compliment Madame Fougeray on her aim," he said. He spoke in an cool, conversational voice, willing to brave the umbrage of Claire Fougeray, if not her father. "I thought that Cousin Claude looked quite fetching with a *serviette* –"

"Why the hell don't you shut up?" Ray said in English.

He saw Sophie and Ben glance at each

47

other with surprise, but they couldn't have been more startled than he was.

Jules stared open-mouthed at him. "What?" He spoke French.

Every one of Ray's many inhibitions called on him to mumble an apology. Instead, he translated his remark for Jules' benefit, although everyone at the table spoke fluent English.

"*Fermez,*" he said with his most precise accent, "*ta bouche.*"

Then, in the stupefied silence that followed, he did something even more amazing. He stood up, tossed his napkin onto the table, and strode – not walked, strode – across the room to where Claire Fougeray sat alone, staring dolefully at her untouched and congealing *entrecôte chasseur.*

"May I sit down, mademoiselle?"

She lifted her head briefly, but not so briefly that he failed to see the glimmer of tears.

"Of course, monsieur."

He sat, and the astonishing confidence that had swelled his chest and straightened his back suddenly wasn't there any more. What was he doing? What was he supposed to say now? Had he made things worse for the wan, wretched woman across from him by calling attention to her? And what about the attention he had called to himself? The back of his neck burned; were they all still staring mutely at him?

How would he explain to them that he'd merely surrendered to an irrational and momentary urge, that he hadn't intended by any means to... Or had he? There was a strange tug at the corners of his mouth. A guilty grin? Jules had had it coming, and it had felt remarkably good to deliver it. It had felt splendid, in fact. No wonder so many people seemed to enjoy being rude. There was definitely something in it.

"I want to apologize for my cousin's behavior," he said.

"Oh, no," Claire said, and looked at him. A tear broke loose and ran cleanly down her cheek; she wore no makeup. "It's I who should apologize. My parents... It's only when my father drinks that – that..."

"There's no need for you to apologize, mademoiselle." He smiled at her, rather smoothly, he thought. "Since we've already been introduced, and we're relatives, after all, perhaps we might call each other by our first names? I'm Raymond."

"Claire," she said softly.

"Do you live near here, Claire?" he asked.

"I live in Rennes, with my parents."

49

"Ah. Well, that's not far."

She looked briefly at him again. Far from what, he was afraid she was going to say. He was struck by how very clear and calm her eyes were. Beautiful, really; melancholy and intelligent.

"No," she said, "not far. Rennes is very nice."

"I'm sure it is."

They sat stiffly while he searched for something to talk about. Perhaps he ought to go; she was merely being polite to him, when it was he who had meant to offer politeness. But he continued to sit. Why, he wasn't sure.

"And you?" she said.

"Pardon?"

"Where do you live?"

"Oh, in California; a city called San Mateo. You've probably never heard of it?"

"Ah . . . no."

"No, of course not. Well." He sipped suavely from a water glass, noticing too late the smudge of Madame Fougeray's rich, plum-colored lipstick on the rim. "Yes," he said, "San Mateo. I'm a professor there. Uh, Claire, do you speak English? My French isn't very good. That is," he added with uncharacteristic vanity, "my spoken French."

50

"Yes, I speak it," she said in delightfully Gallic English, "but your French is excellent."

"No, my accent is excellent. Which is a mixed blessing. Everyone thinks I understand much more than I do, and they speak so fast I can't follow them."

She smiled for the first time. "I have the opposite problem. I understand English very well, but my accent is so terrible people think I understand nothing, and shout at me and use sign language."

No, he almost told her, your accent is beautiful, charming; it's like music. His face grew warm. What a thing to say. Where were these ideas coming from?

"You speak English extremely well," he said. "Where did you learn?"

The conversation continued in this painful vein for another five minutes, then petered desolately out altogether. She had just told him that she was an accountant in her father's sausage factory, and he simply couldn't think of anything to reply.

"Well..." he said, pushing back his chair.

"You said you were a professor?" she said.

He felt a swelling in his chest. She didn't

51

want him to go. "Yes, of European and American literature."

Her eyes widened. "Truly? But I'm a graduate in literature myself. Of the University of Rennes."

"You are? But you said you're an accountant."

"Well, yes, my father wants me to work in the factory, but my first love is literature. One day I will teach it too."

"Really? That's wonderful! I'm somewhat of a specialist in French literature myself," he proclaimed immodestly, "especially the nineteenth century. I have a Flaubert novel with me, as a matter of fact. In my opinion he's the finest of them all. Well," he amended judiciously, "of the *early* nineteenth-century French novelists, that is. And of course with the exclusion of the romanticists."

She laughed. "And I've brought a Balzac. I've been reading it for two days."

"Which one?"

"Les Illusions Perdues."

"Ah."

She tilted her head and looked at him, something like a sparkle in her pale eyes. "Oh? Don't you like it? It seems to me a marvelous work, full of the most keen observation."

"Of course it is, but an author isn't a sociologist. I don't believe he should be judged on ability to observe, but on the power of his literary style. Balzac's is rudimentary at best, and he's far too melodramatic for my taste, and too moralistic as well."

"But isn't Flaubert moralistic and melodramatic?"

"Well, no, I don't think I'd say that; at least, not as much. But it doesn't matter; it's the care he takes with each sentence that's so wonderful – with settling for nothing less than the one wholly appropriate word. No one's ever been a more scrupulous writer than Flaubert."

Ray knew his own eyes were sparkling. He was enjoying himself, something he hadn't expected to do until he was safely back in the library stacks at Northern Cal.

"But," she said, "what has scrupulosity –" She giggled delightfully. "Is that a word? What has it to do with literature? A great book is defined by its power to move, not by how carefully the author peers through his Roget in search of *le mot juste*. Of course *Madame Bovary* is a great novel, but it's because Flaubert had something great to tell us, not because he worried every line to get the words exactly right."

Ray grinned happily. "No, I disagree...."

They talked long past the dinner hour, remaining after the others had left and not getting up until the grumbling Madame Lupis began pointedly sweeping up almost under their feet. Ray had one more surprise in store for himself, and that was when he asked Claire if she'd like to walk to Ploujean with him the following morning for a cup of coffee in one of the cafés. If, of course, the weather was fine.

"Tomorrow? But tomorrow is Cousin Guillaume's funeral. It wouldn't be –"

"The next day then?" The boldly inspired Raymond Alphonse Schaefer was not to be so easily put aside.

Claire lowered her eyes. "You'll still be here?"

"Of course," Ray said, deciding then and there.

Claire hesitated, then accepted his invitation with graceful thanks.

Later that evening, when she came to the salon with her set-faced, close-mouthed parents for ten o'clock coffee, she had added a small gold chocker to her plain wool outfit of navy blue and appeared to have put a touch of color on her lips and cheeks. There

54

was even, it seemed to Ray, the hint of a delicate, delicious floral scent when she passed him. She provided little competition to Leona's chic plumage, but the change was noticeable. Ray spoke to her only in passing – earning a suspicious and belligerent look from Claude – but he had no doubt that she had made the effort for him, and the thought made him giddy with pleasure.

He had no illusions about his own attractiveness. He knew very well that he was one of those gray, quiet men who fail to impress themselves on the consciousness of others. People never remembered whether or not he'd been at a particular meeting or cocktail party, and students who had been at one of his seminars in the morning walked by him in the afternoon without recognizing him.

If you asked the people who knew him whether he smoked a pipe (he didn't) or wore a bowtie (he did), nine out of ten would have no idea. Most would have said he wore glasses, although in fact he only looked as if he ought to. A few years before, in a wild fit of self-assertion, he'd grown a beard, which came in a startling, curly red. But except for a single acerbic remark from the dean of humanities when it was at the scruffy stage, no one commented. And when he shaved it off two years later, no one noticed at all.

So when an intelligent, attractive woman made herself prettier for his sake, well, that was something to think about.

When he got up to go to his room she was reading Balzac. He stopped at her chair.

"I'll see you Friday morning," he said gallantly, not caring who heard him say it.

He went humming to bed, taking the stone steps two at a time. He had not bothered to apologize to Jules.

Guillaume du Rocher's funeral went smoothly, conducted with fitting sobriety and according to meticulous instructions left by the deceased. Afterwards, family and servants gathered in the library upstairs, where Monsieur Bonfante, Guillaume's attorney of more than forty years, was to read the will.

Ray had been in the handsomely wainscoted library on earlier visits to the manoir, but he never felt free to explore it, sensing in Guillaume a jealous and forbidding possessiveness. Now, while people settled themselves on chairs and couches, he moved, open-mouthed with veneration, before the thirty-foot-long wall of old books, many of them bound in gilt-decorated leather. Rabelais, Ronsard, Montaigne – my God, the 1595 edition! – Racine, Corneille, de Sévigné . . .

"Isn't it a pleasant room?" Sophie was standing alongside him, her plain, strong face dreamy and soft.

"Pleasant! Sophie, there's a first edition of Montaigne's collected –"

She seemed not to hear him. "When I was a little girl," she mused aloud, "and we'd come to visit the *domaine,* this was where I'd run to. I'd hide here all day if I could. The sun coming in the windows, the dusty smell of the books . . . I could hardly read yet, but there were pictures . . . and sometimes Alain would come and read to me for a while . . . la Fontaine, or Marie de France . . . and, oh, it was paradise. . . ."

Ray smiled at her. Sophie was full of surprises. She wasn't much of a reader, he knew, but then you didn't have to be a reader to love books. "That's nice, Sophie," he said gently.

"Of course," she said, "it usually didn't last long. Guillaume didn't approve of children in his library."

"Or of adults."

They were interrupted by the impatient throat-clearing of Monsieur Bonfante. The reading of the will was about to begin.

5

Georges Bonfante tapped his sterling silver pencil methodically on the surface of the table and waited with a forbearing smile for the last few to settle down. The milk-and-waterish young man with the awful pre-knotted bowtie – that would be the distant cousin from America. Monsieur Bonfante discreetly shielded the small smile he permitted himself. A bowtie, by the good Lord, a green, polka-dotted bowtie and a brown suit, factory-made and fifteen years out of style (if it ever had been in style). Yes, that was certainly the American. Well, if he hoped to emerge any the richer from this little session, he had a sad disappointment coming.

Monsieur Bonfante watched keenly as the young man chose his seat. Monsieur Bonfante was a student of human behavior, and he had already make his prediction. Yes, just as he expected; at the side of the thin, drab young woman who kept her hands in her lap and her eyes on her hands; the Fougeray girl. The observant Monsieur

Bonfante had seen them come into the salon together earlier, and had not failed to notice the pathetically timid smiles they exchanged. Well, well, they would make a fine pair, like a couple from a children's story book: Mr. and Mrs. Mouse. Perhaps they would live in a burrow somewhere and come out to eat Swiss cheese. And have many fine mouse-children.

He tapped his pencil a final time, smiled authoritatively at the faces turned attentively towards his own, opened his attaché case, and removed the folder.

From an old-fashioned metal case covered with flocked black silk he removed his reading glasses. "What we have," he said, "is a holographic will of great simplicity, written and signed by Guillaume du Rocher in my presence on January 19, 1978." He cleared his throat and began to read aloud.

"'This is my will, and I hereby revoke all prior wills. I direct that all my funeral expenses be paid out of my estate. To the university of Rennes I give my collection of mollusks and all materials pertaining to it. To Beatrice and Marcel Lupis I leave an annual allowance of twenty thousand francs for as long as either of them shall live.'"

This allowance was not as munificent as it would have been in 1978. It would provide butter on the spinach; no more. For their spinach they would still have to work. Nevertheless, it was received with a grateful murmur from Marcel and a pro forma dab of Madame Lupis' handkerchief to a rough and perfectly dry cheek.

Monsieur Bonfante smiled once more at his attentive audience. " 'To my cousin René du Rocher, or to his wife Mathilde in the event of his death, or to their descendants in the event of both their deaths, I leave the rest of my estate, except for the following stipulations.' "

He looked up again to catch a relieved Mathilde preening herself. The will could hardly be a surprise to her, but until it is read one never knows. Now she was wondering what the estate was really worth, what it would mean to her. Well, he could tell her and no doubt would. It meant she and René were rich; they now had a handsome home, the means to maintain it, and a yearly income roughly fifteen times René's comfortable pension besides.

" 'This bequest,' " he continued " 'is contingent on the stipulation that the beforementioned Marcel and Beatrice Lupis be allowed to continue in their positions for as long as they wish.' "

"Of course, of course," René murmured to them. "Be delighted to have you."

" 'In addition,' " Monsieur Bonfante read on, " 'the following property is excepted: all of the contents of the room in the Manoir de Rochebonne known as the Library, including all books, furniture, ornaments, and carpets in it at the time of my death. These I bequeath to my well-loved niece Sophie Butts, neé du Rocher.' "

At this there were gasps of surprise, among the most explosive of which came from Sophie herself, who followed it with a look of round-eyed astonishment at her husband.

Monsieur Bonfante smiled tolerantly. "I will be happy to answer privately any questions you may have about any of the terms that affect you individually. In the meantime, are there any general questions?"

His query went unanswered so long that he put the will into his attaché case and prepared his face for the congratulations and smiles required of him. The beneficiaries rose and came to the table to thank him.

Claude Fougeray now made his first contribution: a long, gargling mutter. Head lowered and weaving ominously from side to side, he stared forward, pressed tensely into the tapestried cushion of his chair, like a jack-in-the-box jammed into place by its lid and about to burst the hook. "No," he said.

"Monsieur?" said the attorney with a smile. Mathilde had warned him about Fougeray.

Claude had placed himself apart from everyone, even his wife and daughter, up against the oaken wainscoting near the door, and one fist thumped rhythmically against the three-hundred-year-old linen-fold paneling behind him. His voice was strained, barely audible. "How do I know that's really his will?"

Georges Bonfante had nothing against Claude. He was familiar with the old stories about him, although he himself had been a young man in Lyons at the time. He did not fault Claude for his behavior during the war; what choice did a sensible man have in those days? Nevertheless, he felt his temper begin to swell at the base of his throat. He was not of a retiring disposition, and he did not care to have his ethics impugned.

"It is a holographic will, monsieur," he said frostily. "Made in my presence."

"Holographic, holographic –"

"Made in his own handwriting," Leona Fougeray snapped from across the room.

"In my presence," Monsieur Bonfante repeated yet again, with admirable patience.

Claude shook his head stubbornly. "No, impossible. I know Guillaume; he told me long ago, before the war – The books would go to the Bibliothèque Nationale when he died." He panted twice, like a beast. "Besides, he hated America – ever since the First War, when they came over, so sure of themselves, with their piss-on-you American walk –"

"Piss-on-you American walk?" Ray was heard to murmur perplexedly.

"All this may be so," said Monsieur Bonfante sharply, "but you are speaking of Guillaume du Rocher as a young man, many decades ago. And I fail to see the relevance –"

"He would never leave his library to an American! Not his precious books!" Claude stood up abruptly, swaying on unsteady legs, propping himself with one arm against the wall.

"An American? But surely his cousin Sophie –"

"Not Sophie, her husband! Leaving them to her is the same thing as leaving them to him. Don't you know what they must be worth? How long do you think she'll keep them?"

"Now just hold on a minute there," Ben said, moving a step forward. With her eyes, Sophie appealed to him to stop, which he did reluctantly.

Monsieur Bonfante's fund of patience was exhausted. "I advise you to hold your tongue, monsieur," he said to Claude in his firmest courtroom voice. "However, if you wish to contest Guillaume du Rocher's will, there are legal means at your disposal."

It was a good time to make an exit, but Claude stood blocking the door, head down, breathing as heavily as a bull and giving the convincing impression that he would attempt to gore anyone who took a step. No one moved. Monsieur Bonfante had placed himself in front of the others and was watching Claude closely, a matador shielding his *peónes*.

"Legal means..." Claude repeated, muddled and wandering. He squeezed his eyes shut and passed his hand over his forehead. "Legal..." His eyes opened and fixed cunningly on the attorney. "How do I know it was his *last* will?"

"I have been Monsieur du Rocher's attorney for forty-two years," Monsieur Bonfante said coldly. "I assure you there was never a subsequent will."

"And never *talk* of another will?"

64

Claude stretched his lips in a malicious grin.

"Monsieur, I don't deal in talk." A fine close. Georges Bonfante snapped shut the latches of his attaché case with firm, incontestable clicks. "Ladies and gentlemen, I think our business here –"

"There was going to be a new will!" Claude said, his voice urgent despite the slurring. "What the hell do you suppose this council was going to be about?"

The others shifted and glanced embarrassedly at each other. Leona Fougeray, eyes blazing, appeared to be on the verge of throttling her husband. Claire looked stricken; pale and trembling. Ray took her hand in his and squeezed it.

"I want what's mine," Claude whispered hoarsely. Two viscous tears rolled unevenly down his cheeks.

Claire, weeping, took a step towards him, but her mother held her back with a thin, rigid arm. "He's made his bed; let him sleep in it," she said through clenched teeth.

"For heaven's sake, the man is blind drunk," Jules said, his face pouchy with disapproval. "Why do we stand here arguing with him?"

"Oh, is he *drunk?* " René murmured in his

wondering way, causing Mathilde to raise her eyes to the beamed ceiling.

Beatrice Lupis grunted. "Is he ever sober?"

"Sh," Marcel said decorously. "This isn't your affair."

But Jules had snickered and Claude had heard. "You," he whispered malignantly to Madame Lupis, "don't you dare...don't you ever talk to me like...you fat-assed slut –"

With lithe and shockingly unexpected speed Marcel Lupis stepped forward. The long, olive fingers of his right hand snaked out and grasped the lower part of Claude's face like pincers, clamping his jaws together, squeezing his red lips into a fleshy, wet flower.

"Be quiet, you," Marcel said with all the passion he habitually employed to announce dinner. But his eyes were like gray ice, and when he took his hand away, Claude was silent.

Claire burst suddenly into strangled tears and ran from the library, her hands to her mouth. Ray went after her. An instant later Marcel walked out, followed at once by Madame Lupis, and then by the others.

None of them looked at Claude, whose spongy face was the color of putty except

66

where Marcel's fingers had left ugly, bright-pink dents a quarter of an inch deep.

"Raymond, do stop pacing, and come and sit down. Eat some breakfast. Have a croissant."

"Uh, I'm not hungry, thanks, Sophie. Uh, what time is it?"

"It's 8:50," Ben said, watching him curiously.

"Well, either come and sit down anyway, or go outside," Sophie said. "You're making me nervous."

Ray threw himself restlessly onto the loveseat near the two armchairs in which they sat before the big, bright leaded glass window. Their breakfasts – coffee, croissants, rolls, butter, and jelly – were on a small round table in front of them.

"That's better," Sophie said. She and Ben continued to eat.

Ray crossed his left leg over his right. Then he uncrossed them and crossed his right leg over his left. He wiggled his right foot and sighed. He jiggled the coins in his pocket.

"What time is it now, please?" he asked.

"It's 8:52," Ben said. "Approximately. Would you like to borrow my watch?"

"No, no, I never wear one. Sophie,

just how are the Fougeray's related to us?"

She glanced up from buttering a torn-off end of her croissant. "Astronomically. Geologically."

"Well, but how, exactly?"

She popped the croissant into her mouth and licked butter from her little finger. "Well, let's see. Claude is Guillaume's cousin, you understand. And Guillaume was some sort of distant uncle of mine, and you're my nephew, so –"

"Sorry, hon," Ben said. "I hate to bring it up, but you and Guillaume were fourth cousins."

She looked at him. "Truly? But he's so much older, after all."

"Doesn't matter. your great-great-grand-fathers were brothers, and that makes Guillaume your cousin, not your uncle. And while we're at it, Ray here's your first cousin once removed, not your nephew."

"Don't be ridiculous. He's Jeanne's boy."

Ben shook his head. "And Jeanne was your first cousin. Child of a first cousin is a first cousin once removed."

Ray had heard this argument before, and he was on Sophie's side. She and Ben had always been his aunt and uncle, and that was that. "But what about the Fougerays?" he said. "How are – oh, just for the sake of discussion – how are Claire and I related?"

"Lord knows," Ben said.

"Oh, come on, Ben," Sophie said. "You understand these things. You're a lawyer."

He laughed. "I'm a corporate lawyer. But I think – I *think* – Claire is the daughter of the first cousin of Ray's fourth cousin once removed – Guillaume, that is – only from the other side of the family, so . . ."

"Good heavens," Ray said, "I'm sorry I asked." He sagged back against the seat. Anything beyond first cousins had always been and still was an impenetrable mystery to him.

At that moment, Claire appeared, calm and cool in a belted trenchcoat. Wearing lipstick. Ray jumped up as if he'd been jabbed. After three steps he turned around to Ben and Sophie.

"Oh, thanks," he said. "Er . . . 'Bye." And, with Claire, he was gone.

Sophie and Ben looked at each other, each with a single eyebrow raised. "I'll be damned," Ben said, and got a look on his face that usually meant a homily was forth-coming. But for once he couldn't think of one.

Half an hour later, Beatrice Lupis was laying out *café crème* and croissants for René du Rocher, who was seated in one of the pleasantly situated chairs in which the Buttses had had their breakfast. Mathilde was starting her first full day as mistress of the manoir by sleeping late. René was considering this unusual occurrence, wondering where it might lead, when four men in the dark berets and faded blue smocks that are the workman's uniform of France appeared at the door.

"We are here to begin on the drains, madame," their spokesman announced when Beatrice opened the door.

"The drains?" Beatrice replied, and then smacked her forehead. She had completely forgotten. The ancient household drains had been showing their age in unpleasant ways for some time, but Guillaume, for reasons of his own, had chosen to ignore the problem so that the resourceful Beatrice had taken it on herself to have it attended to. Because no one even knew precisely where the drains were, the first step was the tearing up of the stone flooring in the cellar, and it was this the workmen had come to do.

But this was not the time for it. There was a turbulent exchange between Beatrice and the foreman. Guillaume du Rocher had just been laid in his grave, she pointed out heatedly; surely out of respect for him the work might be postponed for a week?

Certainly, the foreman replied, using his tongue to shift a toothpick from the left side of his mouth to the right. That would be possible, but four days' masonry work had been contracted to begin *today,* and the equipment had been brought all the way from St. Brieuc. He had no choice, he was sorry to say, but to bill them for the contracted labor and equipment costs, whether or not the work was done. They would be happy to come back later, but they would have to charge all over again. It made little difference to him, he explained, and the toothpick moved back to the left. It was up to madame.

But it was monsieur who resolved the matter. René, aware that he was responsible for the *domaine's* outlay as well as its income, came to the doorway and suggested that it might be best to permit the work, inasmuch as it was being paid for anyway. The men would be out of sight in the cellar, after all, and if they kept their noise to a minimum, used the back entrances, and were generally discreet, why, no impropriety would be done.

Beatrice deferred and led the workmen

around the kitchen entrance. René was well-pleased with the results of his timely and authoritative intercession, but before his second cup of coffee had been drunk the foreman was back. His trousers and sleeves were powdered with fine gray dust.

"Monsieur?" He approched, a great deal more diffident than he'd been before; actually wringing his hands, in fact. Had he not left his beret in the cellar he would certainly have been twisting it. The toothpick was not to be seen.

"Monsieur ... we've found ... in the cellar ... we've found ..."

"What, what?" asked René, alarmed.

The foreman swallowed and took another step forward. "In the cellar ... there's a ... a ..."

6

"A skeleton?" Sergeant Denis stopped doodling. He sat straight up in his hard plastic chair and pressed the telephone closer to his ear with his shoulder.

"Yes ... Well, that is, not a whole one. There's no – no head."

"No head. I see. Monsieur du Rocher, is it?"

"Yes. René du Rocher."

This time Denis wrote it down. "And you found it in the cellar?"

"Yes. That is, the workmen did. It was buried in the floor, under the stones. It's been, er, wrapped in paper."

"And you're certain it's human?"

A pause. "Well, we *think* so. Mr. Fougeray, my – one of my guests – said it was."

"A doctor, this Mr. Fougeray?"

"Oh, no. He owns – er, he's a butcher."

"A butcher," Denis said, writing dutifully.

"He said if it wasn't a person, then it might be a large monkey of some kind, perhaps a gorilla."

Oh, yes, Denis thought. A gorilla buried in the cellar of the Manoir de Rochebonne. Wrapped in paper. Well, it had been a foolish question.

"Monsieur du Rocher, please touch nothing –"

"Oh, no, of course not."

"– and lock up the cellar."

"Lock it up? I'm not sure there's a lock."

"Close the door, then." Denis paused. "There is a door?"

"Yes. Well, I'm sure there must be."

"Close it then, and don't allow anyone in. I'll have someone there shortly."

"Fleury," he said when he replaced the receiver, "go on out to the Manoir de Rochebonne – you know the place?"

Fleury looked up from the well-thumbed office copy of *Lui*. "Near Ploujean?"

"Yes. Someone's found a skeleton in the cellar. I want you to keep it secure until the chief gets there. And take some statements."

"Fine," Fleury said, rolling up the magazine and wedging it into its place behind the A-G file cabinet. He stretched. Nothing ever surprised Fleury very much. "You're really going to call Monsieur Giscard on this? It's probably just a goat."

Denis looked up. "A goat? Why a goat?"

Fleury shrugged. "Why a person?"

Sergeant Denis eyed him. He had never understood Fleury very well. "People don't bury goats in cellars." Or gorillas either.

Fleury shrugged. "Isn't Monsieur Giscard at his convention in St. Malo all week?"

"It's not a convention, it's an institute, very scientific, with professors giving lectures. But he'll have to be interrupted."

74

Fleury grinned. "He'll probably appreciate it. He gets grumpy when he's around anyone smarter than he is."

Fleury was right. Four and a half days of relentlessly abstruse scientific lectures had made Monsieur Giscard – that is, Inspector Lucien Anatole Joly – somewhat irascible. And the fact that most of the undeniably brilliant presenters were a decade or two younger than he was had not helped matters. True, there had been some high points: Gideon Oliver in particular was a lucid and engaging lecturer with, thank God, a sense of humor – an attribute not seemingly in great supply among scientists.

Still, what practical value was there in what he had to tell them? In over twenty years of police work Joly had called for the assistance of a forensic anthropologist three times, and not once could he say that it had made the difference between resolving a case and not resolving it. No, when it came down to it everything turned on the application of the well-established methodology of criminal investigation, diligently pursued. Without that, there was nothing, no matter how many forensic scientists you had on your side, gabbling about sternocleidomastoidal insertions, or sarcosaprophagous insects, or carboxyhemoglobin levels.

By the fifth afternoon, he was restless and bored, and he had begun to think up excuses for calling his office. When the message came for him to do just that, he responded with a sigh of relief and left the lecture hall with such alacrity that he stumbled over the legs of the Hawaiian FBI man dozing so comfortably in the aisle seat.

"Pardon, monsieur," Joly said.

"No problem," said the FBI man amiably without opening his eyes.

When he had hung up after talking to Denis, Joly called the public prosecutor, Monsieur Picard, to inform him of the case, as was his duty. This he did, as usual with some resentment. Pleasant and harmless he might be, but Monsieur Picard was not a policeman and didn't think like one, and to be subordinate to him was a raw, never-ending frustration. That was the one thing Joly admired about the American justice system with its impossible decentralization of police powers into thousands of squabbling jurisdictions. At least they were not under the thumb of the damned judiciary.

Picard, never content simply to let the professionals do their work, would figure out some way of interfering, even in a case like this.

As indeed he did. "Listen, Joly," he said after he had heard the details, "isn't that American skeleton expert at your conference?"

Joly was hardly concerned that the gritting of his teeth might be heard at the other end of the line. "Yes, sir," he said, as near as it can be done without opening the mouth.

"Well, I have a wonderful idea. Why don't you talk with him and see if . . ."

Gideon remained at the lectern for a few minutes after his third presentation of the week, answering the questions of a few people who had clustered around him. This was over swiftly, however; the attendees were anxious to take full advantage of the coffee break to fortify themselves for the upcoming session on "Recent Advances in Ionization Analysis by Means of the Gas Chromatograph-Mass Spectrometer."

When they left, he began crating the two skulls and assorted bones the University of Rennes had lent him. (He had wanted to use his own demonstration materials from the anthropology lab in Port Angeles, but the postal authorities there had made uneasy noises about shipping dismembered human remains across international borders, and in the end it had seemed simpler to borrow them in France.) He was feeling cheerful as he packed the bones in polystyrene chips. For one thing the lectures were going well; for another it was very pleasant to be at a conference strictly as a presenter and not an attendee. It meant he could skip sessions when he felt like it. (He always could, of course, but this way he didn't feel guilty.) And inasmuch as ionization analysis exerted less than a hypnotic pull on him and the weather was brightening, he thought he might get a taxi into the Old Town and walk the famous ramparts.

John Lau came up sipping one cup of coffee and holding out a second. "Here. It's good."

"Ah, thanks, John." He sipped gratefully. "Sorry if I spoiled your nap."

John laughed, the sudden, babylike burble of pleasure that always made Gideon smile in return. "Sorry, Doc. I didn't think you noticed."

"Only when you snored."

"Ah, hey, come on. Anyway, it wasn't your lecture. It was that second beer with lunch."

"It was that *third* beer."

The big FBI agent considered solemnly. "That too," he said.

78

"How are you going to make it through an hour and a half of ionization analysis?" Gideon asked unsympathetically. John was an attendee; he wasn't supposed to spend his afternoons walking around St. Malo.

John blew out his breath. "Oh, Christ. I –" He turned and moved a step to the side, with what Gideon had come to recognize as a policeman's instinctive discomfort at sensing someone behind him.

"Pardon me," the man said in a cultivated, nasal voice with only a slight French accent. "I didn't mean to interrupt."

"That's all right." Gideon recognized him; a tall, bald, self-contained man, rather stiff, who could have doubled for Valéry Giscard d'Estaing, except for his gleaming, steel-rimmed spectacles. He had been soberly attentive through Gideon's lectures so far, and had asked several polite, intelligent questions, but always with a discreetly veiled, unobtrusively superior skepticism; a man not inclined to accept anybody's judgment but his own. He was exactly the sort of man whose posture, or way of speaking, or perhaps whose mere presence, brought out Gideon's not-too-deeply-buried insecurities. All he had to do was gaze down his long nose and raise an eyebrow preparatory to making a remark, and Gideon felt like a ten-year-old in grownup's clothes caught out playing pretend-scientist.

"I am Inspector Joly of the OPJ – the Office of Judicial Police," he said, gazing down his long nose.

John held out his hand. "John Lau, FBI, Seattle."

Joly made a formal,straight-backed ghost of a bow to each of them and ceremoniously shook hands.

"Something has come up that may be of interest to you, Dr. Oliver..."

"Any particular reason for assuming it's human?" Gideon asked as Joly pulled the blue Renault out of the parking lot of the new St. Malo Conference and Exposition Center and turned south on the Boulevard des Talards. They skirted the industrial docks of the Bouvet Basin, where huge cranes glided like colossal spiders among the stacked container loads of coal, fertilizer, and wood pulp.

"Yes, the attestation of a butcher," Joly said drily. "Aside from that, there are apparently some hand bones. I assume there wouldn't be any other animals with anything like human hands – aside from the apes, of course."

"As a matter of fact, there are. The

skeleton of a bear's paw isn't hard to confuse with a human hand or foot. Even the flipper of a small whale."

"Ah," said Joly.

John, who had been quick to accept the inspector's invitation to see the French criminal justice system in action, spoke up from the back seat. "Hey, great, we're really narrowing things down. It's either a person, a bear, or a whale. The case is practically solved."

"Not quite," Gideon said, "there's always the possibility of a polydactylous pig; that is, one in which the primary metapodials have shortened and doubled. It's not that unusual, really..."

There was a certain indescribable expression with which John greeted terms like "polydactylous pig," and he made it now, sinking back into the seat cushions with a rumbling mutter. Joly was less demonstrative, but Gideon noticed an almost imperceptible tightening of his lips that suggested the inspector did not approve of lightness in police matters. Gideon sighed and let the subject of polydactylous pigs drop. Narrow interests, these policemen. Touchy too.

"Any ideas who it could be?" John asked as the car swung onto the N137 and the city buildings began to thin out. "Unclosed homicides? Missing persons?"

"We're making inquiries of the local prefect of police," Joly said, "but you have to remember this is an old house, built in the fifteenth century. The bones may have been there for hundreds of years. Besides, well..."

"Besides?" Gideon prompted.

"Well, whenever something like this turns up, there's always the Occupation to consider. You know, there was a lot of Resistance activity in Brittany. And the village of Ploujean was the scene of a mass execution in 1942. That sort of thing – It makes for very strong emotions."

"I'd expect so," Gideon murmured.

"No, not just against the Germans. I mean villager against villager. 'If you and your brothers hadn't blown up that SS motorcycle, my mother and father wouldn't have been shot.' That sort of thing. And – I'll be frank – there were collaborationists as well as Resistance heroes. There were a lot of unsolved deaths; a lot of mysterious disappearances at that time."

"And that's what you think the bones are?" John asked. "A wartime murder?"

Joly extended his lips and shrugged, looking very French. "Who knows? We

82

haven't even seen them. But that would be my first guess, and if it's right, it may be that you won't see the OPJ at its vigorous and unflagging best. I suspect we'll resolve the matter in the quietest way possible, bury these bones again, and leave them in peace."

John was shocked. "But it's a murder! You don't have a statue of limitations on *murder*, do you?"

"It isn't that, my friend," Joly said. "After the war there was a terrible time of retribution. I was no more than ten, but I remember the killings, the trials, the parading of people naked through the streets, the spitting . . . Ah, my God, once –"

But that was as close to revealing his emotion, Gideon realized, as Inspector Joly was likely to come. He closed his mouth, then went on more impassively. "Well, it's been almost fifty years now. The old wounds are closed. No one wants to open them again." He smiled thinly. "And our good German friends fill our hotels as paying guests."

They sat in silence as the Breton coast's wide sky and low dunes gave way to the rolling hills of the Rance estuary, and then to the somber heaths and dark little forests of the interior. At an intersection with a narrow, graveled road, a primitive wooden sign with the word "Ploujean" pointed left. Joly turned, and in two or three miles they came to a metal plaque at the entrance to a still narrower road lined with old plane trees: *"Manoir de Rochebonne, XVème Siècle, 1000 m. à Droite."*

"You're kidding!" Gideon exclaimed. "Is that where we're going? Rochebonne?"

"You know it?" Joly said, surprised.

He did indeed. A couple of years before, while he was still teaching at Northern California State, he'd spent most of the summer working on an Upper Paleolithic dig in the Dordogne, near Les Eyzies. At the invitation of Ray Schaefer from the Comparative Lit Department, who was passing the summer "on the family *domaine*," he'd driven up to Brittany to join him for the weekend. He'd gone somewhat reluctantly (he was rarely comfortable staying at other people's homes, and the picture Ray had drawn of his Uncle Guillaume was highly forbidding), but to his surprise it had been a relaxing and stimulating two days.

The elegant old building, deserted except for the three of them and two servants, had been a great place to loll around in after the dusty cave site in the south. Ray had been his shy, likable self, and Guillaume du

Rocher, once his aloof and frigid shell had been cracked, had turned out to be fine company.

Unlike many shell collectors, he was a well-read student of marine biology and biology in general, and over dinner the second night he and Gideon had had a table-thumping, highly entertaining debate over whether or not the Neanderthals were entitled to a twig on the Homo branch of the hominid tree. They had parted warm friends, to Ray's amazement, and had continued a sporadic correspondence consisting mostly of articles from scholarly journals overlaid with yellow highlighting and emphatic marginal notes.

"Yes," Gideon said. "I know Rochebonne." He had, in fact, planned on dropping by the manoir during the weekend. "I also know Guillaume du Rocher, and I have a hunch he's not going to be too keen on a bunch of policemen wandering around his house and digging up his cellar."

"You were friends?" Joly asked with an odd inflection

"Yes, in a way." He glanced at the inspector. "Did you say 'were'?"

"I'm sorry to tell you, Dr. Oliver.... Guillaume du Rocher is dead."

"Oh, no," Gideon murmured. He was sorry but not surprised. With his war-ruined body, it was amazing that Guillaume had lived as long as he had. "Of what?" he asked.

"He was caught by the tide in Mont St. Michel Bay while collecting seashells. On Monday, I believe; the day the conference started. There was a report filed."

Gideon nodded, smiling faintly. Well, there was a sort of rightness in that. Certainly Guillaume would have preferred it that way, out there on the ocean floor, rather than having his wrecked kidneys or liver give out while he was in a hospital bed buried in tubes. It was too bad, though; Gideon had been looking forward to re-opening the debate.

They turned through the open gate of iron grillwork set between two tall stone gateposts with carved spheres on top, the only opening in a low wall of lichen-stained granite blocks. To the left what had been a small kitchen garden was being substantially enlarged. Workmen were setting in the walls of a raised bed, and piles of lumber and black earth littered the ground.

Otherwise, everything was the same. The manoir itself was set at the back of some 200 feet of pea-graveled courtyard, a gray stone building as starkly beautiful as he re-membered, with five slender stone chimneys,

86

and a complex jumble of smaller wings branching off behind.

Much of the front was covered by ivy – a solid, rippling mass of green when he'd been here in the summer, but now just beginning to break out into rust-colored new leaves, so that the thick, gnarled, old vines could be seen clinging to the stone blocks. The only signs of ostentation were the early Baroque decorations carved around the window casements, all curlicues and rosettes, looking sheepish and subdued in the otherwise classical façade. An ancient, eroded stone coat of arms, possibly older than the building, had been fitted into the wall above the arched doorway.

With a crunch of tires on gravel, Joly pulled the car to a halt directly in front of the door. John looked up at the coat of arms as he got out.

"A *poodle?*" he said after a moment.

"A lion, I think," Gideon said. Not that it didn't look like a poodle.

"A lion," Joly confirmed, "wearing the collar of the Order of St. Michael. A family emblem, I suppose. They hadn't seen many real lions in those days."

"I can see that," John said.

The bell-pull was answered by a large woman in a vast brown housedress, who opened the thick door six inches and peered uncongenially at them.

"*Bonjour,* Beatrice," Gideon said.

She craned her head forward to see him better. "Ah," she said, her eyes brightening, "the gentleman with the good appetite!"

Gideon laughed. "It's nice to see you."

"OPJ, madame," Joly said sternly, showing her his identification. "May we come in, please?"

As soon as they walked through the vestibule and into the salon, a small man with glowing pink cheeks and a scant moustache hurried to them. "I'm the one who called the police, Inspector," he said with pride. My name is René du Rocher." He held out his hand and Joly shook it, again with a slight stiff-backed bow.

Du Rocher gestured around the room, in which several people sat in clusters. "These are members of my family. My wife –"

Joly cut him off unceremoniously. "Perhaps first you would be good enough to show us the remains, monsieur."

"Of course, Inspector. Certainly." He led them briskly through the room. One of the men, vaguely familiar, smiled at Gideon in a particularly friendly way. Stoop-shouldered and slight, there was something about him that reminded Gideon of Ray

Schaefer, so perhaps it was a relative he'd met when he'd visited Rochebonne before. If so, he'd forgotten completely. A little self-consciously, he returned the smile in passing.

The big cellar was damp-smelling and gloomy, lit by four plain bulbs dangling from a wire stapled to the disquietingly sagging ceiling. Against one of the rough stone walls was an ancient, rickety worktable on which was an untidy package of what looked like rotted white butcher paper, much soiled by blood, or earth, or both. The package had been opened and spread out under a table lamp to show a jumble of brownish-yellow bones.

At the near end of the room some of the big rectangular paving stones had been raised and tossed haphazardly into a pile, uncovering a bed of earth about twelve feet by three. Into this a two-foot-wide trench had been cut, but it had come to a halt after only a yard. A pick and two spades still lay where they had been dropped onto the mounded dirt. Around the brief trench a chalk line had been drawn.

"A body outline for a skeleton wrapped in a package?" John said. "You guys are *thorough.*"

Joly looked at him for a moment, his bare

89

upper lip growing longer than ever, but decided not to reply.

"Good afternoon, Fleury," he said to a small, heavy-lidded man in a buttoned-up suit and a red scarf wrapped several times around his throat. "Nothing's been disturbed?"

"Not if you don't count the crew from the lab," said Fleury, who gave the appearance of treating his chief with sleepy, skeptical amusement, until it became apparent that the sardonic V's of his eyebrows were permanently set that way. "They were here for an hour."

"And?"

"The usual. They crawled around on their stomachs picking up invisible things with tweezers and putting them in their little plastic bags, but I don't think they found anything. Aubin said he thought it was something from the war, maybe even before."

Joly nodded. He went to the empty trench and squatted on his haunches, first carefully hiking up his trousers. He wore stocking suspenders, a fact that struck Gideon as being in keeping with what he surmised of the inspector's approach to life. After a few moments of peering at the empty hole – if there was anything to see, it escaped Gideon

– he got up and dusted off spotless, gray-clad knees that hadn't come within ten inches of the soil.

"Shall we have a look at the remains?" he said. "Perhaps we'd better establish at once that we're not dealing with a polydactylous pig."

"We're not," Gideon said. "I can see that from here."

"From thirty feet away? All I can see are some ribs." They began to walk towards the table.

"Those are enough to show it's what's left of a two-footed animal." As always, Gideon slipped with ease into his teaching mode. "Four-footed animals have ribcages shaped more or less like buckets to support the internal organs. But in bipedal animals, naturally, the insides don't weigh against the ribs; it's the pelvis that supports them, so the ribs have wider arcs to give the organs more room."

"Ah," Joly said. "Yes, I see."

"Those –" Gideon nodded at the bones. "– have rounded arcs, so it has to be two-legged. And since there isn't any other large two-footed animal – apes are basically quadrupeds and built that way – it has to be a human being."

"How about an ostrich?" John said.

Joly frowned at him, but Gideon laughed. "Or an ostrich," he allowed.

At the table, John grasped a corner of the crumpled paper between two fingers. It broke off. "Pretty old, all right."

"Mm," Joly said, "yes. It's hard to tell if the brown on the wrapping is blood or earth. The lab will find out." Absently, he fingered a piece of decayed twine that crumbled into powder under the pressure, then scanned the bones. "Well, Professor, there isn't much here. None of the criterion-bones, as I believe you called them: no skull, no pelvis, no long bones.

"No." Gideon pulled a portable heater a little closer and studied the earth-stained bones without touching them. A ribcage, including the vertebral column and both scapulas, on its back, with the ribs now collapsed one upon the other like parallel rows of dominoes and shreds of dried brown cartilage holding some of the joints together; most of a right hand underneath it, also still tenuously articulated by withered cartilage; a scattering of additional hand and foot bones. They had been there a while, all right; there was no trace left of the distinctive candle-wax odor – the smell of the fat in the marrow – that exuded from bones for many years after the soft tissue had rotted away.

And the bones had coarsened and begun to crack with the temperature changes of many summers and winters. So it had been there twenty years at least, and possibly more.

Definitely more. There, in the fragile scapulas and clavicles, small pockets of calcium phosphate had been leached out by the acid soil. Make it thirty years at least...no, forty, and maybe more yet.

But not too much more. There was none of the mineralization – the "petrification" – that fifty or a hundred years in this soil would almost certainly produce. So: more than thirty, less than fifty. Joly's guess of wartime murder was probably right.

"You're right about it being old," he said. "I'd say it's been here forty to fifty years. And you're sure right about it being a funny kind of collection. There's only about a third of a body here, assuming it's all part of one body, but the bones aren't even contiguous. Hands, feet, and torso."

"So where's the rest of it?" John murmured. He tapped the stone floor with one foot and answered himself. "Under here, too, you think? In another neat little package all tied up with twine?"

Joly shook his head, frowning. "If you're going to bury a body under the cellar floor,

93

why bother to carve it up? Dismembering a corpse is a messy, cumbersome business."

"So I've heard," John said mildly.

Joly continued to frown. "Torso, hands, feet. It's hard to understand the purpose."

"It doesn't seem so hard," John said. "They could have chopped the body up in little pieces, maybe to move it from upstairs to down here without anybody knowing – you know, a few pieces at a time – and then just wrapped the chunks into packages that'd fit under individual stones. You know; randomly."

"Perhaps," Joly said without conviction.

"Well, you're going to have the rest of the floor dug up, aren't you?"

"Very likely."

"*Likely?* I mean, Christ, you've got a third of a corpse here –"

"I shall want," Joly said stiffly, "to talk first to some of the people upstairs. We'll see where that leads." He turned to Gideon, who'd been poring over the bones. "And what can you tell us, Professor?"

"Hard to say much just yet," Gideon said. "As you said, the most useful bones aren't here. But it's definitely an adult. The epiphyses are all closed, and ossification's complete. Not elderly, though; no obvious bone buildup in the synovial joints, and not

94

much burnishing of the articular surfaces either."

"An adult," Joly said. "Someone from twenty to sixty, say?"

"Twenty to fifty."

"I see." He waited for Gideon to continue, but Gideon had nothing to add. "And that's all it's possible to tell?" Joly asked. This, his cool gaze said, was hardly the bravura performance he had been led to expect from the Skeleton Detective of America. "Are there no clues as to race? Sex, height, identifying characteristics? Cause of death . . . ?"

"Sorry," Gideon said with a touch of irritation. Policemen, he had learned, fell neatly into two categories in about equal measure: those who expected miracles from him, and those who expected snake oil. Joly hadn't seemed the type to expect miracles. "Give me a couple of hours, Inspector. I need to spread these out and have a good look at them."

"All right, two hours. Fleury, you'll come with me. Mr. Lau, perhaps you'd find it interesting to join me? I'm sure," he added, coolly polite, "it would be most helpful."

John shook his head. "Not with my French, it wouldn't. I think I'll stay down here with the doc. Maybe I'll learn something." He laughed suddenly, and a hundred little wrinkles folded into well-used laughter creases around his black eyes. "I might have missed a few points during the session today."

7

With his head cocked, John watched the two of them mount the steps. Then he looked at Gideon. "He doesn't like me."

"Oh, he likes you, all right. But you *were* crowding him on digging up the floor."

"Yeah, I probably was, but, holy cow –"

"And he probably thinks you're a little frivolous for a cop."

"Me?" John said with genuine surprise. "Frivolous?" He shook his head. "Nah, he just doesn't like me. I can't understand it."

"I admit, it staggers the imagination," Gideon agreed, and began to lay out the bones in roughly their anatomical relationship, to see just what he had. Ribcage first. Everything was there: twelve pairs of ribs, sternum, both scapulas, both clavicles, seventeen vertebrae from the fifth cervical through the second lumbar. The highest and lowest vertebrae were scarred with crude gouges; in cutting up the body, someone had hacked his way through the obvious places – through the throat just under the jaw (that is, between the fourth and fifth cervical vertebrae), and through the fleshy waist just above the hip bones (between the fourth and fifth lumbar vertebrae).

He picked up a loose vertebra, the first lumbar, and ran his thumb over the bottom edge of it, then did the same with the second. "Ah, here's something. Look, there's just the start of some osteophytosis, here on the synarthrodial aspect of the centrum –"

"Doc...!" As far as Gideon knew, there was only one circumstance that ever brought a whine to John Lau's voice.

"Oops, sorry," Gideon said quickly. "I meant this lipping around the rim, can you see? This sort of rampart..."

"Well, why didn't you say it in English in the first place?" John grumbled, as he had many times before. He looked hard at the bone and brushed his fingers along the rim. "Okay, I feel it... Yeah, right there," he said with pleasure. Intolerant of scientific jargon he might be, and not at his best during long lectures, but he was an eager learner, always interested. "What is it, arthritis?"

"That's right; the kind of wear-and-tear

arthritis that gets us all in time. Part of the normal ageing process. Most people show it pretty distinctly in the lower back by the time they hit forty, and it gets to be more noticeable – and more troublesome – as they get older."

"Forty," said John solemnly, as one hand crept around to his lower spine. "Jesus." He was forty-one, six months older than Gideon.

Gideon put the bone back down. "Since the lipping's just started, I'd say he's under forty and over thirty. Maybe thirty-two, thirty-three. That ought to please Joly." He grinned. "I'm not sure the inspector's too happy with me either."

John nodded. "Yeah, well, you're pretty frivolous for a professor. He probably doesn't like it when you sit up on the desk while you lecture. Hey, did you say 'he'?"

"That's right. It's a male."

"So how come you told Joly you didn't know the sex? And –" His eyes narrowed, "– didn't you say today you couldn't be positive about the sex unless you had the pelvis, or the skull, or what was it, the head of the femur . . . ?"

"That's right," Gideon said, surprised. "I'm impressed."

John shrugged modestly. "Something

98

must have woke me up for a minute. But how do you know it was a male?"

A reasonable question, but difficult to answer. The problem was that it was hard to explain, other than to say that after almost fifteen years of dealing with the human skeleton, his eyes and fingertips simply told him so; this sad litter of bones had supported the body of a man, not a woman. But he couldn't quite face telling Joly – who had been so resolutely attentive at the conference, and who had asked such laboriously penetrating questions, and who had taken such regular notes in a no-doubt tidy and meticulous hand – that he just knew; it was a matter of intuitive, unquantifiable feel.

John, yes, but not Joly.

"I just know," he said.

John nodded his acceptance. Once, a long time ago, he had been in the snake-oil camp, but he'd learned to trust Gideon's judgment on skeletons almost as much as Gideon did.

Most of the time.

"Doc?" he said half an hour later, while Gideon was pondering the meaning of the beadlike nodules on the ends of the ribs. They rang a bell, but he wasn't sure what kind of a bell. They were something he'd seen in textbooks. What was it they were called? Prayer beads, was it? That didn't sound right.

"Hm?"

"You done with this part?" He pointed to an oblong, ridged plate at the front of the chest cavity.

"Uh-huh. For the moment."

"Well, I think you missed something."

"What?" Gideon said abstractedly, still thinking about the bony lumps on the ribs.

"This." John touched the platelike bone. "This is the sternum, right? The breast-bone?"

"That's right" Gideon said, puzzled. "So?"

"Well, *look* at it!"

Obediently Gideon looked. "What about it?"

"*This,* for Christ's sake!" John said. "Are you kidding me or something? The guy's been shot. Even *I* can figure that out!"

Gideon, who enjoyed John's outbursts of forensic enthusiasm, examined the round, smooth hole in which the tip of the agent's index finger rested. "No," he said quietly, "that's just the sternal foramen. Perfectly natural."

"*Natural!*" John shot Gideon one of his old snake-oil looks. "I've seen sternums before, you know; they don't have 'perfectly natural' holes drilled right through the middle of them. There aren't any holes," he added accusingly, "in the ones you're using in St. Malo."

"No, but that's because most people don't have one. There are a lot of variable foramina in the skeleton – sternal, frontal, mastoid – Just minor defects in ossification that show up once in a while."

John was silent for a few seconds, continuing to regard him doubtfully. "Yeah, maybe." He made an irritated sound. "How can you be so sure, anyway? I mean, you haven't even looked at it under a magnifying glass or anything."

Gideon pulled himself up to his full height and looked eye to eye at John. "Does the Skeleton Detective of America," he asked scornfully, "need a magnifying glass to tell a sternal foramen when he sees one? Look at how smooth the edges of the hole are. That shows it's developmental. Bullets don't leave nice, smooth holes. Round, maybe, but not smooth."

"Sometimes they do," John said doggedly. "On the way in they do."

"No, they don't. They might leave an even, beveled perimeter, but not a soft, rounded one like this. Besides –" He flicked off the brown, onionskinlike shreds of cartilage by which some of the ribs still hung on to the sternum and turned it over. "– it's equally smooth on the back. Have you ever seen an exit hole like that?"

John's perseverance finally flagged. He sighed. "No, I guess not...Hey, wait, couldn't it be a *healed* bullet wound?"

Gideon opened his mouth to speak, but was cut off.

"And don't tell me they don't look like this, all smooth and round, because you're the one who showed me they do. And what's more –" He noticed Gideon's smile. "What's the joke?"

"A healed bullet hole smack in the middle of the chest?"

"Sure, why not? The heart's on the left side, right? So a bullet exactly through the center *might* miss it. It might get the spinal cord and stuff, I guess, but a guy could still live, couldn't he?" He didn't seem to have convinced himself. "Or couldn't he?"

"John, the heart *is* in the center of the chest. Most of it's on the left side, yes, but just how much varies. If you want to be a hundred percent sure of hitting somebody in the heart, the place to shoot him is in the middle of the chest. You can't miss. And if you shoot him in the heart he dies. Always."

"Yeah, all right," John muttered, "but still..."

"Anyway, a healed perforation looks different because you get a bony scar tissue building up around it; the edges of the hole thicken. Now, this hole, as you see –"

"All right, all right, forget it. Jesus Christ, do you know what a pain in the ass a guy is who has to be right all the time?"

"I don't *have* to be right, I *am* right," Gideon said with heat. "Maybe if you stayed awake during those lectures the FBI paid all that money to send you to, you might know some of these things."

"Yeah, well, maybe if they didn't put me to sleep I would."

They glared momentarily at each other and then burst into laughter with the ease of old friends who'd been over similar ground more than once, and John stretched and said: "Hey, I'm starving. We forgot about lunch, and it's already five o'clock."

"Already?" That was depressing. In over an hour he had learned next to nothing. "Well, let me see what else I can find before Joly gets back... But I don't think I'm going to come up with a hell of a lot."

"Don't worry about it. You always come up with something weird. Joly's gonna just love it."

But results, weird or otherwise, were few. It was almost as if a prudent murderer, anticipating the attentions of a physical anthropologist, had carefully removed everything that might be useful. Without the skull, the pelvis, or any of the limb bones, he couldn't even make a guess as to height or weight.

Well, maybe a guess. One could get a ballpark-type stature estimate from the length of the vertebral column, and he did have the vertebral column – except for the little matter of the top four and bottom three vertebrae. That left him with seventeen out of twenty-four, a little less than seventy percent of the total, to which he could apply Dwight's old table of coefficients and extrapolate ("fudge," John said, and he wasn't far wrong) the body height.

When he finished clicking buttons on his calculator, the result was 175.31 centimeters – about five feet, eight inches, give or take an inch or so either way. So that was something. He stood looking at the bones, thinking, his pencil eraser tapping his lips. True, the 175.31 centimeters really was little better than a guess; he needed *all* the vertebrae, or a femur, or a tibia to come up with a defensible estimation. But his practiced eye, not burdened with the requirement of scientific defensibility, told him 175 centimeters wasn't far wrong. This was a small-boned man who had stood five-feet-nine at most. And he'd been slight; the near-feminine delicacy of the clavicles and scapulas – which in muscular men were ridged and roughened by the pull of tendinous muscle insertions – suggested gracility, perhaps even frailty. Assuming that he wasn't obese (bones held no information about body fat), his weight would have been somewhere around 130 pounds; 145 at the outside.

These conclusions were too tenuous to pass on to Inspector Joly, who made his appearance at the end of exactly two hours, which left embarrassingly little to tell: The remains were those of a male. (The proportions of the clavicles, scapulas, and sternum, while not completely reliable sex indicators on their own, were enough to provide credible support for Gideon's intuition.) The probable age was thirty-two to thirty-four. Dismemberment had been performed with a knife at the shoulder, hip, wrist, and ankle joints, and at the fifth cervical and fourth lumbar vertebrae.

Only one point seemed to rouse Joly's interest. "A knife," he said. "Do you mean it literally? Not an axe? Or a cleaver?"

"Maybe a cleaver, but he was cut up, not chopped up. If you chop a man's foot off with an axe you naturally do it at the thinnest part of the lower leg, just above the ankle bulge." A slow, undulating shiver rolled up his spine. What a hell of a thing for a reasonably serious, moderately scholarly professor of hominid evolution to be chatting indifferently about.

"Well," he went on, doing his best to ignore this unprofessional reaction, "that bulge isn't made by the foot bones, it's made by the leg bones – the lower ends of the tibia and fibula – so if you chopped through the narrow point, you'd get the last inch or two of those bones in with the foot bones. But all we have here are the foot bones. It's the same with the other cuts. They were made between and around bones, not through them. You can't do that swinging an axe."

Joly stroked the skin behind his ear with a finger. "You know, one of the men upstairs is a butcher. He boasted about once having studied medicine. You don't suppose . . . ?"

"One of the men upstairs? This happened forty, fifty years ago."

"He was in the area forty or fifty years ago. He's been gone since. Claude

Fougeray." He said the name with slow, thoughtful emphasis, and repeated it. "Claude Fougeray. Not an endearing man."

"This is done pretty crudely," Gideon said. "It doesn't suggest any anatomical knowledge."

"I believe he only studied for a year or two."

"Even a first-year med student would do better than this. So would a butcher."

Joly nodded. "All right. Is there anything else you can tell me?"

"Not at this point, but I'd like to have another look at these and bring a few more tools. Something might turn up."

"Of course," Joly said. He did not look overly hopeful. "By the way, our Mr. Fougeray expressed interest in coming down here to watch you at work. Would you object?"

"Why would he want to?"

"Morbid curiosity, I have no doubt, but he seemed to feel that his medical skills might make him helpful. Or perhaps his butchering skills. He pointed out rather smugly that he was the one who diagnosed the bones as human."

Gideon didn't think much of the idea, but he couldn't come up with a valid objection. "Fine, as long as he stays out of the way."

"Good, I'll tell him. I want to be there when he comes." He rubbed his hands briskly together. "Now. The bones will remain here, with the room sealed, until Monday, when our forensics people will pick them up. Will that be time enough for you?"

"Sure, I'll come out tomorrow morning. I don't have any lectures scheduled, and there isn't anything particular I planned to do."

A sudden, unexpected image of Julie jumped into his mind, and he almost allowed himself a rueful smile. To be in France with nothing particular to do! It would have been different a few years ago, but a few years ago he hadn't met Julie. Now, the idea of grand sights and great meals depressed him if he couldn't enjoy them with her.

He chided himself, a man of forty so lovesick that being away from his bright, laughing, beautiful wife of a little more than a year turned everything gray and dull. He didn't approve of it; being that dependent on anyone else was rotten psychology. But how terrific it was to have someone to miss so much. After Nora had died, he had thought for four long, black years that it could never happen to him again. But it had. In the person of a robustly pretty supervising park ranger at Olympic National Park.

It had really come home to him on this trip. When he'd agreed to speak at the conference he'd been sorry, of course, that she'd already committed herself to a week-long seminar for National Park Service supervisors at the Grand Canyon training center, but it hadn't dampened his anticipation of the plesures of France. And yet here he was, glad for the diversion of some rat-gnawed, soiled old bones in a dank cellar ... with Paris a few hours away.

How absurdly adolescent, he thought proudly. And now he did permit himself a little smile, while John and Joly were preceding him up the cellar steps and couldn't see.

8

As the three of them walked down the hallway past the entrance to the salon, the stoop-shouldered, teacherish-looking man who'd smiled at Gideon before looked up from his chair and offered another diffident, tentative grin. With a start Gideon realized it wasn't someone who looked like Ray Schaefer, it was Ray Schaefer. He returned the grin enthusiastically, and Ray came out into the hall to shake hands, watched curiously by the knot of people in the salon.

"Ray, I didn't recognize you before," Gideon told him unnecessarily. "You've taken off the beard."

Ray blinked at him in what seemed to be happy astonishment. "You remember my beard?"

"Sure I do. It was bright red; you looked terrific – like a pirate."

"Well...!" Ray laughed, delighted, and blushed spottily. "A pirate! Well, now... What in the world brings you to Brittany, Gideon?"

"There's a forensic sciences meeting in St. Malo. Ray, I heard about Guillaume. I think you know how sorry I am."

"Yes, well... these things happen, I suppose. He really enjoyed meeting you, you know. And he wasn't the kind to take to many people."

Gideon introduced John and Joly, and they all nodded and smiled, or perhaps Joly didn't quite smile.

"Yes," Ray said, "I've already met the inspector." The awkward smiles continued for a few moments.

110

"How are things at Northern Cal?" Gideon asked.

"Oh, fine, just fine. Yes, I'm doing a new seminar on Restoration comic dramatists next semester. You know, Etherege, Wycherly, the whole rollicking bunch. Who knows, maybe even Vanbrugh and Farquhar."

"Ah," said Gideon.

"Huh," said John.

"Mm," said Joly, gazing down his long, thin nose. "Will you excuse me? I see that Fleury is finished with his report, and I want to go over it with him."

The others watched him go. "He interviewed me for ten minutes," Ray said. "I'm afraid he didn't like me very much."

"He seems to do that to people," Gideon said. "My working hypothesis is that it has something to do with his upper lip."

"It could well be," Ray said thoughtfully. "Do either of you read Henry James?"

John shook his head. "Not on purpose."

"Well," Ray said, unoffended, "there's a passage in *Portrait of a Lady* in which he describes communicating with Caspar Goodwood as being like living under some tall, austere belfry that towers far above one, striking off the hours and 'making a queer vibration in the upper air.'" He laughed.

111

"Doesn't it make you think a little of Inspector Joly?"

"A *lot,*" John said with feeling.

Ray looked happily up at Gideon. "I don't believe I've seen you since you left Northern Cal. Did I hear you and Julie are married now?"

"Yes, we are. Look, I'll be coming back tomorrow morning. Why don't we have lunch together and get caught up on things?"

"Oh, I'm sorry, I'm er, busy for lunch." Ray blushed again. "What about coffee when you get here?"

"Fine. Nine o'clock?"

"Wonderful. Let's just –"

A wan, pale-haired woman with soft, hesitant eyes in a face too worn for her three decades had come unobtrusively down the stairs and stopped, startled to find strangers.

"Oh! *pardon* –" She saw Ray then, and her face came alive. "Raymond." She said it with a slight tremor, pronouncing it the French way, liquid and delicious. Suddenly she didn't look so wan.

"Why, Claire," Ray said. His rounded shoulders had squared the moment he saw her. He tugged cavalierly but without effect at the ends of his bowtie and shot a quick,

112

proud glance at the two men before he went to her and took her hand.

"Claire Fougeray," he announced awkwardly. "Gideon Oliver and John Lau. John and Gideon, Mademoiselle Claire Fougeray." He beamed and fidgeted.

That, Gideon thought with interest, satisfactorily explained the business about lunch. He was frankly surprised; he'd long ago given up on his meek, unimposing, and – well, a little dry – colleague's chances for romance, but it looked, happily, as if he'd been wrong. He smiled at the two of them. "I'm glad to meet you, mademoiselle," he said, meaning it sincerely.

Ray stood back contentedly as she shook hands. "Oh," he said suddenly, with a new smile. "And this is my uncle, Ben Butts."

"Cousin," said the blue-eyed man with the gray hair and the soft Texas accent who had come into the hallway from the salon. "That is, cousin's husband. But the boy here just won't accept that." He grinned and squeezed the back of Ray's neck affectionately. "Look, everybody's dying of curiosity in there, but nobody's got the nerve to come out and say so. Why don't you bring your friends inside and tell us what's been going on in the cellar instead of whispering about it out here?"

113

"But we weren't talking about that at all," Ray said.

"All right, then," Ben said agreeably, "at least invite them in to sit down and have a drink. They could probably use one after two hours down there."

"That sounds good," John said, and Gideon agreed.

"Oh..." Claire said, drawing back. "I must go. I can't stay..."

"Don't be like that, honey," Ben said gently. "Nobody in there's going to hurt you –"

But with a murmured excuse, she was gone, trotting quickly back up the stairs.

Ben watched her go with a sigh, and exchanged a troubled look with Ray. "I sure wish we could get that girl to come out of her shell a little. I'm afraid we have a few frictions here at the old manoir," he said to John and Gideon, "just like normal families do. Ray, did I ever tell you what my Uncle Beau Will'm said about families?"

"No," said Ray, beginning to smile, "I don't believe you did."

"Well, my Uncle Beau Will'm," Ben said, slipping into an East Texas drawl, "that is, my Uncle Beau as was married to my mother's sister Essie, he said ain't no problem at all keepin' peace in the family,

114

just so long's you don't ever make the mistake of tryin' to get 'em all together."

While they laughed Ben bowed them into the salon and Gideon had his first good look at the room. It was here that he and Guillaume had had their lively discussion over coffee and local brandy, observed by a bemused but entertained Ray. Everything was exactly as he remembered – the high ceiling with the warped, orange-painted beams, the rough, hammered-iron chandelier with its anachronistic little light bulbs shaped like candles, the great Louis XIV table in the center, the leggy rubber plants, the age-browned tapestries of barely visible stags and skirted hunters. It felt somehow wrong that they should all be unchanged, while the vital, incisive Guillaume, who had seemed the very heart of the manoir, breathing life into it, should be dead. Indeed, the people in the room – introduced by Ray as Ben's wife Sophie, and Mathilde, René, and Jules du Rocher – struck him even before he spoke to them as intruders who had no right to be there. Ben was right, he decided; he could stand a drink. Something to eat too.

The amiable Sophie Butts quickly set him more at ease. A graying woman with an open, mannish face, she moved over on the couch with a smile and patted a place beside her.

"*Bonsoir, madame,*" he said politely to Mathilde, who informed him that he might as well speak English. She and her husband had spent many years in London; Jules had been born there. Since Guillaume's death, as a matter of fact, French had generally been spoken at Rochebonne only when addressing the servants . . . or certain distant relatives who found it difficult to comprehend English.

Within a few moments, Marcel, as inscrutable and silent as he'd been two years before (Did he recognize Gideon? There was no way to tell), had brought Dubonnets for him and John, and for the next twenty minutes, while he sipped and munched hors d'oeuvres, he answered questions about the bones in the cellar.

"And was he actually *beheaded?*" Jules du Rocher asked. "And his hands and feet cut off?" The puffy Jules had shown a morbid interest in the more lurid aspects of the case. For some minutes, with his little eyes glittering, he had held a half-consumed salmon-and-olive canapé in one hand, forgetting to eat it.

"Well, the body was cut up, yes," Gideon said, looking at him with distaste.

Fascinating," said Mathilde, who evidently didn't share her son's sensational interests.

"But who was it?" René asked. "Why in heaven's name was he buried in the cellar? Who killed him?"

Gideon shrugged. "The police will have to figure that out. About all I can hope to do is give them a description that might help. And so far I haven't come up with anything useful." Here he was equivocating a little, but it didn't seem like a sensible idea to broadcast even the few specific conclusions he'd reached. "But maybe I can find out a little more tomorrow."

"How?" Jules asked. "What can you do that you haven't done already?" As he spoke he waved one hand before his face, saw the canapé in it with visible surprise, and popped it into his mouth, shoving it the last inch or two with a fat thumb.

"Jules," Mathilde breathed.

"Well," Gideon said, "of course the police are still looking for more bones, and if they find the pelvis or the skull, there's a lot we might be able to tell. Still, even if not, a closer look might turn up, oh, some old injury like a healed fracture that might help in identification... Or maybe signs of disease, even a childhood disease –".

"A childhood disease?" Ben echoed.

"Can you really tell that from the bones?"

"Depends on the disease," Gideon said, having taken advantage of the question to toss down a quick triangle of smoked trout on toast. He was careful not to push it in with his thumb. "A lot of them leave permanent signs on the skeleton: TB, rickets, polio... And then there can be signs of operations too – oh, for mastoiditis, say."

He downed a shrimp-and-egg-decorated cracker while they digested this. John, he noticed enviously, was putting canapés away at a far steadier rate, being unencumbered by conversation.

When Beatrice announced dinner, Mathilde, who looked as if she had hoped to avoid this awkward situation, unenthusiastically invited John and Gideon to dine with them. When they declined, saying they would be leaving with Joly in a few minutes, she expressed her regret with a warmly genuine smile and left for the dining room, followed by all but Jules, who stayed in his chair hoping for a few more of the grisly details.

"Dr. Oliver? Monsieur Lau?" It was Joly, standing in the entryway, plainly disapproving at this fraternizing with the household. "I think we can go now, please."

At the doorway he turned to Jules. "Oh, monsieur – I haven't seen Monsieur Fougeray for a little while. Perhaps you would be good enough to tell him he is welcome to examine the bones tomorrow at ten o'clock?"

Jules drew his soft body together and lifted a rudimentary chin. "I will see to it," he said coldly, "that Marcel informs him."

"A Nazi *what?*" John asked. He was in the front seat this time, Gideon in the rear, as Joly drove them back to St. Malo.

"*Obersturmbannführer,*" Joly replied, turning off the graveled road onto the highway. "It's equivalent to a lieutenant-colonel. SS *Obersturmbannführer* Helmut Kassel. You remember the executions in Ploujean that I mentioned? They were on his orders. And among the dead was one Alain du Rocher, who, if you take it on the word of the people in that house, was the nearest thing to an angel you're likely to find on this earth."

He extended his lips to accept the Gitane he had just lit at the dashboard. "Perhaps he was. In any case, according to what they said, Guillaume du Rocher – your old friend, Dr. Oliver – killed the Nazi in retribution for his cousin's death. Certainly, there is no question but that Kassel disappeared with

119

no trace in October 1942. I think that now we have some reason to think that Guillaume –"

"– buried him in the cellar," John said.

"So it would seem. No one appears to know for sure what was done with the body, and Guillaume, they tell me, hadn't talked of it for over forty years. He didn't happen to mention it to you, Dr. Oliver?"

"Not a word. I was only here for a couple of days. We talked about phylogenetic relationships between the Middle Pleistocene hominids and the western Neanderthals."

"Hey, no kidding," John said. "That must have been a blast. I'm sorry I missed it."

It *was* a blast, Gideon remembered. Afterwards, the ailing old man had told him he hadn't enjoyed an evening so much in years, and Gideon had believed him. He thought about Guillaume some more, staring without seeing at the lights of the big trucks flashing by on their night hauls to Rennes. "Inspector," he said, "do you know just what it was that happened to Guillaume?"

"He was drowned in the tide."

"Yes, but do you know how it happened? Did he have an attack of some kind? A stroke?"

"No, I don't think so. He was rather far out collecting shells, and he didn't become aware of the tide until it was too late for him to get back. When he began to run, he stepped into some quicksand. It's very treacherous there."

"Mm."

"Exactly what is it that bothers you?" Joly asked after a pause.

"It's just that he didn't strike me as the kind of guy who'd go out there without knowing exactly when the tide was coming in and exactly when he'd have to start back. He was fascinated by the tides. He had some kind of theory about biannual cycles, and he kept tide schedules going back a dozen years."

"When was it you saw him?"

"Almost two years ago."

"Ah. Well, as I understand it, his health had declined since then; his alertness too, I'm sorry to say. He might easily have become confused."

"I suppose so," said Gideon, unconvinced. "Still –"

"Dr. Oliver," Joly said briskly, "I can assure you there is nothing questionable about Guillaume du Rocher's death. He was simply caught unawares. Half a dozen witnesses saw it, one with binoculars. Afterwards his body was found buried in the sand up to the hips. It's happened many,

121

many times before, and it will happen again. The bay is famous for it."

"I guess so."

John turned around. "Okay, Doc, let's hear it. What's your theory?"

"I don't have one," Gideon said truthfully. "It's just that... hell, I don't know. It doesn't sound right."

"Perhaps we would do better," Joly said with authority, "to discuss the case at hand – the skeleton in the cellar. Several of the people at the manoir remember Kassel; their descriptions corroborate one another, and I am hoping that your investigation will bear them out: a tall, powerful man, very Aryan in appearance –"

"*What?*"

Joly's cool eyes flicked at him in the rear-view mirror. "Pardon? Have I said something –? Ah, of course. You prefer not to know who it is you're trying to identify. I apologize; you told us on the first day of the seminar."

"Well, that's true. Forensic anthro's like anything else. You tend to find what you're looking for. But –"

"Still, inasmuch as it's almost certain that the bones are Herr Kassel's..." Again he glanced at Gideon. "You think not?"

The words were courteous enough, but

122

even in the small mirror the afflicted expression in Joly's eyes was unmistakable: What have I done that God has seen fit to inflict this difficult man on me?

"I think not," Gideon said, and told him straightforwardly about his height and weight calculations. "Five-feet-nine, tops. A hundred and forty pounds, tops. There's no way anybody could mistake him for 'tall and powerful,' Inspector.

Joly considered this without pleasure. "Don't forget about the psychological component, Dr. Oliver. We're dealing with memories forty-five years old. Isn't it likely that people's image of this feared, powerful commandant has been warped by time into something even more terrifying than he was?"

"That's true," John said, on Joly's side for once.

"Sure, but this guy was built along the lines of Ray Schaefer. Do you think even forty-five years could warp that build into an Aryan superman's?"

"Yeah, but don't forget about the fudging component, Doc," John contributed. "You said down in the cellar you weren't sure about the height and weight, didn't you?"

"I didn't say I wasn't sure, I said the

indicators didn't provide technically cogent data."

"Oh, the indicators didn't provide... Well, that's different. That's a whole 'nother story. Excuse me."

Gideon sighed. "Okay, okay, you're right. I can't prove it, but my gut tells me this was a little guy, not a big one. Is that better?"

John hooked an elbow over the back of the seat and turned around, his dark eyes round. "I'm *right?*"

"In principle."

"Oh, in principle." He swung back around to the front and nodded sadly. "You had me shook up there for a minute. I thought I was just plain right."

If Joly found this exchange entertaining he didn't show it. "Dr. Oliver, to speak frankly, it seems to me that you're going out of your way to be obstructive –"

"Obstructive?" Gideon repeated, offended. "You asked me in to give my opinion, and that's what I've given. If you've already made up your mind who that skeleton is, you don't need –"

"No, no, I'm sorry," Joly said hurriedly. "I didn't mean it that way. It simply occured to me that with all the available information pointing to its being Kassel... Well, I find myself wondering if your *modus operandi* perhaps involves a certain skepticism, a need to quarrel with the obvious, to make the simple complex . . ."

"Every time," John said cheerfully. "That's his MO, all right. That's how he got to be the Skeleton Detective of America."

The look that Joly shot him made it icily clear that he knew when he was being put on and it didn't amuse him. He exhaled smoke through his long nose and ground out his cigarette in the ashtray. "Perhaps we'll learn more tomorrow," he said curtly. "I'm having the rest of the cellar excavated, of course."

"Of course," John said, and wisely held his peace.

Each with his own thoughts they said no more until Joly swung the blue Renault off the N137 at the St. Malo exit.

9

Gideon was one of those people who could wake up at a set time without an alarm clock, but it was an instinct he never wholly trusted. As a result, he usually set an alarm before going to bed and generally wound up jerking awake ten minutes before it went off,

125

thus allowing him to punch down the button and avoid being shaken out of his sleep by the alarm itself. Thus also losing him ten minutes' additional sleep that he wanted dearly at the time. It was one of those little problems he had yet to get around to figuring out.

But he was surprised the next morning when the alarm went off while he was still asleep. He slammed the button down twice before he realized it was the telephone. Blindly, he reached for it, his heart racing. He didn't like telephone calls in the middle of the night; that was the way he'd learned that Nora was dead. As he groped for the receiver he saw the time on the glowing clock dial and relaxed: ten after seven. Not the middle of the night at all. Still, damn early.

He growled something into the telephone.

"Oh-oh, sounds like he hasn't been fed yet. I didn't wake you up, did I?"

"Julie?" He smiled and fell back against the pillows, closing his eyes again, letting her voice flow over him. "I love you."

He'd already called her twice in the five days he'd been in France. They'd talked and laughed for almost an hour each time, like a couple of kids with crushes. He hadn't yet had the courage to inquire about the bills.

126

"I love you too. I miss you horribly. When are you coming back?"

"Wednesday. I keep telling you."

"I know, but I like to hear it. Four more days." She sighed. "That's still a long time."

"Mm, I'm glad you miss me. Are you home now? How did the supervisors' seminar go?"

"I just got back from Arizona an hour ago. And I know all about effective supervision now. It's nothing but a matter of providing a climate conducive to the maximization of intra-group cooperation."

"I always thought it had something to do with planning, delegation, that kind of stuff."

"That shows how out of date you are. How's life in St. Malo? Still pretty dull?"

"Well, no, as a matter of fact. Remember the Guillaume du Rocher I mentioned to you? They've found a dismembered skeleton in his basement, and the police have asked me in. What are you laughing at?"

"It's amazing. This always happens to you, doesn't it? So tell me about your dismembered skeleton." He could tell from her voice that she was settling herself comfortably.

He went over it with her briefly.

"Everybody," he concluded, "is convinced it's this SS officer Kassel that Guillaume killed in 1942. Even John thinks so. But I'm just as positive it isn't. Maybe I'll find out more today."

"What does your friend Guillaume have to say about it?"

"Guillaume's dead. He drowned Monday, the same day I got here. The funeral was a couple of days ago."

"Oh, I'm sorry, Gideon. I know you liked him." She was quiet a moment. "Doesn't it strike you that there's something funny about that?"

His eyes popped open in surprise. "It sure does, but what makes you think so?"

"Well, I was just thinking... It's an awfully big coincidence; here's a body lying hidden under the house for forty or fifty years. Then when it finally gets found, it turns out that the person who's supposed to have done it got buried the day before. How convenient."

"You know, that's a good point," he said admiringly. "I never thought about that."

"The bones are found," Julie went on, "the victim is identified, the killer is identified, and the case is all wrapped up – all in one day. Only the only persopn who can confirm it – or argue with it, I bet

128

– just died. And you never thought about that?"

"No."

"You're slipping, Dr. Oliver. I think marriage has made you soft. When you get back I'm going to have to keep you less contented."

"Just try it," he said, then got himself more comfortably stretched out on his back and got down to the sweet, serious business of telling her just how much he missed her. And how he was going to show it when he got home.

An hour later, while John went lamenting to Professor Wuorinen's final lecture ("Larval Invasions of Calliphoridae in Unburied Corpses from Two to Four Weeks Old." *Many graphic color slides)*, Gideon was picked up at the hotel and driven to the manoir by a sharply dressed, intense young man with red hair and elevator heels, who introduced himself as Sergeant Denis. Ray met them at the thick oak door and politely invited Denis to join them for coffee.

"No, thank you, monsieur," Denis said, as firmly as if Ray had suggested a double brandy. He bobbed a Joly-style bow and went to break the police seal on the cellar door and get the workmen started digging.

"Well, let's go sit down," Ray said.

"I've asked Beatrice to bring us some coffee."

With luck Beatrice would not take Ray's request in too narrow a sense; he was ravenous, although he'd breakfasted in the hotel restaurant at eight. Delicious as the French *petit déjeuner* of croissants, rolls, and *café au lait* was, its staying power was an hour and a half at most. The French, realizing this, often had a second breakfast at midmorning to tide them over until lunch, and if Beatrice were to offer him something along that line, he would not turn it down.

In the window alcove of the salon were the same people he'd met the evening before, as if they'd been there all night, leaving only to change their clothes. Now, however, it was an ample breakfast they were putting away, and Beatrice's croissants looked a lot better than the ones at the Terminus.

Ray and Gideon walked past the group, which was deep in conversation (except for Jules, who was sucking in croissants as quickly as he could smear them with jam and butter), and headed towards a pair of chairs in the far corner, but René caught their eye with an amiable smile and waved them over. There was no polite escape. With a small shrug between them, they joined the others.

130

This time it was Ben who moved his chair to make room for them.

Beatrice got there at the same time they did, and, happily, she had not forgotten his good appetite. With the steaming pitchers of milk and coffee there were two big baskets; one of croissants and one of rolls, both of them warm and fragrant – altogether the best combination of smells to be found in France. Maybe in the world.

"We've solved your mystery for you," René announced, sprightly and pink-cheeked.

"Oh?"

"*Obersturmbannführer* Kassel of the SS. That's who it is. It must be."

"Yes, I heard something about him." Gideon glanced down to break open a roll. "Tell me, do you remember what he looked like?"

"I'll never forget." The shadow of a cloud rippled over René's bland face. "No one could, who was here when the trouble came. Very handsome in the German way; very cold, very Aryan. A blond giant..."

"You know," Ben pointed out, "you might be overstating this 'giant' thing a little, which maybe could mislead Gideon. You were a kid then, and to a kid every grown-up looks big and strong."

131

"René was sixteen," Mathilde said. "That was not a child in those days. Besides, I remember the SS man very well too. And I was . . . somewhat older." After a moment she added: "At that time." Just in case anyone thought it might still be true.

"Well, what about the bones, Gideon?" Sophie asked. "Do they fit the description, or don't you have enough to go on?"

He hesitated. He had more than enough to go on, and no, they didn't fit the description, whatever Joly might think. But he was saved from having to hedge by someone making an entrance into the salon. Six pairs of eyes swiveled in the newcomer's direction with candid hostility. Even Ray, to whom glowers didn't come easily or often in Gideon's experience, managed a creditable one.

"Claire's father," Ray whispered to him. Gideon, whose back was to the doorway, turned out of curiosity.

Claude Fougeray, as Joly had said, was not an endearing man, at least to look at. Short-necked and squat, radiating belligerence, he stopped at the entrance of the room to return the collective antagonism with a goggling, malevolent stare of his own. Then he muttered an ugly laugh and made his way past them to the empty dining room.

Good God, if that was Claire's father, no wonder her eyes had that haunted look.

In the salon the conversation had stopped, so that the clink of carafe against wineglass in the other rom was audible, then the hollow gurgle of liquid being poured, and even the three wolfish gulps that followed. There was another muttered, contemptuous laugh, and the process was repeated: clink, gurgle, glug, glug, glug. And again the clink . . . Gideon shuddered. It was 9:15 A.M.

"Tell me, René," Sophie said, her voice brighter and louder than before, "what will you and Mathilde do? Will you give up your job in Germany and come and live at the manoir?"

"Well," René said, "we haven't really –"

"Of course we will," said Mathilde. "It may take a few weeks to put things in order, however. It's quite difficult at the moment without an automobile to get about in. Guillaume's Citroën is still in the car park at Mont St. Michel, you know. I was hoping, Raymond, that you might go there and drive it back."

"The car? Yes, of course. But how would I get there?"

"Take someone else's car, of course."

"But no one else *has* a car, my dear," René said. "Marcel picked everyone up

133

at the airport or the train station in Dinan."

Mathilde shrugged crossly. She was not interested in details. "You can take a taxi to the train station, I suppose, and go from there, or perhaps you can rent a car. It's all *very* annoying. I can't imagine why Guillaume kept only the one car here. In Frankfurt we have –"

"Ha!" Behind Gideon, Claude had returned to the entrance to the salon. No one looked in his direction.

"– three automobiles and could easily do with another. It sounds ostentatious, I suppose, but –"

"Ha!"

Even Mathilde faltered. "– but as a matter of fact . . . as a matter of fact . . ."

"Ha!" There was a startlingly loud crash.

Gideon spun around in time to see Claude's half-filled wineglass drop to the thinly carpeted stone floor and smash a few inches from where the carafe had splintered a moment before.

"Jesus Christ!" Ben Butts cried hoarsely. "What is it? Claude . . . !"

Claude's body was rigid, arms spread, fingers clawing convulsively at the air. *"Ha!"* he cried. *"Caah!"* From one corner

134

of his stretched lips a fine white froth seeped, as if his mouth were full of soap. His bulging eyes heaved.

"Oh, my God," Sophie murmured. "He can't breathe."

"Do something!" Mathilde commanded all-inclusively. "He's having a heart attack!" *And,* her tone implied, *on my Aubusson carpet.*

Gideon, as paralyzed as the rest of them, finally pulled himself out of his chair and moved towards the stricken man. Before he got there Claude jerked as if an electrical current had pulsed through him, grunted through clenched teeth, then abruptly threw himself down on the floor, onto his back, like a circus performer who would momentarily spring unaided to his feet, all in one movement.

He didn't spring to his feet, of course. He didn't move at all, except for his outflung arms, which settled gently to the floor at his side in a quiet motion of terrible finality. His eyelids were lowered halfway over glazed and unfocused eyes. When his mouth fell open a moment later, a gob of foam welled from it and slid down his cheek towards his ear.

Head down, hands clasped behind his back, Joly listened to Gideon's brief description of what had happened. When it was done he nodded once and stepped from the vestibule back into the salon to address the assembled household, who sat, edgy and subdued, in the alcove. Only Leona and Claire, in seclusion in their rooms, were absent.

"Ladies and gentlemen, "he said matter-of-factly, "I shall want to speak with each of you in the next few hours. After that, I expect to ask for your cooperation in remaining in the vicinity for the next several days."

"But we're supposed to fly to the States tonight," Ben said.

Others began to protest too, but Joly cut them off. "If any of you find it an extreme inconvenience to remain until – let's say Tuesday, three days – please inform me when we speak privately. But I hope that won't be the case. It would create annoying and time-consuming difficulties for me and for yourselves. Madame," he said to Mathilde, "is there a room in which it would be convenient for me to hold interviews?"

"I suppose so," Mathilde said grudgingly. "Guillaume's study is right across the hall."

"And someplace other than here where people might wait comfortably? I'm afraid

136

I must ask all of you not to return to your rooms for the moment."

Mathilde fixed him with a penetrating eye. "Are your men going to search them?"

"Yes, they are."

She sighed her displeasure. "There are some chairs at the landing near the central staircase."

"Thank you. Fleury, please escort everyone as Madame du Rocher directs, and wait with them."

There was some muttering but they went meekly, except for Mathilde, who expressed restrained indignation at these high-handed police methods in her own home.

"Oh, and get somebody here from Pathology," Joly called after Fleury. "Dr. Fouret, if he's available."

"I hope he's a *real* doctor," Mathilde grumbled with a last scathing look at Gideon over her shoulder. Gideon spread his hands apologetically. His tentative, conspicuously amateurish attempts at CPR had not met with her approval. Nor with his own, but Claude had been so obviously beyond the reach of cardio-pulmonary resuscitation or any other earthly assistance that nothing would have helped in any case. Not even a real doctor.

So said Dr. Loti, the elderly physician –

Guillaume's doctor of many years – who had been summoned by Marcel after Claude's shocking attack.

"Well," he said to Joly, coming from behind the folding screen that had been set up around Claude's body and snapping shut his black leather case, "your professor friend here is right about the cause of death. I'm sure your laboratory will confirm it." He nodded at Gideon. "The smell of bitter almonds; very good, young man."

Joly's glance at Gideon was not especially grateful.

"Look, Inspector," Gideon said, "this is your case. I don't want anything to do with it. I don't know anything about it. I just happened to be here."

"So it seems."

"All I know about bitter almonds is what I read in Sherlock Holmes. I don't even know what a bitter almond is."

"Mm." Joly turned to Loti. "Do you have any idea how quick death would have been?"

"Within minutes, probably only a very few. Cyanide is one of the most rapidly lethal of all poisons. It disrupts the oxygen-carrying capacity of the blood the moment it's ingested."

"Then we can certainly assume that it was
138

in the wine," Joly mused. He stood looking at the crime-scene crew taking their photographs and bustling around the corpse on their knees. One man was dusting the pieces of the broken carafe with black powder. "Are you getting any prints?" Joly asked him.

"Yes. More than one person's, I think."

"Good."

"But you know," Gideon volunteered, "you wouldn't have had to touch the carafe if you wanted to put poison in it. In fact, you'd be crazy if you did."

Joly gazed down his nose at him for a long moment, his lips pursed. "Thank you," he said.

"You're very welcome." Funny the way policemen never seem to be particularly appreciative when obliging laymen point out self-evident facts to them. "I think," he said prudently, "that I'll get out of here and take another crack at those bones."

Inspector Joly did not object.

When the manoir had been built, the stairwell in the southeast corner had evidently been housed in a massive tower. The tower itself had disappeared long ago, probably in some nineteenth-century remodeling, so that there was no sign of it from the outside. Inside, however, the worn stone steps still spiraled in their old cylindrical casing, and the landings were big, hexagonal chambers of bleak, gray stone, sparsely decorated with gloomy fragments of Greek and Roman statues, and furnished with a few appropriately austere wooden chairs and benches.

Fleury had taken the family members to the landing on the ground floor, through which Gideon had to pass on the way to the cellar, and there they stood or sat, alone or in small, grim clumps, looking put-upon, annoyed, or bewildered. There didn't seem to be much in the way of grieving, Gideon noted. Not surprising, given his own brief acquaintance with Claude.

Ray (one of the bewildered ones) approached him tentatively. "It wasn't a heart attack, then? I mean, with the police here and all . . . ?"

Gideon led him a little away from the others; out of hearing. "It looks like the wine was poisoned, Ray."

When his friend seemed more bewildered yet, Gideon said gently: "It looks like he was murdered."

"As if," Ray murmured automatically, off in his own world, "in both instances. Or 'as though.'" He frowned dreamily while

140

Gideon's words made their way through. "Murdered," he finally said. "But why would anyone want to –" Guile was not one of Ray Schaefer's strong points, and Gideon saw his eyes widen at some unwelcome thought in the midst of his conventional response. "– to kill Claude?" he finished weakly and predictably.

Gideon studied him for a moment. "Ray, if you know something, you ought to mention it to Joly."

"Oh, I don't know anything," he said, dropping his eyes to stare at his toes. "Nothing important; nothing that could matter." He paused and considered. "It's just...well, there was some trouble during the war."

"The war? You mean the Second World War?" He looked at Ray with interest. There were an awful lot of World War II vibrations bouncing around the Manoir de Rochebonne.

"Well, yes, sure. In 1942." Ray wriggled and shifted. "Oh – it's just that Claude had a chance to warn some people that the Nazis were going to arrest them, but he didn't do it and the SS executed them. One of them was my Uncle Alain – my cousin, rather; Sophie's and René's brother – and I guess there were some hard feelings."

141

"Yeah, I can see how there just might be."

"Well, I mean *really* hard feelings." He hesitated, then gave his mild version of a what-the-hell shrug. "The thing is, Sophie absolutely adored him, and she's never forgiven Claude. They never even got Alain's body back from the Nazis."

"I see."

"And Mathilde was engaged to him before she married René. And –"

"Listen, Ray, if you're thinking about holding this back because you think it'll protect Sophie or Mathilde –"

"Me?" Ray said miserably and uttered an implausible laugh.

"– don't do it. Tell Joly what you know."

"But I don't – Gideon, it was almost fifty years ago."

"Ray, don't hide anything; it can wind up hurting whoever you're trying to help. Believe me."

"Whomever," Ray said, and retreated into a mute and uncharacteristic mumpishness.

10

With his slim, elegant fingers steepled before
his lips and his elbows on the plain metal
desk in Guillaume du Rocher's study, Joly
read aloud from the note lying on the blotter
in front of him. It had come from the bureau
in Mathilde's room.

"'I have reached a decision on a matter
of singular family importance,'" he read.
"'We will discuss it at Rochebonne on 16
March.' You have no idea what he was
referring to?"

Mathilde fingered the necklace of heavy
gold links at her throat. "I'm afraid I don't,"
she said flutily. "You do realize he sent the
same note to everyone."

Joly unsteepled his fingers. "You, your
husband, and your son flew here from
Germany – your husband giving up several
days of work – without knowing why you
were coming? Merely on your cousin's
instructions to do so?"

"Yes, Inspector. Others came from
considerably farther. There was nothing
strange about it. When business matters of

importance to the family arose, Guillaume would simply send for us, and we would come."

"But you arrived Sunday, the day before. You had many chances to talk with him. The subject never arose?"

"*Every*one arrived Sunday," Mathilde said patiently. "*Every*one had many chances to talk with him. I should be very surprised if any of them know any more than I do about it."

"Not even Claude Fougeray?"

Mathilde's upper lip curled very slightly. "Claude least of all."

"Claude and Guillaume were not on good terms?"

"I believe Claude Fougeray had not set foot in the manoir in over forty years."

"And why was that, madame?"

Ah, a hesitation, a fleeting shift in the focus of her eyes, a gathering of resources for equivocation.

"Oh, he had some sort of falling out with Guillaume – ages ago, in the forties. I never knew the details. I was quite small at the time."

You were seventeen at the time, madame, Joly said to himself, but he decided to let it go for the moment. There were more immediate matters.

144

"Madame du Rocher, can you think of anyone who might have wanted to kill Claude Fougeray?"

Mathilde's eyes lit up with happy malice. "Well, there *is* someone who comes to mind, but . . . no, it's ridiculous, and I'm not one to tell tales . . ." Her glittering fingers rose again to her necklace as she paused demurely.

With a small sigh Joly delivered what was expected of him. "Permit me to decide that, madame."

"Very well, Inspector," she said promptly. "I understand that most murders are committed by one's closest relatives. Isn't that so? Well, that's where I should look if I were you." She rested her topmost chin on the next one down and eyed him meaningfully.

Joly did not enjoy coaxing, and he was not very good at it. And he didn't care for Mathilde du Rocher.

"If you have something to say, please say it clearly," he said sharply.

She glared at him, as if deciding whether to punish him by holding back, but in the end her instincts won out, as he was sure they would. How often could opportunities like this fall into her lap?

"Leona Fougeray," she said flatly, letting him know that he had taken the joy out of it

145

for her, "is having an affair with a man in Rennes; an elderly, immensely wealthy widower who is eager to marry her. He is in his dotage, as I need hardly point out – or haven't you met Leona?"

"Briefly, madame. I should think she would find divorce a more delicate avenue than murder." Damn. Sarcasm wasn't going to get him very far. Did he used to be more tolerant of mean and boring people, or was it his imagination?

"More delicate, perhaps," Mathilde replied evenly, "but far slower, and with the disadvantage of requiring dealings with obstructive petty *fonctionnaires.*"

He looked at her with new respect.

"In addition," she said. "Monsieur Gris is a devout Catholic. He would never marry a divorced woman. But a widow – well, that's a different story."

"May I ask how you come to know this? Is it common knowledge?"

"In our family? I don't think so. *I* certainly have never talked about it; except with my husband, of course." She glanced challengingly at him, but there was nothing to read in his eyes. "However, I happen to have a friend in Rennes who keeps me informed. You can rest assured that it's true."

146

"I have no doubt of it." He stood up. "Thank you for your help." Joly was known among his colleagues for his abrupt interview terminations, which often shocked informants into giving more information than another twenty minutes of questioning might bring. He walked around the desk to the door of the study and opened it.

Mathilde watched him without getting up.

"Is there something more you wish to tell me?" he asked with a small smile.

"How," she replied, "is this to be paid for?"

The smile disappeared. "Pardon, madame?"

"Am I expected to maintain the people you've ordered to remain here? Food is not free, and I'm sure you're aware that it's going to be some time before the estate is formally settled –"

"I didn't *order* them to stay here, I asked for their cooperation," Joly said, drawing a finer point than he liked. "But I'm sure that if you speak with Monsieur Bonfante he'll arrange something."

He sincerely hoped so. A complaint from the commanding Mathilde du Rocher to Monsieur Picard, the public prosecutor, was not something he wanted to think about. And

147

now that he had a fresh murder on his hands, things would be getting even worse; there would be a *juge d'instruction* riding herd on him as well. Pity the poor French detective. Did John Lau appreciate how simple his life in the FBI was? Joly doubted it.

He bowed Mathilde out, went back to the desk and jotted a few more sparse notes on the lined pad on which he had put down a word or two from time to time. Then he turned to the list of names at the front, placed a check mark before Mathilde's, as he had already done before those of René, Beatrice, and the resolutely taciturn Marcel. With a finger to his lips he studied the remaining names, then got up again and called to Fleury.

"Will you have Madame Fougeray come down, please?"

Another formidable woman, Leona Fougeray. Not in Mathilde's way; Mathilde was imposing the way a cannonball is imposing – heavy, dense, solid. Leona had the formidability of an arrow, or better yet a poison dart – quick, thin, brittle, full of venom. Vivid as a magpie in a black-and-white striped suit with enormous square shoulders that made her neat, dark head look tiny, there was not even a pretense of the

148

mournful widow about her; no hint of tremor, no tastefully restrained anguish over the fact that her husband's body had been carted off to the police morgue barely half an hour before. In fact, she had spewed a stream of abuse each time Joly had mentioned Claude.

"No, how do I know what my husband meant?" she said, her Italian accent strong despite a quarter-century in France. "I haven't paid attention to him for years. Half the time he was raving from wine, the other half he was raving just from natural stupidity."

"Perhaps," Joly said, "but his remarks this time were very specific." He glanced at his notes. "At the reading of the will he claimed that Guillaume had planned a *new* will, did he not? He said that was the purpose of the council."

She turned down her mouth. "He said, he said. Pipe dreams. How could he know what Guillaume planned? You think Guillaume confided in him? If he did he'd be crazy. For forty years we never heard from him; not once. You know the first time I ever saw the great Guillaume? Last Sunday." She shrugged. "Not such a treat."

"Your husband also said – to you, before Guillaume died – that the others had a

149

surprise coming, that he knew some things they didn't know."

Her mobile eyebrows went up. "You know a lot."

"You don't know what he meant? You don't know the reason for the council?"

Again she grimaced. "I told you, they were pipe dreams. Who knows what Guillaume's letter meant? But my husband – oh, it was very clear to him. Guillaume, in his old age, was full of remorse for cutting him out of his will back in the Dark Ages. He was going to make us millionaires." she laughed curtly. "Look, is it all right if I smoke?"

With gratitude, Joly approved her request. He lit her American Virginia Slim, then a Gitane for himself, and took a cardboard paperclip container from a drawer to use as an ashtray.

"Madame Fougeray, just why was your husband cut out of the will?"

"Hey, how old do you think I am?" she said with more distress than she'd shown over the murder of her mate not two hours before. "I was born in 1934. Claude robbed me from the cradle. I didn't marry him until 1952. How could I know what happened at the *manoir*" – she said the word with derisive affectation – "right after the war?"

"Do you mean he never spoke of it to you?"

"Oh, he spoke of it to me all the time."

Joly wondered sourly if she were mimicking him. "And just what did he say?" he asked, his patience beginning to fray.

"Ah, just that the family turned Guillaume from him for no reason at all – only that they wanted to keep the estate among themselves."

"And do you believe that?"

"Of course I don't believe it," she said contemptuously. "There's more to it than that."

"But you don't know what."

"No, why should I care? I told him we shouldn't even come here. And now somebody's killed him for his greed." She nodded to herself, blew out a haze of smoke, and ground out her barely smoked cigarette in the box. "I thank them."

Joly, who had a keen sense of propriety, was offended. "Madame," he said stiffly, "whom can you think of that might have wanted to kill your husband?"

Leona threw back her dark, tight-skinned head and laughed. "If you want to know all the people in the world who hated his guts, you're going to have some long list." She stared at him hotly. "You can start with me."

Joly took a final pull from his own cigarette and put it neatly out. "Very well, madame," he said equably, "we'll start with you."

By 11:30, Joly was tired and out of humor. He was getting nowhere, and each person he interviewed seemed more irritating than the one before. This, he knew, came largely from fatigue, but there could be no question that Jules du Rocher was a singularly unappealing young man, fat, pouty, and given to simpering, gossiping, and other disagreeable behaviors.

Joly interrupted him while he was expounding his theory that Ben and Sophie Butts might well have poisoned Claude Fougeray out of fear that he would challenge Guillaume's will and deprive them of the valuable Rochebonne library. This thesis had been enthusiastically advanced following other helpful ideas pointing to the possible guilt of Claire, Ray, Leona, Marcel, and Beatrice.

"As to the reason Guillaume du Rocher called all of you together," Joly cut in wearily. "I suppose you have no idea."

"Oh, no," Jules replied, readily switching topics. "I know, all right."

Joly looked skeptically at him. "Oh?"

152

"He was going to sell the manoir to a hotel chain – Swiss, I think, or Swedish – and he wanted to tell the family about the arrangements."

"And how do you alone come to know this, monsieur?"

"He told me on the telephone last week. He said no one else was to know, so I didn't tell anyone."

Under Joly's steady gaze, his plump, smooth cheeks colored sullenly. "If you don't believe me, you can check the telephone records. Well, can't you?"

Joly nodded.

"And ask Beatrice. She put the call through. She *told* me he wanted to tell me what it was about. Go ahead and ask her, if you want to. Anyway, why should I –"

"All right," Joly said. "All right." Now that he thought about it, Bonfante, the attorney had told him that a Swiss hotel concern had been after Guillaume for years to sell the place. He sipped at the coffee Beatrice had brought him ten minutes before; lukewarm then, cold now. "Why only you and no one else?"

Jules shrugged. "It's the way he wanted it, that's all. He told me lots of things before anyone else knew about them. I was his favorite, you know."

153

Joly let this improbability pass. "And why were the Fougerays, who were not his favorites, invited to this particular family council after all this time?"

"That's just what *I'd* like to know," Jules said, and laughed as if he'd made a joke. He looked meaningfully at the small plate of butter cookies Beatrice had brought along with Joly's coffee.

"Please," Joly said, gesturing at the untouched cookies. "Now, these 'arrangements': What sort of arrangements?"

Jules stuffed two cookies into his mouth one after the other, tamping them in like tobacco into a pipe. He licked the residue luxuriously from his thumb and forefinger (leaving them glistening, Joly noted with displeasure) and sighed like a man who'd just gotten a desperately needed fix. "Something about investing the proceeds, or capitalizing the profits, or some such thing," he said, chewing. "I'm afraid I didn't listen very carefully. I don't have a mind for finance, you know. Poor Father will never understand it, but I live for the arts." He dropped his eyes modestly. "I'm a novelist. I'm working on a book now."

"Ah," said Joly, not caring to encourage this subject.

"It deals with the struggle of a banker's

154

son to actualize his spiritual potential in a world of crass materialism and greed," Jules volunteered.

Joly studied him for some sign of joking, but failed to find any. Jules' eyes, which the young man seemed able to keep from the remaining two cookies only with difficulty, fell on them with a look of open longing.

Joly pushed the plate towards him. "Help yourself, please. I'm not hungry. Now, is there anyone else you can think of who might have wanted to kill Claude?"

Jules crammed the first of the cookies into his mouth and got his damp fingers securely around the second before answering with a smirk. "Is there anyone who didn't?"

Twenty feet below Joly and Jules, in the ancient cellar, Gideon was working tranquilly in the warmth of the portable heater, using the ten-power magnifying lens he'd neglected to bring with him the day before. He had pulled the goose-necked lamp down to three or four inches above the tabletop and twisted the head so that the light shone horizontally across the bones, highlighting texture and irregularities. Hunched over them, the lens against his cheek and his face only a few inches from them, he slid each segment by, millimeter

155

by careful millimeter. Claude Fougeray and
Lucien Joly faded peacefully from his mind.

After an hour he finished his meticulous
scrutiny of the vertebrae and straightened
up with a grunt and a grimace as his own
vertebral column creaked back into the
unlikely S-shape that was its normal and
precarious human condition – the penalty,
as he told his students, for going recklessly
around on your hind legs when you have a
cantilevered spine begging for support at
each end.

So far he'd found nothing. No skeletal
oddities to make identification easier, no
signs of cause of death. Only the tiny, scoop-
shaped gouges of rodent incisors that had
been chewing away for most of the forty-odd
years the bones had been there. He stretched,
groaned luxuriously, rubbed the back of his
neck, and walked over to the work crew.

"Finding anything?" he asked Sergeant
Denis.

Denis shook his head with disgust. "But
if there's anything here we'll find it." His
eyes flashed with determination.

Gideon accepted him at his word. Denis
was obviously a man who took his work
seriously. He had been down there all
morning, closely overseeing the three-man
work crew – who proceeded nonetheless at

156

their own leisurely pace, ignoring with tolerant good humor the younger man's exhortations towards speed and care. So far, moving outward from the original trench, they had taken up the big paving stones from about a third of the cellar floor and were now digging through the compacted, sour-smelling earth to a depth of about three feet. He watched them for a few minutes, long enough for the crick in his neck to smooth out, and went back to the table to get on with his own work.

His slow, tedious examination of the hand and foot bones produced nothing but more mouse nibbles. The same for the sternum, clavicles, and scapulas. He was almost finished with the ribs, and had about given up hope, when he finally found something. It was on the fifth rib of the left side, midway along its length; a crease across the narrow top of the bone, about an eighth of an inch deep. It wasn't a normal indentation, and it wasn't an anomaly either, like a sternal foramen.

And it sure as hell hadn't been made by a mouse. Not scoop-shaped, this time, and not one of a parallel row of two or three. Just a single notch that didn't belong there, all by itself, with a distinctive V-shaped cross-section and edges of telltale sharpness and clarity.

A knife wound. And from the broad, wedgelike shape of the notch it had been a large knife with a blade that thickened markedly as it neared the haft. Single-edged too; otherwise it would have nicked the underside of the rib above it as well. Most likely a big kitchen utility knife or a chef's knife. Or maybe a wartime bayonet, given the time. And of course the breadth of the V made it clear that it had been no mere prick, but a deep, murderous thrust between the ribs.

Without doubt, it would have punctured the left lung, and then...He chewed thoughtfully on his cheek. Now exactly where the hell would a knife slipped in over the middle of the fifth rib go? It was hard to visualize; not as obvious as it seemed. The middle of a rib is not in the middle of the chest, but far around to the side; closer in fact to the back of the body than the front.

With the fingers of his right hand Gideon found the angle of Louis, the easily palpable bump on the upper segment of the sternum. That was where the second rib attached, and from there he counted downward to the fifth. Then he worked his way slowly along it,

158

probing with some difficulty through the thick pectoralis muscle that covered it.

In the far corner – the very far corner, as far from the moldering remains on the table as they could get – the workmen were sitting on the floor, leaning comfortably against the wall and watching him. Freed from the eagle-eye of young Sergeant Denis, who had gone off to lunch, they had produced a meal of their own: tumblers of red wine from a plastic, screw-top liter-bottle, an aromatic, crumbly goat cheese, and hunks of bread torn from a couple of baguettes. For the moment, however, they had suspended conversation and even swallowing to watch with rapt gazes as the American fingered his way so engrossedly across his own chest.

Gideon nodded at them and groped onward. The middle of the rib was higher than he'd remembered – it was easy to forget how sharply the ribs curved upward – front to back – and directly under the arm. Deep in the armpit, in fact. Seemingly a hard place to reach with a knife, but not, he had learned in these last few days, an uncommon site for a stab wound. The victim throws up his hand to ward off a thrust or a blow, the delicate, vulnerable axilla is left unprotected, and the knife strikes home. There was almost no other way to open the armpit to attack. That meant, of course, that there had been a struggle involved here, or at least that the victim had tried to fend off his attacker.

He folded a piece of paper and inserted the sharply creased edge into the cut in the bone. Judging from the downward, slightly forward angle, the blade would have entered at the tangle of nerves and veins that made up the brachial plexus and then sliced through the thin, ineffective barriers of the serratus anterior and intercostal muscles, nicking the rib on the way. Then into the left lung and through the tough pericardium.

And finally, inescapably, deep into the pulsing, muscular sac that drove the entire circulatory system: the left ventricle of the heart. Death, certain and immediate.

He turned again to the brown rib on the table and grazed his thumb delicately along it. Three inches farther forward, on the same surface, there was something else: a tiny burr, so inconspicuous he'd missed it before. Once more he leaned over the bone with the magnifying glass.

"So? Is it as fascinating as all that?"

Gideon started. Absorbed, he had forgotten that lunchtime had come and gone, forgotten to be repulsed by the grisly scenario he was constructing, forgotten pretty much where he was, and he hadn't noticed Joly come downstairs, walk across the room, and stand for some time observing him. Looking up, he was startled to see that Denis had returned too, and the workmen were busy digging again.

Joly's head was tilted slightly back as usual, the better to stare down his nose.

"Well, I've been able to come up with a little," Gideon said.

"Ah? Joly's raised eyebrow was a terse expression of skepticism. Restrained, polite, even tolerant, but skepticism all the same.

"He was murdered –"

The smallest of smiles from Joly. "Ah," he said again, and took off his glasses to polish them with a crisply folded handkerchief.

"Stabbed to death," Gideon said. "By a right-handed assailant. During a struggle." He hesitated, then finished up: "With a kitchen knife," he said confidently. In for a dime, in for a dollar.

Joly slowly refolded his handkerchief, as if it were very important that it be done along the original crease, and put it back in his pocket. "All this from a single rib?"

"That's right, Inspector." Well, more or less. Some of it was a little on the speculative side, but Joly's air of amused superiority was

161

getting under his skin a little, and he thought a show of strength was called for.

Joly lit a cigarette and sucked in a long pull, studying him all the while. "Perhaps we might go over it one point at a time?" he asked nasally, while ropes of blue smoke poured from his nostrils. "Stabbed, you say. The rib shows some sort of scratch?"

Gideon showed him the nick. Joly looked at it for a long time, using the magnifying lens. Unlike Gideon, he didn't hunch over it, but stood rigidly erect, head lifted, and gazed down his nose at it as he did at all things. Then he went on to examine the rest of the rib and some of the other bones as well. The cigarette was a third of the way burned down before he said anything.

"I see many nicks and cuts . . ."

"Mice."

Joly looked up at him in that long, slow way Jack Benny used to eye Rochester or Phil Harris after they'd nailed him with a zinger. Only the inspector had more nose to stare down, which made it all the more effective. "All of them? Every single one but this one alone?"

"That's right."

"But this one alone is from a knife and nothing else."

Gideon explained about the U-shaped
162

incisors of rodents and the V-shaped cross-section of knives.

Joly nodded economically, listening with his head tilted to one side, and looked through the lens again. He touched the gouge with a cleanly manicured thumbnail. "Why not another animal? A dog that might have got at the bones, perhaps, or a cat? Or," he said with a smile, "do they too have scoop-shaped incisors?"

"No, cone-shaped. Or rather the canines are cone-shaped, and since carnivores bite with their canines, they leave a set of cone-shaped holes. Ragged ones, very recognizable. No, this is definitely from a knife. Look." He handed the bone to Joly. "Run your finger along the back of the cut – that is, the part on the inside of the rib. Feel the roughness?"

Joly did as instructed and nodded.

"When a knife – or an axe – cuts through bone," Gideon said, "it drives the compact bone before it so that there's some chipping at the exit. It's liked sawing through a block of wood; you get splintering at the back."

Joly fingered the cut again. "All right, let's say that it was a knife or other sharp instrument –"

"A knife, Gideon said, then added: "I

163

think." He was beginning to feel a little sorry for the inspector and a little over-pontifical.

Joly breathed in, then out. "And not an axe, for example? Didn't you say a moment ago it would affect the bone the same way?"

"Sure, but there's no way anything as gross as an axe could have chipped just the top of one rib; there'd be other damage."

Joly conceded. "Yes, you're right," he said, and blew out smoke. He ran his long-fingered hand lightly across the few fine, short hairs on the top of his head. In his own way he was enjoying himself, Gideon realized, even if he hadn't won a round so far. After a morning of evasive answers from reluctant interviewees, this string of direct and unconditional responses was probably refreshing.

"Your conclusions are quite helpful and interesting, Dr. Oliver," he said, not yet willing to throw in the towel, "but I should tell you that I still have a few reservations about them."

That makes two of us, Gideon thought, but he wasn't quite ready to admit it yet.

Joly continued: "For example: I haven't heard you suggest that there is anything that tells us exactly *when* the wound was caused."

164

"No, there's no way to know, but why should that make any difference?"

"Because," Joly said mildly, "if it was made by the pick of one of the workmen who came upon it yesterday, there would be some question about its being the cause of death. No?"

"Oh, I see what you mean. Well, actually, we *can* say for sure –"

With a sigh the policeman interrupted him. "No, let me guess. No doubt, bones that have lain in the ground for some time become discolored, as these have done. And a cut that was made yesterday would show as fresh white against the brown. Am I correct?"

"You are," Gideon smiled, not unhappy to have Joly finally score a point, "and there's something else too." He set the rib on the table directly in the path of the slanting light and found the little burr with his finger. Then he handed Joly the lens. "Look there."

Joly looked, his eyes narrowed against the cigarette smoke. "It appears to be an imperfection of some sort...a little curlicue..."

"A curlicue of bone; that's just what it is. Live bone responds to a knife a lot like wood, as I said, so if you carve a thin slice

165

off it, the slice will curl away, like a shaving."

"And dead bone is different?"

"Right. You couldn't carve a curling slice off that rib *now* any more than you could off a piece of porcelain. What you're looking at is a place where the blade scraped against the bone when it was living."

Joly straightened up and put down the lens. "But this is in a different place. What does it have to do with the other cut?"

"Oh, I think we can pretty safely assume it was also made at the time of death – there's been no healing of either cut – and that it happened when the knife was pulled back out. The direction and angle of the slice suggest that the knife was probably twisted a little, and –"

" *'Probably'?* " Joly pounced with dry elation on the word and leveled the two fingers in which he held his cigarette at Gideon. " *'Suggest'? 'Safely assume'?* Can you mean you actually admit to some uncertainty? Fallibility, even?"

Gideon laughed. "No, I just didn't want to seem cocksure."

Joly looked at him, then emitted what was for him a full-throated laugh: a series of four staccato barks. He dropped his cigarette on the stone paving and ground it out with his

166

heel. "There's a restaurant you might enjoy in Dinan. What do you say to lunch?"

11

After the hours in the dingy cellar, Dinan was a welcome change, an old, pretty town surrounded by ancient stone walls almost hidden by gnarled ivy and bright green lichens, and dominated at one end by the handsome, brooding keep of its medieval castle. The town center was straight out of the fifteenth century, all cool, clean, gray-brown stone. The streets were cobbled with it, the ramparts and the crooked, cramped old houses made from big blocks of it. No wood, no stucco, no brick; only stone. But there were enough perky little trees in planters, enough minuscule gardens, enough tiny shops and restaurants to make it all cozy and appealing in a smaller-than-lifesize way, a Disney World rendering MiddleAgesLand.

Joly parked the car outside the walls, along the Promenade des Petits-Fosses, and they walked through the old portal, then down twisting alleys, to the Grill-

Room Duguesclin just off the Place du Champ-Clos.

"You'll like it, I think," Joly said. "Traditional Breton cooking, though it's run by a family of Iranians, strangely enough."

The sign outside said *"Grillades sur Feu de Bois,"* and the grill turned out to be a huge, open fireplace of stone that was the centerpiece of the plain dining room, with a lively fire throwing out a campfire aroma that had Gideon salivating before the door closed behind him. On a wide, blackened grate set over the fire, portions of meat and fish sizzled under the teeth-flashing, showy supervision of two lean, brown young men. A radio on the counter behind them softly played Simon and Garfunkel.

"No," Gideon said, mostly to himself, as they sat at a pleasingly rough and heavy wooden table, "I don't think so."

"I beg your pardon?"

"Not Iranians. They're dolichocephalic, all right, but only moderately so, with pretty delicate cranial morphology. And the *ossa nasalia* are practically flat, which should settle it."

"Why, yes," said Joly, "that should certainly settle it."

"Moroccans, maybe, or more likely Algerians."

168

"And to think," Joly said, "that yesterday a performance like that would have made me smile."

"You're smiling now." Not that it was easy to tell, but by this time Gideon could recognize the slight compression of the lips combined with the barely visible upturning of their corners as a Joly smile. The cool, constantly assessing eyes hardly came into it.

"Ah," Joly said, "but it's a different sort of smile. I must confess that even this morning my first reaction to your findings was that you were –" He shrugged. "–well, wishfully extending the implications to be made from rather scant data – a sort of artistic exuberance, quite understandable under the circumstances.

Gideon laughed. "Inspector, where did you learn your English?"

Joly bowed his head stiffly, accepting it for the compliment it was.

Over a first course of *palourdes* – steamed clams on the half shell, drenched with garlic butter – Gideon explained the rest of his findings. Joly poked single-mindedly away at his clams but nodded with appreciation from time to time.

"Some of it *was* artistic exuberance," Gideon admitted. "I *think* it was a kitchen knife, but I wouldn't want to bet my life on it. And as for the murderer being right-handed –"

"Ah, yes. The angle of the notch on the rib, I suppose? It suggested that the thrust was delivered from in front of the victim, and since it pierced his left side . . ."

"Right. I mean, correct."

Joly dabbed at his lips with a napkin and sipped from a glass of Muscadet. "Well, I would consider that a fairly reasonable inference, at least until other evidence presents itself." Which was about how Gideon felt about it too, now that his earlier flush of belligerence had passed.

When the main course came, the conversation lapsed while they dug in. Joly was an enthusiastic eater, and if his grilled trout was as good as Gideon's flame-charred fresh sardines there was reason for his enthusiasm. By the time the cheese plate was brought, Joly had had a second glass of wine and was loose to the point of actually leaning against the back of his chair. A good time, Gideon thought, to find out what had been going on upstairs while he'd been in the cellar.

"How'd your investigation go this morning?"

Joly nodded silently, as if that were an

answer, and went on trying to cut his way through a rocklike wedge of Cantal.

"Making progress?"

Shrug. Noncommittal grunt.

"Not solved yet, I take it?"

"Not yet." Coherent speech this time. A distinct improvement.

"Suspects?"

"Oh, yes."

"Well, it certainly is fascinating getting all this information right from the horse's mouth." He bit into a roll spread with soft, tart Banon.

Joly smiled. "Everyone in the manoir is a legitimate suspect." He hesitated, then apparently decided to trust Gideon after all. "The wine carafe was placed on the sideboard by Marcel at about ten o'clock last night, when Claude took the previous one up to his room. Between then and nine o'clock in the morning, everyone had ample opportunity to drop a few hundred milligrams of cyanide into it. With or without fingerprints."

"So much for opportunity. Any leads on *why* he was killed?"

Joly had succeeded in separating a hard crescent of cheese from the wedge and using his fork to place it on his bread. He looked up at Gideon without raising his head, so

171

that his eyebrows were lifted and his forehead wrinkled. Unexpectedly, he burst into his machine-gun laugh; a real one, the kind in which his eyes participated.

"In my long and distinguished career, Dr. Oliver, I have rarely seen so many credible motives." He put down his fork and leaned forward. "In less than a week, Claude Fougeray has antagonized everyone within reach." He began to count on his fingers. "He held Jules du Rocher up to ridicule as a braying and cowardly fool, which he no doubt is; he brought the docile Marcel Lupis to white-faced and violent rage by insulting Madame Lupis; he disparaged Ben Butts' honor; he – Now, what have I forgotten?" His right forefinger paused over the fourth finger of his left hand and came down. "Oh, of course he's devoted a lifetime to bullying and mortifying his wife and daughter. And Leona Fougeray, who makes no bones about her delight that he's dead, is not a woman I would care to provoke."

Joly gave up counting and slowly twirled his wineglass by the stem, staring at the dregs. "Ah, and in what must have been a memorable scene at the reading of Guillaume's will, he implied strongly that he would challenge it; this in front of a roomful of people who benefited substantially from its provisions."

Gideon listened with increasing respect as Joly went on to elaborate. A lot had been uncovered in a very few hours. "Are people usually this forthcoming?" he asked.

"About each other, yes," Joly smiled. "Especially about their relatives. If it's damning evidence you want, I often say, talk to your suspect's family."

Gideon smiled too. It sounded like something Ben's Uncle Beau Will'm might say.

Joly continued to rotate his glass thoughtfully, then drained the little left in it. "But you know, I can't say that I put much faith in Claude's being murdered as revenge for offended dignity or impugned honor. Or even to avoid the bother of divorce. It simply doesn't happen very often."

"Which leaves the will. You think somebody killed him to keep him from contesting it?"

Joly squirmed a little. He didn't like being pinned down. "Not exactly. The possibility of a successful challenge was small to the point of absurdity. There were simply no grounds. The lawyer Bonfante carefully explained that to everyone after the reading. Why should someone risk murder in such a case?"

173

"What did you mean, 'not exactly'?" He poured himself and Joly some wine from the half-bottle of new Beaujolais they'd ordered to go with the cheese; the policeman held up his hand when the glass was a quarter full.

"Well, I think there's something else going on beneath the surface – something that they haven't been so forthcoming about. Claude Fougeray, it seems, declared loudly and at every opportunity that the reason Guillaume had called them all together was to announce a *new* will he was going to prepare; presumably with Claude himself as the major beneficiary."

"Do you think it might be true?"

The inspector swirled the wine in his glass thoughtfully. "Not really. So far I've found nothing to suggest it was anything more than wishful thinking. And Bonfante says Guillaume hadn't mentioned his will in years."

"But you're not completely sure about it?"

"I wonder about it, yes."

"You think the attorney might be lying?"

"Georges Bonfante? No, no, I've known him for years. And if you're thinking he himself might make an interesting suspect, I'm afraid he won't. He hasn't been near the manoir since the reading. Neither have any

174

other outsiders, I might add. So our suspects, if not our motives, are finite and well-defined. A nice, old-fashioned mystery."

Gideon tried some of the ash-impregnated Montrachet on a piece of roll, scraping off most of the grit and doing his best not to think about the horrifying lesions he'd seen in the teeth of prehistoric peoples who'd consumed ash with their food as a matter of course. But taking care of your teeth was an everyday concern. How often did you meet up with a really first-rate Montrachet?

"What *was* the reason Guillaume got them all together?" he asked.

"Ah, your mind runs like mine," Joly said; clearly a compliment. "According to Jules it was to discuss the selling of the manoir to a hotel chain."

"According to Jules?"

"Jules was the only one he told, apparently. He was the old man's great favorite, it appears; they were very close."

"Jules?" Gideon said with surprise, remembering the soft young man who had slavered over the thought of severed heads and hands.

Joly smiled wryly at his expression. "Yes, it seems an inexplicable lapse in judgment
175

by a man otherwise well known for his discernment. How is that Montrachet?"

"It's delicious, but I hope your teeth have thick enamel."

He offered the wine bottle again but Joly declined. "Thank you, no. I've already had too much. I generally limit myself to a single glass at lunch."

"Look, Inspector," Gideon said, pouring a little for himself, "I'm confused. Let's say Guillaume *had* been planning a new will –"

"I don't think it's likely. Claude was given to deluding himself."

"But let's say he had, and the estate was going to go to Claude instead of the others . . . Well, Guillaume died five days ago, right? Without making a new will. It was over and done; what connection could there be to Claude's murder?"

Joly swallowed a small piece of bread and cheese and dabbed at the corner of his mouth with a napkin. "Yes, that's true."

"Well –" Gideon put down his glass. "Hey, are you saying that you think there was something fishy about Guillaume's death after all?"

This was dismissed with a wave of the hand and a sour expression. "I hope that wasn't a pun. Why do you persist in

176

returning to this? What reason would anyone have to kill Guillaume?"

"For the money in the will," Gideon said. "A lot of people must have been champing at the bit to get their hands on their shares."

"Surely they could wait another year or so."

"Another year?"

"You didn't know? That's all he was given to live by Dr. Loti, and that was some months ago."

Gideon very nearly blurted: "I'm sorry to hear that," which would have been pretty peculiar under the circumstances. "No," he said instead, "I didn't know."

"Well, it's common knowledge. Dr. Loti's a good physician, but he isn't the man to have if you want to keep secrets. Now, does that satisfy you?"

"I suppose so," Gideon said doubtfully. But with or without a plausible motive, Guillaume's death just didn't sit right. Not that he expected to convince Joly.

" 'I suppose so,' " Joly repeated with a smile. "A man who doesn't give up easily. Still you're right in a way. There is, as you say, something fishy here somewhere; something they know but they're not telling me, something not quite..." He searched for a word and came up, surprisingly, with:

"...kosher. Something in the past, I think. I've begun to wonder if it might not have something to do with the SS man's murder."

"Maybe, but – I hate to keep bringing this up, but that isn't Helmut Kassel down there with the notch in his rib."

"Perhaps not, perhaps not." Joly nodded abstractedly; his attention was wandering. "Do you mind if we don't stay for coffee? I think I should be getting back."

Gideon lifted his wine to finish it, but for the second time he checked it in midair and put it back on the table. "Something in the past, did you say? Inspector, didn't anyone tell you about Alain du Rocher? About how Claude was responsible for his murder?"

Joly's expression made it amply clear that nobody had. Head down, he listened, scowling, to Gideon's explanation, not pleased that the information had failed to surface during his interviews. And also, Gideon thought, not too thrilled about having to get it from the Skeleton Detective of America.

"Perhaps I'll have a little more wine after all," he said when he'd heard it all. He poured about a tablespoonful into his glass, rolled it around the bottom, and drank it

178

grimly down. "Strange that no one should think of mentioning it to me."

"Well, maybe they just wanted to keep an old family scandal quiet. Maybe they forgot about it, or didn't see any connection."

Joly tilted his head back and barked. "Yes, and maybe oysters grow on trees."

They had agreed to pay for their own lunches, and Joly, who thought he might have been overcharged, carefully compared his bill to the prices written on a blackboard behind the grill. But he had trouble reading the posted prices, tilting his head up, then down, and finally raising his glasses slightly and peering along his nose at the chalkboard.

"I have had these damned bifocal lenses for a week," he muttered, "and I'm no more used to them than on the first day. I still can't see anything, except through the bottoms. It's very hard on the neck. May you never have to wear them, Dr. Oliver."

Gideon's cheeks burned suddenly. And well he deserved to blush. All those smug and uncharitable observations about Joly's haughty posture and down-the-nose stare, and it had turned out to be a matter of new bifocals, not stiff-necked pomposity at all. Or only a little. Even the inspector's wide, clean upper lip suddenly looked more human, less invulnerable, than before.

"Inspector," Gideon said, "do you suppose we know each other well enough for you to call me by my first name? It's Gideon."

"Oh," Joly said, groping through his coin purse, "yes, of course. Mine, ahum, is Lucien."

Gideon had the impression it was something he hadn't told many people.

When they got back to the manoir they were met by an excited Sergeant Denis, who herded them breathlessly into the cellar. Another find had been unearthed, this one not wrapped in a package, but simply dumped into the ground about ten feet from the first; nine pieces in all, soiled and discolored. Not bones this time, but articles of military dress.

A pair of cracked, black boots with straps over the insteps; a leather, Sam Browne-style belt, also black, with a disk-shaped buckle; a shoulder cord of braided metal; some tarnished medals and military insignia; and a peaked, black cap. And on the cap, darkened by time but still glinting malevolently after all these years, the SS Death's Head, lovingly molded in dull white metal.

Gideon and Joly looked at each other over the head of the thrilled and garrulous Denis.

"Son of a gun," Gideon said.

"*Voilà,*" said Joly.

12

"So, you were wrong," John said philosophically. "It's not like it never happened before, you know."

"I'm not wrong," Gideon maintained. "I don't make that kind of mistake with skeletal material; you know that."

"What about those bones they found scattered along the Massachusetts Turnpike near, where was it, Stockbridge? Remember? You were sure as hell wrong there."

"True, but that was an understandable mistake, a minor misinterpretation."

John stopped walking and stared at him in mock incredulity; or perhaps it was outright incredulity. "Telling us the bones belonged to a five-to-seven-year-old when the guy was really thirty-two is a minor misinterpretation?"

"Well, Jesus Christ, John, the guy turned
181

out to have cleidocranial dyostosis. You know how rare that is?"

"I don't even know *what* it is."

"His ossification schedule was all screwed up. How was I supposed to know that? All I had to go on were a couple of maxillary bones and a clavicle –"

John played an imaginary violin.

"Come on, John, that was just my preliminary report, anyway. When they found the rest of the post-cranial skeleton I came up with the right age, didn't I? Well, didn't I? I practically identified the guy for you."

"That's true," John admitted, and they began walking again. "But you don't have very much to go on down in the cellar either. Remember, you were the one who said it was just a gut feeling. Maybe this Kassel was a huge guy with little hands and feet. Maybe he had polio as a kid and his spinal column shrunk up or something. Isn't that possible? Couldn't you be wrong about his size?"

"No," Gideon said. He shook his head back and forth as they continued their slow pace. "Absolutely not. Uh-uh. Nope."

"Well, as long as you keep an open mind." John's twinkly child's laugh burbled out and Gideon laughed too.

They had been walking around the pond

behind the manoir for almost an hour, along the gravel path cut into the terraced bank. The early March twilight had come while Gideon had filled John in on the day's events, and above them, on a knoll, the great stone building loomed, silhouetted against what was left of the light, its complex, steeply pitched roof angles and tall stone chimneys as featureless, black, and sharp as paper cutouts. In the rear courtyard, a few stunted, gnarled oak trees, still bare, were outlined against the empty, rose-gray sky.

In all, Gideon mused, downright sinister-looking; a fine setting for skeletons in the cellar and murders in the drawing room. Or the salon, as they called it.

"Let's go around one more time," John said. "I've got some ideas about Fougeray's murder." They went a few steps in silence while he arranged his thoughts. "From what you said, Joly's got more motives than he knows what to do with."

"Right. Everything from Alain's death almost fifty years ago right up through some muddy insinuations Claude tossed around when they read the will. Plus the fact that he antagonized everybody in the place from the first day he got here. Joly hardly knows where to start."

"Well, I think maybe I do. The first thing

he needs to do is find out when the murder was planned. If the killer didn't set it up until this week, then it might be on account of something new. But if it got planned *before* this family council ever started, then obviously Claude got killed on account of something that happened before."

"I suppose Joly'd agree with you, but how is he supposed to figure out when it was planned?"

"By finding out when the cyanide got bought."

"And how –"

"How is he supposed to find that out? By using those little gray cells these French detectives are supposed to have so many of."

"Belgian, not French. Poirot was Belgian."

"Big deal; same thing. Look: If the murder was planned ahead of time, then the killer could have gotten hold of the cyanide ahead of time. But if it got planned since this family meeting started, then he had to get it in the last few days, right?"

"I suppose so," Gideon said, his interest deepening. When John started sounding like a cop he was generally on to something.

"What do you mean, you suppose? People don't go around with a vial of cyanide on

184

them in case they just happen to run into somebody they'd like to bump off. They get it for a reason. So all Joly has to do is find out if this particular cyanide got bought before this week or not. If it got bought before, then the murder was *planned* before; it has to be one of the *old* motives, not a new one, and nothing Claude did or said after he got here had anything to do with it."

"Of course," Gideon said after a moment. "You're right."

"Sure I'm right. What are you sounding so amazed about?"

"I'm not amazed. I'm just wondering how Joly would go about figuring out when the cyanide got bought."

"For starters he could check with the pharmacies and chemical supply outfits in the area to see if any's been bought in the last week."

"Would a chemical supply place keep a list of the people who buy cyanide?"

"In France, who knows? Back home, it's different from state to state. In a lot of places the buyer has to sign a 'poison book.' But even if they don't do that here, how much of a job could it be to check it out? You're only talking about a radius of maybe fifty miles with no big cities in it, and how many people buy cyanide?"

"I don't know. What's it used for aside from murder?"

"Poisoning rats and moles; that kind of thing – but not much any more, at least in the States. Also, I think they use it in metallurgy; you know, silver plating. I don't know for what else. Not much."

Gideon nodded. "Why fifty miles? Why not a hundred, or five hundred?"

"Just a rough figure. I'm guessing whoever did it wouldn't want to disappear from sight for too long while he bought the stuff, just in case it made him look suspicious later on, and fifty miles is about as far as you could drive and still get back inside of two or three hours."

"Yeah, I guess . . ." Gideon stopped John with a hand on his forearm. "John, nobody drove anywhere. There wasn't a car available. Guillaume's the only one here, and it's still at Mont St. Michel."

"Is that right?" John's face was masked by the dusk now, but Gideon heard the quickening in his voice. "That makes it a whole lot easier. You'd just have to check in these little towns right around here."

"No, someone might have gotten a taxi to Dinan and bought it there or even taken a train from there to somewhere else."

"Sure, but how many taxis could there be

186

around here, and how many passengers could they get? This is the boonies, Doc. It'd be a snap to check out. Hey, you think Joly's thought about all this?"

"Probably," Gideon said as they began walking toward the manoir again. "He seems pretty sharp to me."

"Yeah, but you never know. It's funny how little things can get by you. You think I ought to mention it to him?"

"Sure," Gideon said. "He really likes it when you tell him how to do his job."

Joly had been faintly irritated to begin with, having been interrupted while interviewing Sophie Butts in the study, and he listened to John with his head bent sharply down, his back poker-straight, impatiently jiggling his toe. But in the end he was appreciative.

"Thank you," he said politely. "Of course I've already begun canvassing local suppliers of cyanide, but I must admit that I hadn't thought of all this."

"You would have," John said magnanimously. "You've just been up to your ears."

"Very true. Oh, and you'll both be interested to know that Claude's death by cyanide poisoning has been confirmed. Potassium cyanide, in solution in the wine.

187

The level in his blood was nearly five percent; it's a wonder he lived as long as he did." He bowed lightly in Gideon's direction. "It might well have gone undetected, Dr. Oliver – er, Gideon. Cyanide poisoning is easy to miss unless one is looking for it. It's a good choice for murder, as a matter of fact."

"Well, thanks, uh, Lucien; there was that bitter-almond smell. Pretty hard to miss."

When Joly had gone back into the study, John turned slowly to Gideon.

"*'Lucien'*?" he said wonderingly. "*'Gideon'*? What's going on?"

"You just have to know how to handle him, John."

"Maybe," he said, nodding. "But you know, I think the guy's finally starting to appreciate us."

On their way out they found Ray moping aimlessly around the courtyard, kicking at pebbles. It seemed as good a time as any to bring up something that Gideon had been wanting to ask him.

"Ray," he said without preface, "what was Guillaume doing out in Mont St. Michel Bay when he died?"

"Guillaume?" Ray's sandy eyebrows rose. "Looking for shells. I thought you knew."

"I heard, but how do you *know* that's what he was doing?"

"He told us – the night before, at dinner. He said we'd have our meeting the next day, but it'd have to wait until the afternoon. It was going to be the first good day for collecting since October, and he was going to be out in the bay all morning. Why do you ask?"

"Look," Gideon said, "does it make sense to you that he'd let the tide catch him by surprise? Would a guy as clear-headed and systematic as that go out there without checking the tide table?"

Ray frowned. "I suppose it *is* a little surprising, but – well, you know, everybody says he's been getting absentminded; he's almost eighty. I mean he was."

"Did he seem to be getting absentminded to you?"

"I don't know. Maybe a little, but he was as intimidating as ever; I can tell you that." He peered worriedly up into Gideon's eyes, then John's, then Gideon's again. "Gideon, you're making this sound awfully ... sinister. Why, you're saying that Guillaume's death wasn't an accident either, aren't you?"

"I don't know, Ray," Gideon said kindly. "The police don't find anything suspicious in it, if that makes you feel better."

189

Ray sighed. "This is all extremely traumatic."

Gideon nodded sympathetically. Not as traumatic as it was going to get, an uneasy hunch told him.

"Doc," John said as Gideon drove slowly between the gateposts and swung the rented Cortina to the right, the headlights picking out the trunks of the roadside plane trees like twin rows of colorless concrete pillars, "you're doing it again."

"Doing what?" Gideon wondered blamelessly.

"Sticking your nose into something that isn't your business."

"Me? Surely not."

"Look, if you think there's something funny about Guillaume's death, just tell Joly. Don't run your own private investigation."

"I already told him. He doesn't agree."

"But you know a little more now. Maybe –"

"John, no offense, but I'll take care of this myself. Don't worry, when and if I have something to tell Joly, I'll tell him. I'm not doing this to get in his way, you know."

"I know. You're doing it to find an excuse to avoid going to any more lectures on sarcosaprophagous bugs. Jesus, I didn't

190

know I could say it." He laughed and stretched. "Hey, tomorrow's Sunday. No school. We got any plans?"

"Nothing firm. We were going to spend some time in St. Malo – the old part: walk the ramparts, see Chateaubriand's tomb, Jacques Cartier's tomb . . ."

"Tombs," John grumbled. "Great. Sounds like your kind of holiday."

"All right, what do you say if between tombs we drop in on Dr. Loti? He lives in St. Malo."

"Who's Dr. Loti?"

"He's the one who came out to look at Claude's body. He was also Guillaume's doctor, and I thought I might ask him a question or two. Want to come along?"

"What happened to taking care of this by yourself?"

"I didn't say I couldn't use a little moral support from my friends. Besides, I know you; you think there's something weird going on too."

John considered the idea for some seconds. "To tell the truth, Doc, I don't. But what are friends for?"

The next morning, as they breakfasted in the dining room of the Hôtel Terminus, a *commissaire* of police from one of the
191

southern provinces came up to shake hands with them.

"I'm very sorry," he said to Gideon in correct but tentative English. "I cannot stay for the second week. I have enjoyed the program very much."

"Problems back home?" John asked, policeman to policeman.

"Letter-bombs," he replied gravely. "Two last week to local politicians."

"Anyone killed?"

"Both recipients were killed. And two bystanders injured. It's terrible; like a plague. Like guns in America. France is afflicted with it."

"I didn't know that," Gideon said.

"Oh, yes. Everywhere: Paris, Marseilles, even St. Malo. These damned..." His pale, lined face flushed angrily, then set. He bowed and left.

Gideon drank the last of his coffee. "Whose turn?"

"Yours," John said, and slid the bill to him.

Gideon signed it, put down his room number, and the two of them walked out to the hotel lobby.

"Letter-bombs suck," John said.

"I'm not too keen on them myself."

"No, I mean there are some kinds of killers

you can almost sympathize with. But shredding a guy's face through the mail, when you can be a thousand miles away ... not giving a damn if someone else opens it up and gets his eyes blown out or his hand torn off – you just spend another ten bucks for a couple of ounces of commercial explosive and a cheap detonator, pack it in a manila envelope, and send off another one. Ah, it sucks."

"John, I agree with you. You don't have to get graphic."

When they stopped at Reception to leave their keys, the man at the desk pulled a thick, plain manila envelope out of a rack behind him. It was heavily stamped, but there was no return address. Just "M. Oliver, Hôtel Terminus, 20, rue Nationale, 35400 St. Malo," penciled on the front.

Gideon and John glanced at each other and laughed with a marked lack of conviction.

"Uh, when did it come?" Gideon asked. "I wasn't expecting anything."

"It was in this morning's mail. An express delivery. Is something wrong?"

"Wrong?" Gideon said. "No, of course not." He lifted the envelope – gingerly – and carried it carefully from the desk, resting it on both palms like an unstable soufflé. It was

193

stiff and heavy, about a quarter of an inch thick.

"John," he said, walking very slowly and keeping his eyes on the envelope, "am I being overly paranoid?"

"I don't know about 'overly,' but, yeah, I'd say you're being paranoid. Who'd want to kill you?"

"That's what Ray said about Claude Fougeray," Gideon muttered.

"Come on, you're just spooked because of what that French cop said. Let's get out of here. We're supposed to be in that doctor's office in twenty minutes."

"No, wait up a minute." The bar, which extended into the lobby, wasn't open yet. Gideon set the envelope face-up on one of the round, plastic-topped tables and looked at it. John was right; if not for that brief discussion with the *commissaire*, he would already have torn it open and been on his way to St. Malo. All the same . . .

"John, let's say I thought this thing might be a bomb –"

"For the sake of argument, you mean."

"Right. Is there any way I could check it out, or would I just have to put it in the bathtub and turn on the water? Or call the police?"

"No, there's a kind of commonsense

standard routine you go through, if it makes you feel any better. You look at the point of origin and the sender. If they're unusual –"

"It doesn't say who the sender was. The point of origin's Marseilles, according to the postmark." He frowned at John. "Marseilles?"

"Okay, so who in Marseilles would want to send you a letter-bomb?"

"Nobody. Nobody in Marseilles would want to send me anything. I don't know anyone in Marseilles."

"Mm," said John. "Well, moving right along, you check the handwriting on the address. If it looks disguised –"

"Block letters," Gideon said grimly.

John laughed. "Okay, block letters. Boy, you really think someone's trying to blow you up, don't you? Well, you could check it for flex."

"Flex?"

"You bend it – but only a little. A lot of these things have spring tension mechanisms in them, and they feel kind of springy. Sometimes you can even hear the metal creak."

Gideon delicately picked up the envelope by two corners, lifted it to the level of his ears, and very gently –

"Hey!" John shouted. "Go bend that

thing somewhere else! What are you trying to do?"

Gideon put it back down and gave John what he thought was a first-class imitation of Inspector Joly's Jack Benny gaze. "I thought," he said, "that this was mere paranoia on my part."

"I just think," John mumbled, "that if you're really worried about it, maybe you ought to call Joly's office."

"If *I'm* worried about it," Gideon said with richly satisfying contempt.

Joly was at Rochebonne, and neither Denis nor Fleury was at the *hôtel de police*. The sergeant on duty was not so much unsympathetic as incurious, reeling off bored, monotonic questions like a recording: Has someone threatened you? Do you have reason to think someone wishes to harm you? What reasons do you have for thinking this package might contain a bomb? The answers did nothing to arouse his interest, and Gideon was told he needn't bother to bring the object to Dinan. Merely leave it with Sergeant Mallet at the *hôtel de police* in St. Malo. The sergeant would be happy to take care of it, and the police would be in touch with *le professeur* in due course.

Glad it had not been Joly he'd talked to,

Gideon hung up sheepishly and thought seriously about opening the damn envelope and forgetting about Sergeant Mallet. But in the end, having set (he thought) the wheels of the *Police Judiciaire* in motion, he felt it would be better to follow through.

The envelope was duly left at the police station with Sergeant Mallet, or rather in his absence with a harassed young policeman who was trying to mediate a noisy argument between a stall-owner from the Place Poisonnerie and a motorist who had allegedly run over a fish. (Gideon might have mistrusted his translating abilities but for the indisputably flattened sea bass on the counter.) And by 9:30 A.M., only half an hour late, they were in Dr. Loti's office in St. Malo's elegant old Place Guy-la-Chambre, just inside the ramparts at the St. Vincent Gate.

13

Dr. Loti's consultation room was a Frenchman's version of Norman Rockwell's idea of what a doctor's office ought to look like: ageing books, heavy old mahogany furniture, a few comfortably faded red-plush chairs stuffed with horsehair, a worn, good carpet on a gleaming wooden floor, a big desk of golden oak. Pierre Loti himself looked something like an elderly Michelin Man, large and cheerful, with a round, pneumatic-looking torso. He sat behind his desk, fingers interlaced comfortably on his vest-clad abdomen, leaning back in his wooden swivel chair and staring at the ceiling while he talked. And talked.

"Forgetful?" he said. "Do you mean, was he senile? Did he have Alzheimer's disease? Did he lose track of where he was, so that he had to be led home? No-no-no-no." His wattles jiggled as he shook his head.

"On the other hand, it's true that he'd been getting a little absent-minded with time, yes. A little impatient with the needs of others, a little set in his ways. A man of a certain age has a right to it, don't you think so?"

"I certainly do," Gideon said politely. Dr. Loti was no more than five years younger than Guillaume had been, if that.

"Certainly," Dr. Lot agreed. "But you know, a good many people don't know the difference between a mind that's empty or confused, and a mind that's truly 'absent'; that is, somewhere else, concentrating quite efficiently on some abstract or distant problem and ignoring the immediate trivialities of the moment." He nodded, tilting himself a little further back in the chair, pleased with the way he'd put it.

So was Gideon, who tucked this appealing perspective on absent-mindedness away for the next time he had to defend himself for unthinkingly dropping a batch of letters he'd just received into the next mailbox he passed. That or something equally trivial.

"In that sense of the word," Dr. Loti rambled on, "yes, I think you could say Guillaume was absentminded. Enough so, regrettably, to cause his death."

"You think he was concentrating so hard on his collecting that the immediate triviality of the incoming tide caught him by surprise?"

Dr. Loti chuckled softly. Not many people can chuckle convincingly, but Dr. Loti was an exception. His eyes closed and his shoulders shook, and a low rumble vibrated comfortably out of his belly. "Well, yes, I do. Of course. What else?" In half an hour, this was his most succinct response.

"What's going on?" John asked Gideon. "You going to let me in on this?"

"Sorry," Gideon said. The physician's

maundering French, punctuated by throat-clearings, chuckles, and snufflings at a cigar that was out more than it was lit (Dr. Loti seemed to enjoy it either way) had been taxing his ability to understand, and he had neglected to translate for a few minutes. He summarized briefly.

John shrugged. "Makes sense."

Yes, it did. On logical grounds he still had little reason to think there was anything more to Guillaume's death than everyone said there was. There was only the intuitive, nagging feeling that it just didn't sit right; strolling out into the most dangerous bay in Europe without a tidetable simply didn't sound like Guillaume du Rocher, regardless of where his mind happened to be at the time. It wasn't much to go on, even with the provocative but conjectural questions Julie had raised.

"Just one more question, Dr. Loti –"

"As many as you like, as many as you like. It's Sunday morning; no patients." He leaned expansively forward to get the soggy, dead cigar stub from his ashtray and stick it in his mouth, the better to consider the next question.

"I was told that Guillaume only had a year to live. Is that accurate?"

"Close enough. I told him so at his last

examination in January. Maybe one year, maybe two. His kidneys weren't functioning properly, his spleen, his liver...The damage he'd suffered during the Occupation was finally taking its toll." He picked a few moist shreds of tobacco from his lips and chuckled reminiscently. "But knowing him, it would probably have been closer to two years. He was quite something, Guillaume du Rocher."

"Mm." Nothing was leading anywhere. As Joly had cogently pointed out, with Guillaume so close to dying anyway, why would anyone kill him? Not for an inheritance, certainly. He began to get himself ready to admit to John that his trusty intuition might have overstepped itself this time. It wouldn't be the first time, as John would be sure to point out.

"Look," Dr. Loti said, "let me show you something. You're interested in these things." He billowed out of his chair and over to his oak file cabinets, emitting as he went a faint, clean scent of lavender. He rummaged for a moment, then waved a sheaf of X-rays at Gideon and began slipping them one by one into the clips of a shadow box on a side table; the only touch of modern medical technology in the office.

"Just look at this," he murmured happily

to himself as he got the transparent photographs up, sat down in front of them, and flicked on the fluorescent lights behind them. "It's astonishing. Look at that ... Just look at this..." He motioned John and Gideon nearer.

"You go ahead, Doc," John demurred. "You can explain it to me later."

"Now," said Dr. Loti to Gideon, "you know your bones. What would be your prognosis in this case?"

"I'm not too good at reading X-rays, Doctor. I don't –"

"Never mind. Just for fun. Pretend you're a physician. What's the diagnosis?"

Gideon sat down next to him and leaned forward to study the two rows of photographs. He couldn't make much of the muzzy gray shadows that represented the soft tissues, but he could see that the pictures were all of one person, and the condition of the bones made him wince.

"So what would you say?" Dr. Loti urged. "Will he live?"

"Will he live? I'd say he was already dead." He pointed at various photographs. "Six, seven fractured ribs; crushed left maxilla, shattered orbit – my God, some of the pieces aren't even there." His finger skimmed the bottom row. "Crushed right humerus, fractured left ilium...And the *legs!* It looks like a tank ran over them... You're not going to tell me this is Guillaume?"

Dr. Loti laughed and nodded proudly. "Taken August 16, 1944; the first time I ever saw him, in the hospital in St. Servan – two days after the liberation of the *cité.* And you're right, in a way. An ordinary man would have been dead twice over. Oh, he wasn't far from it. He'd been under the rubble of a building on the Place Gasnier-Duparc for ten hours. Ruptured spleen, punctured lung, lacerated liver, crushed larynx...And every wound was septic. He was raving, delirious, hallucinating; for days he didn't know who he was. A sensible physician would have given up. But me, I persisted." He gazed fondly at the transparencies.

Gideon gazed too. Guillaume's visible scars, shocking as they'd been, had given no idea of the devastation beneath. "It's amazing that he lived."

"Not only lived, but recovered, insofar as a man with such injuries can recover. But a missing eye, a paralyzed arm, a few metal pins and struts – these were mere annoyances to Guillaume. Overcoming physical dis-advantages was nothing new to him. As a child his health had been very delicate, you know."

"No, I didn't. But didn't you say you didn't know him before 1944?"

"Yes, but I saw the family records later. Of all the du Rochers, he was the only one who was a sickly child: rickets, asthma, rheumatic fever. They had little hope for him, but in the end he was a bigger success than all the rest of them put together. Well, he didn't let his war wounds stop him either. As soon as he was well enough, he went back to pursuing his business and he prospered. He died a much richer man than his father, did you know? When he retired in 1975 he was still going to Paris three times a week. He was on nine boards of directors. And he managed to live a full life besides."

Dr. Loti leaned forward, exuding lavender, mouthwash, and damp cigar. "You know what I mean when I say a 'a full life'?" His eyes twinkled.

"Uh, yes . . ." Gideon said uncomfortably. He wasn't anxious for a clinical description of Guillaume du Rocher's sex habits. "Well," he said, standing up, "thanks very much for your time, doctor."

"My pleasure, young man." The physician flicked off the lights behind the X-ray display glass, stuck the cigar in his mouth, and rose to extend his hand.

The hand remained extended. Gideon was staring, transfixed, at the now-opaque photographs. For some minutes he had been looking at them inattentively, not really seeing them, but when the bright light behind them had suddenly gone out, it had left a set of negative after-images, dark where they had been light, light where they had been dark. It was those fading images in his mind, not the photographs on the glass, that he was staring so hard at. The third X-ray from the left in the upper row, a ventral view of the thorax; that dark, round shadow . . .

"Dr. Loti," he murmured, "would you mind putting that light on again?"

The physician did as he was asked, then turned his bland moon-face curiously up to Gideon.

Gideon waited tensely while the fluorescent lamp flickered and then caught with a hum. The X-rays jumped into sharp focus, and there was the spot, not dark now, but leaping out at him, white against the frosted glass behind it. How could he possibly have missed it?

He pointed at it. "That spot – What is it?"

"This?" Dr. Loti said, obviously puzzled. "You don't know? I would have thought –"

"I have trouble reading these things," Gideon explained again.

"Really?" The physician looked at him doubtfully. "Well, that's a sternal foramen."

"I understand, I understand!" John shouted over the piercing, salt-heavy wind that had cleared the St. Malo ramparts of other tourists and now drove the big breakers of the English Channel against the base of the walls fifty feet below in great, spuming surges. "A sternal foramen. Like the one on the guy in the cellar. What's the big deal?"

"The big deal," Gideon shouted back, his face turned away from the wind, "as I keep trying to tell you, is that this just about proves the body in the cellar isn't any German officer – he's a du Rocher. Or at least he's related to Guillaume du Rocher."

"That I *don't* understand. What are you saying, that everybody who's got a sternal foramen is related to everyone else who's got one?"

"No, of course not, but congenital features like that tend to run in families. Do you have any idea what the frequency of sternal foramina is?"

"No, what?"

"Well, I don't know exactly –"

This earned a grunt and a sidewise glance.

"– but it's rare; from what I've seen, maybe once in a hundred people. So what kind of likelihood is there that two once-in-a-hundred possibilities would show up in the same house just by chance, one on Guillaume and one on the body in the cellar?"

John thought it over as they continued walking. "I don't know. What?" he finally said.

Gideon made a grumpy noise. John had a way of picking peculiar times to be literal-minded. "Guess," he said.

"Once in two hundred?"

"Once in ten thousand."

"No kidding," John said, most of it carried off in a sudden gust.

"Yes. You multiply the probabilities. John, what do you say we get down off these damn ramparts and go someplace we can talk without yelling at each other?"

"Fine, what are you getting mad about? You're the one who wanted to come up here."

True enough. A breezy walk around the top of the famous fortified ramparts of St. Malo had seemed just what was needed to think through what they'd heard in Dr. Loti's office. But the offshore breeze had become nasty and the sky had darkened, so that the sea to the west was now iron-gray and ominous. And the views of the stately, slate-roofed town within the walls, so lovingly rebuilt after the war, lost their charm and turned gloomy and flat. And it was going to rain any minute; a cold, dismal March rain blowing in from the Channel Islands.

At the Bastion St. Louis they took the stone stairway down and went in search of a restaurant, the post-breakfast hollow having made its growly appearance some time before.

"How about here?" Gideon suggested.

John looked doubtfully at the signboard set up on the sidewalk. *"Dégustation de crêpes,"* he read slowly. "Really sounds appetizing."

"It's just a pancake house."

"Yeah, but who wants pancakes? Don't you want some real food for a change?"

"John, I know it's tough to accept, but you're just not going to find a Burger King in St. Malo."

"Well, what about –"

"And I'm not going into another pizza place for at least two days. Besides, Brittany's famous for pancakes. Everybody eats them here. They're unbeatable. Trust me."

So he'd read in the guidebooks, and so it turned out to be, fortunately for his credibility. At a counter in the dining room a slickly self-assured cook poured dipper after dipper of batter onto a round griddle over a gas ring, smoothed out the buttery liquid with two casual but precise swipes of a push-stick, and flipped out thin, tender, perfect pancakes at the rate of two or three a minute. These were topped with fillings by an assistant, folded deftly into omeletlike rectangles, and delivered steaming to the customers almost as fast as they came off the griddle. John and Gideon had their galettes – dark, pungent buckwheat pancakes filled with creamy white cheese, ham, and tomatoes – less than a minute after sitting down.

They wolfed them happily down and ordered more before leaning comfortably back to take up where they'd left off.

"Not too bad," John admitted. "Okay, so those sternal foramens prove Guillaume and that skeleton were related?"

"Yes." Gideon washed down the last of his galette with a mouthful of hot chocolate. "Well, maybe not exactly *prove*. It's a matter of probabilities –"

John's eyes rolled up. "Oh, boy."

"Look, John, there's no way to prove anything like this from bones and X-rays. But when you run into something that can happen by chance only once in ten thousand times, you have to assume something *other* than chance is operating. And in this case the only reasonable possibility is a genetic relationship between Guillaume and the skeleton in the cellar."

"What about coincidence? If it could happen by chance one out of ten thousand times, why couldn't this be the one time?"

"It could, but the chances of your being wrong are nine-thousand-nine-hundred-and-ninety-nine out of ten thousand. Not a great bet. Anyway, do you really believe in coincidence? I don't mean abstractly; I mean as a factor in a murder case."

John poured himself a little more beer from his bottle of Kronenbourg, sipped, and considered. "No," he said. "I don't. I don't know any cops who do."

"Okay, that's settled. Now all I have to do is convince Joly."

The fresh pancakes had arrived; a cheese-filled galette for Gideon, and a sweet dessert crêpe stuffed with cream and sugar for John.

"Why should Joly be hard to convince?"

210

John asked after a test-bite that apparently met his standards. "The guy's peculiar, but he's not dumb."

"Well, for one thing, there's the little matter of the SS paraphernalia that was buried in the cellar. For another thing ... Well, I can't think of another thing, but Joly will."

"The SS stuff." John put down his fork. "I forgot all about it. How do you figure that, anyway? You think one of the du Rochers joined the SS? The Germans had Nazi police units made up of local nationals in the occupied countries, didn't they? And Guillaume was in the Resistance, right? Maybe he killed this guy because –"

"Uh-uh. You're talking about the *Milice*, I think. They had second-rate uniforms, nothing like the flashy German SS. Denis did some checking; this stuff was definitely bona-fide *Allgemeine* SS, straight from Berlin, and the rank insignia were *Obersturmbannführer*. Helmut Kassel's rank."

"So then what do you think ..."

"I don't know what I think. At this point it'd be nothing but speculative inference anyway."

John's hand went to his heart. "Speculative inference! Jesus, Doc, far be it from

211

me to suggest that a man such as yourself would stoop to engage in speculative inference."

"All right," Gideon said, laughing, "maybe I've done it from time to time in certain rare circumstances, but in this case I just don't have any data to go on. But I don't care *what* else they find down there. Those bones belong to a du Rocher."

John nodded slowly. "So the question is: Who?"

"Oh, I think I know who."

John's eyebrows lifted.

"Alain du Rocher," Gideon said.

John's eyebrows remained suspended for some second. A forkload of crêpe and crème Chantilly also paused inquiringly. "The guy the Nazis killed? The one Claude didn't warn?"

Gideon nodded.

"That's crazy."

"John, it all fits. He was living right there in the manoir during the war, and those bones got buried down there right about the time he was killed. And it just happens to turn out that nobody seems to know where his body is."

"Yeah, but –"

"And those bones *look* like du Rocher

bones; the same proportions and con-
formations as Guillaume's, and some of the
same features; I could see it in the X-rays.
And remember when I said the bones made
me think of Ray? It's a look that runs in the
family."

"What about René? He's built like a
doorknob. So's Jules."

"Well, sure. You can't expect everyone in
a family to look alike, but where you can see
it, it's distinctive."

"Yeah, but I still don't see why it's got to
be Alain. Why not somebody else in the
family?"

"How many du Rochers do you think
disappeared without a trace in 1942?"

The fork finally finished its journey and
John chewed thoughtfully. "Okay, I agree
with you: We're not talking proof here, but
it makes a lot of sense. Hey, wait a minute.
If Alain got killed by the Nazis, what's he
doing in Guillaume's cellar?"

"Yeah, that's a slight problem."

"I'd say it's gonna take some world-class
speculative inference."

They had finished eating and ordered
espressos before either spoke again.

"Doc, you gonna tell all this to Joly?"

"Sure, not that I'm looking forward to it.
I know he appreciates us, but I'm not sure

213

how much he enjoys these new and startling developments every few hours."

"Well, then, what would you say if I pass it along for you? I was thinking of dropping by Rochebonne this afternoon to sort of see how things are going anyhow. If you don't mind visiting those tombs by yourself."

Gideon swallowed the tiny portion of coffee in two rich, bitter sips. "Tell you what: Why don't I ride over there with you? You can drop me off at Ploujean."

"Ploujean? What's at Ploujean?"

"Joly said there's a plaque to the six men the Nazis executed."

John studied him over the rim of his cup. "You're going to do some more burrowing into things on your own, aren't you?"

"Well, things have gotten a little more interesting, and –" At John's expression he hurriedly altered course. "No, honestly, what is there to find out in Ploujean?"

"Doc," John said with a sigh, "every time you start thinking you're a detective, I wind up having to bail you out."

"John, I don't think I'm a detective. All I want to do is – well, pay my respects to Alain, I guess. See what the monument's like. That's all."

And it was, more or less. But if something came from it that would be fine too. You never knew.

14

The plaque was easy to find. Ploujean had only two dusty streets, intersecting in a T, and at the center of the T was a small, bare plaza of brown gravel, and at the center of the plaza was a granite boulder surrounded by a black wrought-iron fence. On the granite was a plain rectangular plate of patinaed bronze with a few lines of simple, raised lettering.

16 OCTOBRE 1942

EN HOMMAGE AUX COMBAT-TANTS DES FORCES FRANÇAISES DE LA RESISTANCE DONT LA LUTTE ET LES SACRIFICES ONT JALONNE LA ROUTE DE LA LIBERATION DE PLOUJEAN.

FRANÇOIS-RENE BRIZEUX
CHARLES KERBOL

215

AUGUSTE LUPIS
HENRI DE PILLEMENT
JEAN-PIERRE QUEFFELLEC
ALAIN DU ROCHER

Gideon turned slowly from it and looked at his watch. Two-thirty; in half an hour he was supposed to walk to the manoir and meet John for the drive back to St. Malo. Thinking about what he'd just read, he strolled towards Ploujean's only café, a tiny awninged place that looked out on the square. Had he learned anything from the plaque? Yes, he thought, maybe he had. *"La lutte et les sacrifices,"* it said – "the struggle and the sacrifices." There was no reference to executions; not even a mention of the Nazis. Why not? Was it simply the dignified restraint of a little village that had had enough of blood and passion? Or was it conceivable that Ray and his family had the story wrong? That Alain and the other five had not died at the hands of the SS, but in some other way? If so, new possibilities arose as to how his body had wound up in Guillaume's cellar.

"Sans prétensions," it said on the fly-blown window of the café, and the interior lived up to its promise. A few rough wooden tables and chairs – not folksy wooden but

216

utilitarian wooden – gritty floor, no menus, fly-bown travel posters on the wall (Venice, Costa del Sol, Miami). Three elderly men sat at one of the tables nursing a carafe of red wine. From the attentive, quiet way they watched him come in, he knew they'd been talking about him. Ploujean's Café de la Paix, unlike its Paris namesake, was hardly on the tourist track and any stranger was no doubt worth serious and protracted consideration, particularly one who took the time to study their memorial.

"*Bonjour,*" he said, and the three nodded in unison, swiveling their heads to watch him go by and choose a table.

He ordered *cidre bouché,* Breton cider, which the barman brought to him in a bottle with a blue earthenware bowl instead of glass.

"The men whose names were on the plaque," Gideon said conversationally in French as the bottle was set down. "How did they die?" Talk stopped abruptly at the other table.

"Executed, monsieur," the barman said.

"By the Germans? The SS?"

The barman looked at him as if he were simple-minded. "Of course, monsieur."

So much for that half-formed line of thought. Easy come, easy go. Still, it was worth following a little further. "Do you know what became of the bodies?"

"The bodies?" the barman said, looking at him as if he were not only simple-minded but dangerous. "No, monsieur. You're American?"

"Yes. I've heard that the SS colonel who was in charge at the time was assassinated by the Resistance. Is that true?"

"So I've heard," said the barman nervously. "Thank you, monsieur."

He went back to the bar, leaving Gideon embarrassed and selfconscious. Asking sensitive questions of strangers in foreign places, particularly under scrutiny, was not something that came naturally to him. It was a good thing, he thought, as he had many times, that he'd switched to physical anthropology during his first year in graduate school. He'd have made a hell of a cultural anthropologist.

He drank some of the tart, cool cider from the bowl, turned his chair slightly away from the other table, and looked up at the black-and-white television set on a metal shelf over the bar. Out of the corner of his eye he saw the barman go to the table with the three men to report on his bizarre conversation with the newcomer. He drank some more cider. There was a Bugs Bunny cartoon on

218

television. Bugs was wearing a waiter's uniform (consisting entirely of a jacket with a towel over the arm). On a tray behind his back he had a cigar with a sputtering fuse sticking out of it. He was bending solicitously over a seated Elmer Fudd, who was elegantly dressed in quilted smoking jacket and ascot.

"Permettez-moi de vous servir, monsieur," said Bugs urbanely. *"Voulez-vous encore un cigare?"*

But Elmer wasn't about to be had. *"Non merci,"* he said, *"je suis bien á mon aise."*

What would "Bugs Bunny" be in French, he wondered idly – *Lapin Fou? Insecte le Lapin?* He didn't find out. The oldest of the three men had come to his table and sat down. He was about eighty, a small man with eyes like shiny coffee beans, a nose like a zucchini, and a drooping but exuberant white moustache. His blue smock was covered with dark smudges and the cheerful, pungent aroma of shoe polish was all around him. The wrinkles on his otherwise clean fingers were lined with it, as if someone had carefully traced them with a pen.

"Bonjour," Gideon said again.

"American, eh?" the man responded.

"Yes, I am."

The man laughed. "I knew it as soon as I saw you. I told them." His French was

219

rustic, thickened with a heavy Breton accent and hard to follow. "So you're interested in Colonel Kassel, are you?"

"Well –"

"I can tell you what you want to know," the man said and smiled shrewdly. "I know who you are, you know. I know where you're from."

"Pardon?"

The man laid a forefinger alongside his huge, pockmarked nose and leaned forward. *"Say... Eee... Aah,"* he whispered.

"I'm afraid –" Gideon began in confusion, then laughed. The sounds were letters of the French alphabet. "CIA?" he said. "No, I'm a professor of anthropology. I teach –"

But the man only nodded his head conspiratorially. "Wah...sheeng...ton," he whispered with the same respectful cadence. "Don't try to fool me."

Gideon decided that maybe he wouldn't. "Yes," he said solemnly, "I am from Washington." True enough, on its face.

"Aah," the man sighed with pleasure. "I thought so. I can always tell."

"What do you know about Colonel Kassel?" Gideon asked. He would have preferred being a little less direct and a little more polite, but he supposed that being an agent called for bolder style.

"What do I know?" Under the shapeless smock the thin, old shoulders shrugged. "I killed him."

Gideon blinked. "*You* killed him?"

The man was offended. He turned to his friends at the other table and called to them. "Hey – did I kill him or not?"

They knew immediately what he was talking about, and agreed loudly, with the barman joining in, that Jean-Honoré Bourget had indeed killed him, and no one in the village would say otherwise.

Gideon, sensing that protocol called for it, invited them over and earned smiles and nods by ordering them another carafe of wine. Jean-Honoré wondered politely if he might have a Pernod instead, and this was brought in a slender glass with an ice cube floating in it. He poured some water into it from a squat bottle with an "Anisette Berger" label on it, took a contented sip of the resulting milky-green liquid, and settled happily back to tell them all how he killed SS *Obersturmbannführer* Helmut Kassel.

It was like watching a father deliver a familiar bedtime story to his children. When he couldn't remember a detail, they supplied it for him, so they wound up telling a lot of it themselves, and when they contradicted him on a minor point, he said: "No, truly?"

and went equably along with them. There was a lot of laughter.

But on the major points there were no contradictions, and no laughter either. In retribution for the murders of the six men named on the plaque, Jean-Honoré and three other *Maquis* had done away with the SS man. One of the other three was the local barber, the second was a woman school-teacher, and the third was the leader: Guillaume du Rocher. Only Jean-Honoré was still alive.

Kassel, who had seen himself as a ladies' man, had been lured to an afternoon assignation with the schoolteacher in the Hunadaie forest not far from town. There, they had killed him.

"How?" Gideon asked.

"With a claw hammer, mostly," the old man answered pleasantly. "Edmond wanted to use his razor, but Guillaume said it would be best to have no clean knife wounds." He nodded with approval. "He was right, too."

Working quickly, they had stripped him of his uniform, even his underwear, and dressed him in old farm clothes that smelled of pigs and manure. They carried him a few hundred feet to the road that runs between Ploujean and Plancoet. There Guillaume, whom the Nazis permitted to have a car

222

because of his status and apparent docility, ran over him, making sure that his face was crushed against the asphalt. The body was left in the road to be found by the authorities – some drunken peasant who'd stepped in the way of a transport truck or a speeding staff car – and that was the end of that.

"But wasn't there any retribution? Didn't the Nazis –"

Jean-Honoré grinned. "Not very smart, the Boches."

"Well, you see," one of the others explained, "the last thing the SS wanted was to let it out that somebody with a rank like that might have been assassinated. They didn't want *us* to know, and they certainly didn't want Berlin to know. And as for the regular army, the regular administration, they just wanted the SS out of here, the sooner the better; they hated them more than we did."

"As much, maybe," Jean-Honoré said. "Not more."

"As much," the man agreed. "So in the end they settled for the story that he just disappeared on one of his little trips to somewhere or other; one of his private, unannounced 'investigations' to the Argoat, or the Morbihan, or maybe Normandy. Nobody knew where."

"Anywhere but *this* district," Jean-Honoré said. "Bureaucrats are the same everywhere." He finished his pernod with a sigh, turned down the offer of another, wiped the ends of his moustache between thumb and forefinger, and looked with sparkling little eyes at his satisfied audience.

"What did you do with Kassel's uniform?" Gideon asked.

"What kind of a question is that?" the barman said.

"No, why shouldn't he ask?" Jean-Honoré said. He shot a melodramatically cryptic glance to Gideon. "He has to know many things." Gideon nodded, soberly and mysteriously.

"The uniform..." mused Jean-Honoré, searching his mind.

"You burned it," said one of the others.

"*Burned* it?" Gideon said.

"Oh, yes, that's right..." said Jean-Honoré. "Well, the parts that would burn without making a stink; the cloth parts. The rest Guillaume took away with him to bury somewhere. In his wine cellar, maybe," he said and laughed. "My God, it hurt to bury those boots. You should have seen what we were wearing for shoes."

So that explained that, and much to Gideon's satisfaction. The SS regalia simply had no connection with the bones in the cellar. Two separate murders, two separate burials. No relationship beyond the fact that one had been executed by the other, and the other killed to avenge him. So much for the SS insignia that had so pleased Joly.

But the main questions still remained. How had Alain's skeleton (a third of it, anyway) gotten into Guillaume's cellar in the first place? Where was the rest of it? And now most disturbing of all: What possible connection might Guillaume have had with it? For it was next to impossible that Alain had been dismembered and buried in his cellar without his knowing about it. He sighed. The more he found out, the more confusing it got.

Jean-Honoré decided that perhaps another Pernod might be very nice after all. Gideon bought it, thanked the old man, and shook hands all around, finding himself bobbing up and down as each one popped out of his chair in turn. As he left he heard the barman's querulous voice: "Well, what does he care what happened to the bastard's uniform?"

Gideon glanced over his shoulder as he pulled the door closed behind him. There was Jean-Honoré hunching forward over his

Pernod, eyes glittering, explaining the situation to his attentive cronies.

"*Say . . .*" he whispered knowingly, his forefinger alongside his nose, "*Eee . . .*"

John was right. Joly was beginning to appreciate them, or at least he was getting used to their popping up with astute insights to muddle his investigation into Claude's death. When Gideon got to Rochebonne after a ten-minute walk along the tree-lined road from Ploujean, he found the inspector on a cigarette break from whatever he'd been doing, strolling amicably with John in the courtyard and enjoying the rare spring sunshine. Gideon fell in step with them.

"Alain du Rocher, eh?" was Joly's greeting. Not exactly a full-hearted endorsement of Gideon's deduction, but not a contemptuous rebuff either. Just the mildly amused, not unfriendly skepticism with which he tended to receive ideas other than his own. Gideon was getting used to Joly, too.

"You were right, Doc. Lucien doesn't buy it." So the two of them had graduated to first names too, which was good. John's pronunciation – *Loosh'n* – brought no more than a momentary strain to the papery skin under Joly's eyes. Something like Mathilde's

226

look when he'd referred to "Roach Bone" in her presence.

"It's very hard to see how it can be Alain," the inspector said. "I called our local prefect of police as soon as Mr. Lau – ahum, John – told me what you thought. As a matter of fact, it turns out that Alain du Rocher's height, weight, and age do conform to what you learned from those bones."

"Well, then –"

"But so do many other people's. Bretons are in general shorter and more slender than other Frenchmen, as I'm sure you're aware. And unfortunately for your theory, there's simply no doubt whatever about Alain's execution by the Nazis."

"Yes, I know. That's the one thing that doesn't add up; how he got into the cellar."

"Gideon, he was picked up by the SS at 5 A.M., October 16, 1942, and taken to the *mairie*. Between 10 A.M. and noon the other five *Maquis* were brought in. There were many witnesses, including the prefect himself as a child. None of them ever came out again. No," Joly said comfortably, walking erectly along, hands behind his back, face turned up slightly towards the pale sun, "everything suggests that the bones in the cellar are Kassel's. Surely you see that."

"No, Kassel was run over by a car and

left out in the road near the Hunadaie forest."

It was a sign of just how accustomed Joly was becoming to them that he received this without even a hitch in his step and listened with tolerant resignation while Gideon told him the rest of what he'd learned in Ploujean. It was, in fact, Gideon who stopped in mid-stride.

"Hey, I just remembered," he said. "One of the names on the plaque seemed familiar, but I couldn't place it – Lupis; Auguste Lupis. Aren't Marcel and Beatrice named Lupis?"

"They most certainly are," Joly said with interest.

"You think maybe Marcel's father, or uncle, or somebody might have been executed with the others?" John asked. "That would give him a hell of a reason for wanting to kill Claude."

"Indeed it would," Joly said, and raised one eyebrow minutely. "Just what I needed: another motive. Gentlemen, I can't thank you enough."

15

Wither Man?

Gideon scowled at the title on the cover sheet. One of three master's qualifying essays he'd brought with him to grade at his leisure, he'd put it off until last, but now, after two and a half hours spend working on the others in his room, the time had unavoidably come. He looked gloomily at the writer's name. Tara Melnick. Was it part of some immutable law that in every class, no matter how enjoyable otherwise, there must be one student whose presence made your teeth ache?

Probably so. Just as the president would always have his Sam Donaldson, so would Gideon always have his Tara Melnick. He deliberated longer than he should have about whether to insert the omitted "h", and finally did, but with a heavy heart. He had corrected her spelling before, and had been told for his pains that his slavish concern with outdated rules of orthography and grammar was redundant in the age of WordStar and Perfect Writer. Moreover, she had informed him, it was now commonly agreed among progressive linguistodiametricians – what those were he had been afraid to ask – that individual language variants were valid in their own right as legitimate microcultural expressions.

He shifted in his chair, bored and at loose ends. Graduate students seemed younger these days. And sillier. It was true that at forty he was now twice as old as some of them, but had he ever been as tedious as Tara Melnick?

Tara Melnick. What had happened to the Ruths, anyway; the Dorothys, the Roberts, the Bills? Where had the Taras and Megans and Ians come from? Buried in his work, had he missed some clandestine migration of Celts from across the sea? Did parents get their children's names from *Harlequin* romances?

He stared with distaste at the orange-and-brown wallpaper in front of him. At first he'd liked the bright, sprightly pattern, but then John, who had the same wallpaper in his room, had innocently remarked that it made him think of giant orange daisies wearing sunglasses. Ever since, all those hundreds of daisies had been leering through their shades at him, even in the dark when he was sleeping.

Well, he might as well face it. He turned resignedly to the first page of the paper. "Just who does *Homo sapiens* think (s)he is," it demanded belligerently, "this self-named 'smart primate'? What is this so-called civilization of ours, built on the rape of the air and the water, torn from the innocent, nurturing earth? And what lies ahead for it . . . *if anything!!??*"

He was saved from learning the answer to this alarming question, temporarily anyway, by the telephone's ring. Let it really be for me, he murmured; not a mistake but an honest-to-God, attention-demanding interruption.

He got his wish. It was Joly, very businesslike. "Gideon, there are several things I want to talk to you about. First, we've turned up some more bones in the cellar. I thought you might be interested."

"You bet I am, Inspector!" Gideon said with fervor that must have surprised Joly. With a happy sigh he shoved *Wither Man?* into a drawer and settled back to listen.

"I'm fairly sure they're the remaining parts of our burial, whoever it is –"

"Alain."

"Whoever," Joly said again, which seemed reasonable enough to Gideon. "There's a skull, pelvis, and arm and leg bones. They were in two packages – same paper, same string as the first. Even the same knots."

"Are the bones in good shape?"

"So they seem to me. I've had them carefully packed."

"Damn, it would have been better if I'd seen them *in situ.*"

"I suppose so, but our own people have already gone over them for dust and debris, and so forth. What's needed is a purely anthropological analysis."

"Even so, seeing them in their original context and relationships –"

"I'm sorry, my friend, but it's already done. They have to be shipped to Paris in any case, you see. It didn't occur to me that it would make any difference to you."

"Well, it doesn't matter that much. I'll be glad to look at them for you." So it wouldn't be textbook forensic anthropology, but it was a lot better than *Wither Man?* And if it really was a complete skeleton, he was certain he could unequivocally settle the question of its identity, even to Joly's satisfaction.

"As long as they're boxed," he said, "could you have them dropped off here and save me a trip to –" He was struck with a novel teaching idea. "What about bringing them to the conference center tomorrow morning instead? I'm doing my final session from eight to ten. We could do the analysis right there in class. It'd give the attendees a chance to participate in an actual case."

There was a long pause while Joly weighed the propriety of this.

"Lucien, they're all cops, you know. They're on our side."

"Well, yes, all right," Joly finally agreed reluctantly. "I'll bring them myself."

"And will you bring the original bones too, if you haven't sent them off yet?"

"Of course." Gideon heard the scrape of a match and an intake of breath as he lit up. Then some little tck-ing sounds that indicated he was probing with his tongue for a shred of tobacco between his teeth.

"You said there were several things you wanted to talk about?" Gideon said.

"Yes, there are. John will be interested in this too. We've checked for local sources of cyanide, and there are none. The nearest in Rennes."

"So that must mean –"

"Second, there is no taxi service in Ploujean, but there is one in Guissand – that is to say, the ambulance from the mental hospital serves as a taxi when needed – and it's had six calls in the last week; none of them involved any of our friends at the manoir."

"Which has to mean –"

"Third, I've constructed a time chart based on each person's observations. During the days, at least, no one has been out of sight of all the others for more than two hours at a time; not nearly long enough to get to and from any place where potassium cyanide might be found. Which must mean...?" he prompted.

"That – as John pointed out – whoever did it had the cyanide with him before last week. He – or she – planned Claude's murder ahead of time."

"Correct. It was old business, not new business."

"As old as 1942, do you think? Was somebody settling wartime scores with Claude?"

"I think it's not unlikely. As far as we know, none of them has interacted with him for decades, so what else could it be? Ah, and apropos of that, Auguste Lupis was indeed the father of Marcel. He became quite emotional when I confronted him with it."

"So you think –"

"I think," Joly cut in, "that he's one more person with an ancient, passionate hatred of Claude, that's all. One more in a long list."

"Yes..." Gideon nodded thoughtfully at

the daisies. "But look at it this way: Your list of prime suspects is shorter now."

"Oh? How would that be?"

"Well, if he was killed on account of something that happened in 1942, that probably lets out anyone who wasn't there at the time, doesn't it? Not definitely, but probably. The younger people, mostly; Leona Fougeray, Claire, Jules...Ben Butts too...and Ray," he added after a moment, just so Joly would know that he was being objective, had been objective from the start.

There was a pause. Gideon could picture him, head tipped back, lower lip extended, while he watched the smoke curl slowly upward from his mouth. "Why don't we just say it focuses interest on those who *were* here?" Joly said. "Mathilde and René du Rocher, Marcel, Sophie – all of whom had ample reason to detest Claude. And then there's Beatrice, Marcel's wife; I wonder if she was in the area in 1942. You wouldn't have any idea, would you?" he added dryly. "You seem to have a way of knowing these things."

"Not a glimmer," Gideon said, laughing.

"Well then, I suppose I shall have to find out for myself. Oh, finally – I understand you turned in a small package to the police in St. Malo this morning."

"Package?" He'd been hoping it wouldn't get back to Joly. "Oh, yes, that. Well, the thing is I'd just been talking to this *commissaire* about – well, anyway, I left it with them. Just in case, you know."

"Yes, it's a good idea to be careful. The bomb squad spent a good part of their afternoon processing it."

"They did?" Gideon laughed sheepishly. "All right, let's hear it: What was in it?"

Joly emitted one of his quiet, mournful sighs.

"A bomb," he said.

"Who the hell would want to kill you?" John asked, leaning back in the one armchair. He had brought a bottle of armagnac for nightcaps, but it stood unopened on the table.

"That's what you said this morning," Gideon replied, standing at the window. As in many small French hotels, the Terminus' inside rooms overlooked a small garden that was used in the summer as a breakfast area. "When you said I was paranoid," he added gloomily, looking down on the dimly illuminated tangle of winter-sodden plants yet to undergo their spring cleanup.

"*You* said you were paranoid. I just agreed with you."

236

"Well, we were both wrong. Someone's really trying to get me." He laughed suddenly, dropped backwards onto the bed, and clasped his hands behind his neck, leaning against the covered bolster that took the place of pillows during the day. "All things considered, I'd rather be paranoid. You're right," he added with feeling. "Letter-bombs suck."

"Yeah. What'd Joly think?"

"The same thing, I guess, but he didn't put it in those words."

"Funny. I mean what'd he think it was all about?"

"He thinks somebody at the manoir doesn't want me to find out something about the bones. The Marseilles postmark doesn't mean anything except that it's a good place to get that kind of thing done. He says if you know the right people, for two hundred dollars and a phone call somebody will make a bomb and mail it anywhere you want. You don't know the guy who does it, and he doesn't know you or the person he sends it to. Next to impossible to trace."

"Do you know what kind of bomb it was?"

"He called it an IRA special."

John grimaced. "Too bad; that won't be any help. It's the simplest kind there is. A kid

237

can make one. A little package of commercial explosive, a plain detonator, and a needle. When you open the letter, it jabs the needle into the detonator and blooey. Sometimes. Half the time it doesn't work."

"I'm glad to hear it."

It was odd; this morning when they'd just been guessing about the bomb, and more or less playfully at that, the idea had shaken him, even if he'd felt foolish about it. But now that he knew for sure that someone was actually trying to blow him up, he was more angry than anything else. One of the simpler pleasures of life – opening an unexpected package – was never going to be quite so simple or pleasurable again. And he was angry because it was almost certainly someone with whom he'd recently been chatting so affably at the manoir who had skulked to a telephone and done it, long-distance. It was so damned . . . unsporting.

"So what could somebody be afraid you'd find out?" John asked. "For instance."

"What I did find out. That Alain du Rocher's buried in the cellar. That no matter what that plaque says, and the prefect of police says, and anybody else says, Alain's body was buried – hidden – under the floor of the old family home."

"Let me get this straight. You think he

wasn't executed by the Nazis? You think somebody's trying to cover up a murder in the family? How could that be? How could everybody have the facts wrong?"

Gideon rocked his head slowly back and forth against the bolster, gazing absently at the ceiling. "It beats me, but everybody *is* wrong. Alain's in that cellar, not in some mass grave."

"Maybe they got the body back from the Nazis – to bury it decently, you know?"

"And chopped it into pieces and wrapped it up in butcher paper like so many veal cutlets?"

"No, I guess not." John was silent for a few moments. His chair, tilted onto its rear legs, tap-tapped softly against the wall. "But look: Realistically, why should anybody expect you to find out it's Alain? I mean, who'd even know he had a sternal foramen?"

Gideon laughed. "Don't you remember? I spent half an hour in the salon the other night – while you were gobbling up hors d'oeuvres – explaining what I was doing to anybody who'd listen; how I was sure the body wasn't Kassel's, how it was built like a du Rocher, how I could find out all kinds of things about it, and on and on."

"Oh, Christ, that's right. Smart, Doc."

239

"Brilliant."

"Is Joly giving you police protection?"

"No, I'm just supposed to exercise reasonable prudence, was the way he put it. He said the kind of guy who'd send me a letter-bomb probably isn't the kind of guy who'd take a shot at me in the street, or try to run me down with a car, or anything like that –"

"That's true, he probably isn't. But you know, he's sure as hell the kind of guy who'd put cyanide in somebody's wine, isn't he?"

"I suppose he is. Or she." Gideon stretched and raised himself from the bed. There was a tightness at his temples and a throbbing at the base of his skull. He got headaches so infrequently that it took him a moment to realize what it was. Maybe he *was* shaken. Or maybe he was hungry.

"I think I'll go get something to eat. I missed dinner. How about you?"

"Me?" John said, his surprised laugh indicating how ridiculous the idea was. "No, I had a steak a couple of hours ago." He tipped his chair forward and stood up. "I'll keep you company though."

"That's all right. I wouldn't mind a walk in the fresh air to think things through."

John looked directly into his eyes. "Doc, let's get something straight right now. The conference is over in just a couple more days, and we go home. Until then I'd be a lot more comfortable if you didn't go anywhere without me. Nowhere. Okay?"

"John," Gideon said, bridling, "Joly said reasonable prudence, not –"

"Yeah, but I know you; you're not reasonably prudent. You start poking around –"

"Goddammit, I don't –"

"Look, will you just give me a break?" He chopped at the air, his voice rising. "Just humor me for once?"

For no reason he could think of, Gideon burst out laughing. "All right," he said tiredly, "I'll give you a break." He clasped John's arm briefly. "Thanks."

He pulled his windbreaker from the open coat rack near the door and tossed John his. "So I guess you'll be coming to Mont St. Michel with me tomorrow after the session."

"What's at Mont St. Michel?"

"The Romanesque-Gothic abbey. One of the wonders of the Western world. I wouldn't want to leave without seeing it."

"Yeah, it also happens to be where Guillaume drowned, right?"

"Well, yes. I might like to have a look at the tidal plain too, out of curiosity."

"I'm coming, all right," John said.

"Don't look so glum. There's a famous restaurant there. Mère Poularde. One of the shrines of French gastronomy."

John made a face. "Pancakes again?"

"Omelets."

"You know the first thing I'm going to do when we get back to the States?" John asked, slipping into his jacket.

"Buy a hamburger."

"Damn right."

16

This time when Julie called him at 7 A.M., he'd been up almost two hours, ostensibly getting his notes ready for class, but mostly brooding about letter-bombs, murders, dismemberments, and the all-round nastiness of people.

"Hi," she said. "Isn't it Wednesday there yet?"

It was as if someone had opened a window and let a fresh breeze into a fetid room. Her voice was sleepy and warm, bringing a vivid image of what it was like to awaken next to her in the morning, her warm, naked bottom

242

snuggled sweetly against his thighs and belly, his arm lying loosely over her waist, his face against the silky, fragrant, sleep-damp nape of her neck.

He put down the ballpoint pen and closed Stewart's *Essentials of Forensic Anthropology*. "I wish it was," he said sincerely. "Were," he corrected. That was what came of being around Ray again.

"Me too. It's crazy, but I can't sleep when you're not with me; not very well, anyway. There are all kinds of creepy noises in the house that aren't there when you're here."

"What?" he said, pleased and flattered. "This from a thirty-year-old, self-sufficient park ranger who slept alone her whole life until recently?"

"Well, I wouldn't exactly say my *whole* life. I mean, there were a few nights here and there –"

"Okay, okay, I'm sorry I sounded smug. But it's nice to be needed."

"Oh, you're needed, all right," she said with agreeable warmth. "Gideon, how are you? I've been worrying about you."

"Worrying? Why?"

"Because you – I don't know, you always get into . . . adventures that never happen to anyone else. There isn't anything wrong, is there?"

"Wrong?" He laughed. "No, of course not." What was a bomb in the morning mail to the truly adventurous? Besides, why bring it up now when it couldn't serve any purpose other than to worry her? Later was good enough. If there was going to be any comforting and soothing as a result, he didn't see why he shouldn't be there in person for the benefits. "Not that things haven't been exciting," he said. "Let's see, when did we talk last?"

"Friday night; Saturday morning your time."

"Two days ago. Let me think now. . . . No progress on the Guillaume thing, but it looks as if those bones in the cellar belong to a cousin named Alain who was murdered by the Nazis. Joly doesn't think so, but I'm ninety-nine percent sure."

"But what were they doing in Guillaume's cellar, then?"

"Ah, you cut right to the heart of things, don't you? Nobody knows."

He took the electric coil out of the mug of water he'd been heating and tipped in a little Nescafé out of the jar. "I suppose the only other interesting thing is that we've had a murder; another cousin, a distant one named Claude Fougeray, who everyone blames for Alain's death. He knew the SS was coming for Alain and didn't warn him. Someone put cyanide in his wine. He expired in the drawing room, as a matter of fact, with everyone right there, including me."

He searched without success for a plastic spoon he thought he had somewhere, gave up, and stirred in the powdered coffee with his pen, listening all the while to her quiet breathing. "No comment?"

"I was just trying to decide whether or not you're serious."

"And?"

"I decided you are." Another brief silence. "Aren't you?"

"Sure."

"Gideon, you're absolutely amazing. Never a dull moment. Do you know who did it?"

"No, but we think it might have something to do with Alain's death, which makes most of the older members of the family suspects. They all loved him. Oh, and there's even a chance the butler did it. The Nazis killed his father at the same time; also with Claude's knowledge."

"Claude sounds like a wonderful guy. I agree with you; the murder's probably got something to do with that, all right."

"I appreciate the vote of confidence."

"You're welcome, but actually I was thinking about the cyanide."

"Come again?"

"Didn't the Nazi bigwigs use cyanide to commit suicide if they were caught? Or am I thinking of arsenic?"

"No, you're right. It was cyanide; because it works so fast. Goering killed himself with it in Nuremberg. Himmler bit into a glass capsule too. What makes you ask?"

"I was just thinking that if somebody *was* getting back at Claude for cooperating with the SS cyanide would be a logical choice – you know, a kind of symbol, linking him with Nazi war criminals. Does that make any sense?"

"Well, it seems a little theatrical, but I guess it's a point. I'll mention it to Joly. Any other hints I ought to pass along?"

"You're being snide, but yes, there is something else. You can tell him that Mathilde's husband ... What's his name?"

"René."

"You can tell him that René isn't guilty."

"Fine, I'll sure do that. This morning. Did you want me to give him any particular reason?" He sipped the coffee.

"Uh-huh. You can point out that since he's the one who let the workmen in to dig

246

up the basement – You did tell me that, didn't you?"

"Yes..."

"Then he couldn't have had anything to do with Alain's body being down there, or he'd never have let them get near the place."

Gideon put down the mug. "Julie, that is really a good point! Of course he wouldn't have! I *was* being snide, and I hereby apologize. Abjectly. You're making more progress back there in Port Angeles than I am in St. Malo."

She laughed, delighted. "You really hadn't thought about that yourself?"

"I hadn't even thought about thinking about it." He had another sip of coffee and ran the idea through his mind. "So if it's true that Claude's murder has its roots in the Occupation, and if it's true that it was an act of revenge, and if René's out of the picture...that just leaves Mathilde du Rocher and Sophie Butts. And Marcel, of course. They were all young then, but they haven't forgotten."

"Don't get carried away now; that's a lot of it's."

"There are a few," he admitted.

"Now that I've made my contribution, you don't suppose we could talk about something besides murders, and skeletons, and Nazis for a while, do you? Things are getting creepier than ever around here."

He smiled. "You bet. You all settled down for the night?"

"Uh-huh. I'm in bed."

"Good," he said, his voice softening. "What are you wearing? That silky tan thing, I hope; the one that accentuates that lovely, long, marvelous intra-sacrospinalis sulcus you have."

"Ah," she said with a sigh, "that's more like it."

Joly brought the three hoards of bones to the seminar in separate boxes, and he, Gideon, and John tagged each set with different-colored plastic tape to identify them. Then Gideon had the attendees lay them all out in proper anatomical position.

This was accomplished to his and the students' satisfaction. Of the 200 visible bones of the human body (the other six were ear bones, deep in the skull), 197 were present, mice apparently having made off with three small wrist bones.

Gideon then told them in general terms about the circumstances of the find, discussed the sternal foramen, and pointed out and explained the knife-scarring on the fifth rib.

"Now, what I'd like you to do," he said to the twenty-odd trainees gathered around the table, "is to estimate sex, age, and height on your own, going through the same steps I would; by now you should know what they are. See what you can do with race too. You'll split into three groups and we'll get three separate reports, and then I'll tell you how to see it. Any questions? If not –"

"Hold on one moment, please, Doctor." The speaker was a slender, delicate black police captain from Nairobi; voluble, articulate, and animated. And always ready to argue. "How do we know," he demanded in his machine-gun English, "that these bones are a single individual? They were found in three separate packages. Perhaps they are parts of three individuals. Or two, or four. Who can tell for certain?"

"It's obvious," retorted an officer of the Parisian *Sûreté Urbain* irritably, anxious to get on with the exercise. "We found a hundred and ninety-seven bones, all different. If there were more than one person here there would have been some duplications: two mandibles, two left clavicles –"

"True," Gideon heard Joly say quietly behind him, apparently talking to John.

"No, no, no," the Kenyan said. "To find duplications would indeed prove that there is more than one burial. But *not* to find them does not prove that there is *not* more than one burial." He folded his slender arms. "It is not warranted by the facts."

"That's true too," Joly allowed.

But the class grumbled predictably at the Kenyan: Hadn't Dr. Oliver said a hundred times that science doesn't deal with proof, but with probability? And to find 197 bones without a single duplication –

"No, wait," Gideon said. "Captain Morefu's making a sound point. We can do better than that. As a matter of fact, I have; while you were putting the skeleton together, I did a little matching."

He picked up the fifth cervical vertebrae, which was tagged with blue tape, and the fourth, tagged with green. "Vertebrae are the most complexly shaped and probably the most variable bones in the body, and they nestle into each other more closely than any others do; that's what gives the spinal column its strength. Now, this C4 and C5 were in two different packages; if they were from two different people, they might fit roughly into each other – but not like this."

He held up the small, hollow-centered bones and slipped them against each other.

They fit perfectly; as neat, tight, and inescapably matching as a pair of stackable chairs.

"No. No, Dr. Oliver, no." Captain Morefu was shaking his fine head. "How can I accept this as proof? How can we say with certainty that no two people have ever had greatly similar spinal columns? Many times have I seen –"

"Wait, Captain; give me a chance. There's something else, and it's about as close to proof as we're going to get in this business. If you look at these two vertebrae –" He paused and held them out. "Here, have a look. Tell me if you see anything."

The Kenyan took them, turning them slowly around, frowning hard. After a few seconds he looked up, his face transformed and smiling. "These scratches. They match."

"That's it," Gideon said and explained to the others. "The captain's referring to the cut marks made during the dismemberment. If you hold the adjacent bones together in their natural positions, you can see how some of the marks start on one bone and end on the other. How could that happen unless they were together when the cuts were made? Case closed; We're dealing with a single body."

251

He put the vertebrae down. "Now get going with your analysis. And remember, start with the sex."

"What difference does it make what we start with?" someone wanted to know. "Why the sex first?"

"Partly because you have to know the sex to draw other conclusions from it. Men and women have different proportions, as you may have noticed."

"No shit," one of the Americans said.

"But also," Gideon said with a smile, "sexing a skeleton is easier than anything else, and it's nice to start with something easy. If you just flipped a coin you'd be right half the time. Compared to determining age, there's nothing to it."

"For you, maybe," someone muttered.

"For you too," he said, not quite truthfully. "You've all watched me do it. Now let's get to it."

The exercise went slowly while the groups measured, calculated, and debated. Gideon was itching to have a go at the new material himself, but resigned himself to wait, enjoying the teacherly satisfaction of watching his students put to competent use what they had learned from him.

At a little before ten, the three groups began their reports. They were unanimous in their determination of sex: the skeleton was that of a male. Gideon congratulated them and announced his agreement. A moment's glance at the pelvis had confirmed what he already knew.

The groups also agreed on height; not surprising since all the long bones were there, and the application of the Trotter and Gleser equations was an easy task. But the estimate was surprisingly low: five-feet-four, plus or minus two inches. His own quick and dirty estimate from the vertebrae had been five-eight, and he couldn't possibly have been four inches off. Two, maybe. Besides, Joly had already told him his findings matched Alain's description. The attendees had fouled up somehow. He'd go over their work with them in a few minutes and straighten them out. Odd that all three groups should get it so wrong.

The reports on race were next. Given the complexity – some anthropologists said the impossibility – of determining ancestry from the skeleton, he hadn't been going to ask it of them. But they had wanted to try, using the few simplified guidelines he'd given them (and, he was sure, the various stereotypes about skull thickness, brain-cavity-size, and "primitive" features that many of them had brought with them). Gideon let them go ahead, confident the experience would be instructive if nothing else.

It was. Two of the groups couldn't agree among themselves and gave up trying, their preconceptions in tatters. This Gideon thought of as salutary and not unexpected. But the final group's report was a dandy.

"We have determined," said the grave, slow-spoken female CID inspector who presented their report, "that the remains are those of a person of the Mongoloid race."

"*Mongoloid?*" echoed Gideon.

"Mongoloid," he was assured. "Quite probably northeastern Asiatic."

Anyone but the solid, relentlessly sober Inspector Hawkins and he might have thought his leg was being pulled. "Now where the hell did you get Mongoloid from?" he asked.

Inspector Hawkins was unfazed. "We applied intermembral ratio analysis and got a tibial-femoral index of 81.4," she replied without tripping over a syllable.

Well, she had her theory right, if nothing else. A tibial-femoral index of 81.4 meant that the tibia – the shin bone – was 81.4 percent as long as the thigh bone. And anything less than 83 percent was generally accepted as Mongoloid, reflecting the shortness of the Asiatic lower leg compared to the upper leg. In other races the typical ratio was much higher.

"Did you take the physiological lengths of the bones, not the maximum lengths?" he asked.

For the first time the sturdy Inspector Hawkins faltered. "The . . . ah . . . physiological lengths?"

That explained it, he thought with some relief. For a moment there he'd started to wonder what was going on. As racial criteria went, intermembral ratios weren't bad, but they required trickier measurements than he'd been able to present in class. He'd spent a few minutes talking about the principles involved, but he hadn't expected anyone to try and apply them. Fine, it would be one more good lesson for them to take back: using half-understood techniques was a mistake that could result in ludicrous errors. Better to call in an expert when you weren't sure what you were doing.

"Here, let me show you how it's done," he said, and taking the sliding calipers he moved to the table and picked up the right tibia. "Now, the physiological length of a long bone is its functional length, which you . . ."

His voice faded as he became aware of the odd heft of the bone. Puzzled, he looked more closely at it. Then quickly at the other tibia, and then both femurs. It was the first time he'd really examined them, and after twenty or thirty seconds' study, he was still puzzled.

For one thing, Inspector Hawkins was right, even if she'd gone about it wrong. He didn't need the calipers to tell him that the tibia was quite short compared to the femur. But it was the lightness of these normally dense leg bones that bothered him; that and their shape. There was something odd about them; not wildly odd, but . . . something.

"Strange . . ." he said, more to himself than anyone else, and ran his fingers down the dusty, dry, brown length of a femur.

The class had seen him at work before and they were used to this. They waited patiently.

Not Joly. He stepped up to the table. "What's strange?"

"The bowing," Gideon said abstractedly, continuing to move his hand over the bone. "Look at the shaft. And do you see the torsion in both tibias – just a little, as if someone grabbed each end and gave it a small twist?"

"No," Joly said.

"Do you know what that means?" Gideon went on, still staring at the bones.

256

"No," Joly said again, this time with a wary edge to his voice.

"Oh-oh," John murmured from outside the jellyfish-ring. "Looks like another case of cleidocranial whatsamatosis."

The circle of trainees surged silently forward with interest, all at the same time, like a jellyfish flexing inward.

Gideon looked at Joly. "Inspector, I know who this is."

Joly looked down his nose at him, head tilted back, lips pursed, eyes narrowed. "You knew who it was yesterday."

"I was wrong," Gideon said.

17

There was a ripple of anticipation around the circle. They had been through three sessions with Gideon, and they knew that he was not above the occasional use of a dramatic device to make a point. But this time they waited in vain.

"I think," Joly said, "this is something the professor and I had best talk about alone. I'm sure you understand."

"Good idea," Gideon agreed. What he had

to say was going to test Joly's newly acquired tolerance to its limit, and it would never do for the dignified *inspecteur principal* to have a fit in front of his colleagues.

When they had left, buzzing, Joly closed the door behind them, silently walked the length of the room back to the table, looked at John, looked at Gideon, and sighed.

"I know I'm going to regret this..." He tipped his head towards the table, looked back at Gideon, and elaborately formed his lips into a circle, as if he were about to blow a smoke ring.

"Who?" he said suspiciously.

Gideon decided that the best way to tell him was just to tell him.

"I think it's Guillaume du Rocher."

After a brief moment of stunned silence, John smacked his big hands together and yelped with joy.

Joly's lips continued to form their fishlike O for a few seconds, then wavered and shut. He subsided slowly into one of the scattered chairs with another immense sigh.

"This –" Gideon began.

But Joly was resignedly holding up his hand. "By Guillaume du Rocher," he said patiently, "I imagine you mean...I pray fervently you mean...some long-lost relative – of whose existence only you happen to be

258

aware, of course – who happens to have the same name as the Guillaume du Rocher who drowned last Monday in Mont St. Michel Bay?"

"No, I don't –"

"Because you *can* not mean the Guillaume du Rocher who drowned last Monday in Mont St. Michel Bay, and who was publicly buried in the family cemetery at Rochebonne one day before the first of these bones – these very old bones – were found." A rare plaintive look puckered the flesh around his eyes. "Can you?"

"No, I don't mean that Guillaume either."

"Come on, Doc," John laughed. He too dropped into one of the black plastic-and-chrome chairs. "What do you mean? Who is this guy?"

"What I mean," Gideon said, "is that unless I'm way off base the man who drowned in the bay wasn't really Guillaume du Rocher."

Their expressions were so artlessly baffled – jaws dropping, brows soaring, like a couple of ungifted actors simulating astonishment – that he burst out laughing. In all fairness, he remarked to himself, being the Skeleton Detective of America did have its moments.

"I'm pretty sure *this* is the real

Guillaume," he said with a glance at the skeleton, "and he's been dead since World War II, not since last Monday."

"Well – but –" John stammered. "You said you met him yourself a couple of years ago –"

"What I met was somebody who called himself Guillaume du Rocher."

"And are we permitted to know," Joly asked, recovering his equilibrium, "how you deduced that the man who was known as Guillaume du Rocher for as long as anyone can remember – to his family, his attorney, his servants, his doctor, and scores of others who knew him well – was not the 'real' Guillaume du Rocher?" He pulled out a fresh pack of Gitanes and tore it open; rather testily, it seemed to Gideon.

"I deduced it from the simple fact that these bones belonged to the real Guillaume. Therefore, nobody else could be him, no matter how many people recognized him or think they recognized him. He's been down in that cellar for almost fifty years. At least that's the way it looks to me," he added circumspectly, mindful that less than twenty-four hours ago he'd been telling them the bones were Alain's. "John, do you remember what Loti said to us?"

The ends of Joly's mouth moved slightly

down. He was not pleased to hear that they had been interviewing the doctor.

"Not really," John said. "I got the *bonjour* pretty good, and I got the *au revoir*, but I didn't get too much in between."

"He said Guillaume had rickets."

"Yeah, that's right; you told me." His eyes widened. "This skeleton's got rickets?"

"It sure as hell does. The leg bones show torsion, bowing, shortening – not extreme, but enough. That's why the class came up with such a low height estimate, and it's what messed them up on race. It all adds up to rickets."

And, he was too embarrassed to mention, so did the beading on the ribs that he'd noticed days ago and promptly forgotten. Not prayer beads at all. The "rickety rosary" was what old pathology texts called it, and it should have been a giveaway. But with rickets being so uncommon for the last fifty years, and with this particular case being relatively mild, and with his reference books back in Port Angeles... Given time he could probably come up with a dozen excuses, but the simple fact was that he'd missed it.

"Doc," John said. "Am I wrong, or don't you get rickets from malnutrition? Why would a rich guy like Guillaume have it?"

"It comes from a lack of vitamin D in kids.

It throws off bone metabolism. But people didn't even know what vitamins were when he was born, and plenty of rich kids got it."

Joly had lit his cigarette and come to the table to stare accusingly down at the bones. "Why would a case of rickets prove so conclusively that this is Guillaume? As you said, other people have had it."

"But not any other du Rochers, according to Loti. And this is a du Rocher, all right; the sternal foramen, the skeletal proportions – Who else could it possible be?"

"I believe the same question was asked of me yesterday," Joly observed drily. "At that time the correct answer was Alain du Rocher."

"Well, I was wrong," Gideon admitted again. "I was going with the information I had at the time."

Joly merely looked at him.

"You get new data, you have to modify your hypotheses," John contributed sagely from his chair.

"That's about the size of it," Gideon smiled. "Look, maybe it can be verified. The teeth have had some work done on them. Maybe there are some dental records around."

"After all this time?" Joly said. "I doubt it." He frowned, stroking his cheek, still looking penetratingly down at the bones, as if waiting for them to explain themselves. "All right, let's say you're right –"

"You're wearing him down, Doc," John said.

"Very probably," Joly conceded. He turned to face Gideon through a veil of blue smoke. "If so, it raises a good many new questions. Who killed him? Why? How was it possible to keep it secret all this time? Is there a connection to Claude's murder?"

"I've got a good one too," John said. "If that stuff on the table is what's left of Guillaume du Rocher..."

"Yes?" Joly said, turning.

"....then just who the hell was it who drowned in the bay last week?"

Under self-imposed and mutually agreeable rules John and Gideon gave themselves a break from the proliferating mysteries of Rochebonne and didn't discuss them during most of the drive to Mont St. Michel. But when they stopped for gas at an Elf Station near St. Georges de Grehaigne, John could no longer restrain himself.

"Doc, I've been thinking about it," he said, turning intently towards Gideon, his palms on his thighs and his elbows akimbo. "I don't think it makes any sense. How could anybody get away with it? It's impossible."

"What's impossible about it?"

"Well, what are you saying? That after Guillaume died somebody imitated him for the next fifty years or so and fooled everyone who knew him? It can't be done."

"Why not? Remember, everybody thought he went off to join the Resistance in 1942. When he showed up again – that is, when the fake Guillaume showed up –"

"Come on, admit it. Listen to what you're saying. Does this sound like real life?"

"– nobody had seen the real one for two solid years."

"Doc, Doc, you've been watching too much TV. I'm telling you it can't be done; not really. You can't fool a guy's family, his friends... There are too many little things you can't imitate exactly – his expressions, the way he smiles, the way he walks, and moves, and even stands; the little bits of trivia he knows –"

"Even," Gideon said, "if the new Guillaume's face was so scarred you'd never be able to recognize it? Even with a damaged larynx that changed his voice to a whisper? Even if most of his bones had been pinned back together with 1944 techniques so he walked, and moved, and stood differently?

264

Even if he turned reclusive and hardly talked to anyone any more? Even if he'd already lived at Rochebonne so he knew the routine?"

"Yeah, well, that's a point – but are you telling me his own *doctor* wouldn't know him?"

"Loti never saw him until they brought him into the hospital in 1944."

"What about the rickets?"

"What about the rickets?"

"Well, Loti knew Guillaume had rickets as a kid. Couldn't he see the new Guillaume didn't have it?"

"John, after the crushing this guy's bones went through, no doctor in the world would have spotted a mild case of rickets unless he did a microscopic analysis of the bone tissue. And why would Loti do that?"

"Yeah, but..." John shook his head with frustration. "His handwriting, what about his handwriting? There must have been things around that he signed before. You're telling me that no one ever noticed the difference in –" He stopped and fell back against the seat. "You're going to say that the paralyzed arm was the one he used to write with before the war. Aren't you?"

"I don't know, but I'll give you odds it was."

As Gideon paid the bill and drove back out onto the N176, John watched him thoughtfully. "You're really starting to believe this stuff, aren't you?"

"God help me," Gideon said, "I think I am."

18

Mont St. Michel. Everyone has seen pictures of the towering, medieval pyramid rising on its rocky island out of the sea, but no one can help being astounded at first sight of the real thing. It is like the Grand Canyon; you can look at photographs of it all your life, but the first time you stand on the rim looking down into it the words that jump to your lips are, "My God, I didn't know it looked like *that!*"

"Jesus H. Christ," John said, "I didn't know it looked like that!"

They had pulled the car to the side of the road to stare at it from half a mile away at the foot of the long causeway that connects it to the nondescript town of Pontorson. It was a surprise to Gideon too. He'd been prepared for its size, for its stark beauty, for the way it twisted and rambled upwards, moving higgledy-piggledy through time: at the base, crenellated ramparts dating back to the Hundred Years' War; in the center a colorful jumble of cramped stone houses form the fifteenth and sixteenth centuries; and finally, at the top, the great abbey itself, its eighth-century core altered and enlarged a hundred times in a thousand years, yet strangely balanced and all of a piece.

What the pictures hadn't prepared him for was its raw, gray vigor. Despite the stone traceries, the spires, the arches, Mont St. Michel was rudely masculine; hard, plain, virile. The towers didn't soar, they surged and thrusted; the whole crowded rock was like a living animal, bunched, powerful, restlessly alert.

"So where's this shrine of French gastronomy?" asked John, who never stayed awed very long. "Even an omelet's starting to sound good."

But *Mère Poularde* was closed until the season officially opened on April 1. So were most of the other restaurants on the Grand Rue. They worked their way up the steep, narrow street, growing increasingly pessimistic about the prospects for lunch. "We just can't come to a place like this and eat in one of these crummy fast-food places,"

Gideon said, referring to the tiny shops where chilled-looking vendors sold luke-warm pizza slices and stale-looking sand-wiches wrapped in plastic.

"I can," John said, then stopped abruptly. "Hey, I just thought of something." He chirped with laughter. "Wow."

"What?"

"Well, Guillaume's will isn't worth a damn. Not if you're right about those bones."

Gideon stared at him. As obvious as it was, it hadn't occurred to him. "Of course! It wasn't really Guillaume who made it out, was it? Whoever it was, he didn't have any right to give Guillaume's property away."

"That's the way I see it," John said, starting to walk again. "This gets weirder by the minute. All those people who got something in the will – they're not entitled to it. Boy, there's another great reason for murder right there."

"How do you mean? How would they benefit from killing him?"

"Not him, you."

"Oh," Gideon said. "Me."

"Sure, the minute you figured out that skeleton was Guillaume, that'd be it for the will."

Gideon nodded wearily. There were too

many motives; that was the problem, just as Joly had said, and they kept coming up with new ones. If the invalid will really was behind everything in some way – and that made considerable sense – then any of the heirs who knew Guillaume hadn't really been Guillaume might well have wanted Gideon dead. But *did* any of them know? And even if they did, where did Claude come into it? Why kill him? Not because he'd threatened to challenge the will, certainly; Bonfante had made it clear that he couldn't have brought it off.

Was is possible that Claude knew about Guillaume's murder in 1942 and someone killed him to keep him quite? Not very likely. If he'd known he'd have told a long time ago, instead of fuming for forty years over a will he knew to be fraudulent.

And what about the pretend-Guillaume, with only a year to live? Assuming he was murdered (which even Gideon was beginning to have doubts about), who would benefit in any important way by moving up his death a few months?

No, there was something more than the will involved; more than vengeful hatred of Claude too. Something they were all missing, something at the heart of it that would make everything fall into place. That it had to do in some way with the dark affairs in the cellar of Rochebonne in 1942 he had little doubt. But what, exactly?

"Have you noticed," he muttered to John, "that the more we figure out, the less we seem to know?"

At this point, happily, they came upon a sight that warmed them both: an open restaurant, a mellowed sixteenth-century inn with a hanging, filigreed metal sign over the door. *Le Mouton Blanc*, it said, and underneath, appropriately, was a picture of a contented-looking white sheep. It was the kind of place about which John might have had doubts, but as they approached it, two people came out, and the aroma of *pommes frites* that wafted out after them was more than enough to convince him.

The combination of smells inside was even better, notwithstanding the usual fug of cigarette smoke: steamed seafood, fried potatoes, roasted meat. It was probably just the way it smelled in 1600, Gideon thought with pleasure, except, of course, for the tobacco, which wouldn't have arrived from North America for another few decades. It was about half-full, and at a table near the back were Ray and Claire, with Sophie and Ben Butts.

"Come join us!" Ben shouted as soon as they walked in.

They threaded their way between the tables. "I don't know; you look pretty crowded already," Gideon said with a smile.

"Oh, no, please, we can easily make room," Ray said, looking glad to see them, and Claire murmured something similar.

"Sure," Ben said. "Unless you're rubbin' elbows, eatin's just stokin'."

"And who said that?" Sophie asked.

"I believe it was my cousin Bobby Will."

"I thought your cousin was Billy Rob."

Ben looked thoughtfully at her. "No, Billy Rob's my uncle on my mother's side; married to Clara Bea. Bobby Will's my cousin on my father's side – Willie Bob's boy."

Amid general laughter, a couple of chairs were taken from nearby tables and Gideon and John squeezed in. No one had ordered food yet, but they were almost through a bottle of white wine, and a new bottle with two more glasses was brought. *Sélection de l'Hôtel, Vin de Table,* the modest label said, but it turned out to be a better-than-ordinary Chablis.

Gideon lifted his glass in a salute. "So,"

he said, "what brings you to Mont St. Michel?"

He felt at ease with these four. Of all the people at Rochebonne they were the ones he trusted most: Ray, sweet-tempered and earnest, and altogether above suspicion; gentle Claire Fougeray, thin and pallid, but with a ruddy heat in her cheeks that he guessed was due less to the wine than to Ray's proximity; Sophie Butts, frank and solid; Ben, with his easy way of meandering between homespun adages and lawyerly good sense. If one of them turned out to be a murderer, he was going to be awfully annoyed. And surprised.

It was Ben who answered. "We came down to pick up Guillaume's car and take it back. Seemed like a good excuse for us all to get out of the house for a while, take a train ride, see the Mont before we left." Smiling, he raised his glass to toast the others.

"Are you taking off?" John asked. "I thought Joly wanted you to stay."

"Can't," Ben said. "There are big things on the menu at Southwest Electroplating. Two-million-dollar comparable-worth suit coming up. Anyway, Joly told us from the start we could go after tomorrow. He knows where to find us if he needs us."

"Ben and I are catching a ten o'clock flight

from Paris tomorrow night," Sophie said. "These two will be leaving the next morning, by train from Dinan."

Gideon looked with interest at Ray and Claire. "You're going together?"

"They certainly are," Sophie said happily.

"Oh," said Ray, and cleared his throat. "Well."

"Raymond is being kind enough to accompany *maman* and me to Rennes," Claire explained primly, looking down at her glass. "After that he will be our guest for a few days."

"Well, you know, I don't have to be back at Northern Cal until next week," Ray said, "so I thought ... you know." He tugged at the ends of his bowtie and shone with inarticulate happiness.

Sophie took a healthy swallow of wine and put down her glass. "I don't know about anyone else, but I could eat a horse. Claire, dear, why don't you order for us? Is that all right with everyone?"

That was fine with everyone, and Claire, who seemed in her retiring way to be pleased with a role in the limelight, consulted at length with the waiter before settling on a three-course meal of traditional Norman cuisine. By the time the ordering was done, most of the new bottle of wine had been drunk and the level of conviviality was high. There was a blaze in the fireplace, and outside a passing rain had left the cobblestones of the Grand Rue gleaming, making it easy for Gideon to enjoy the pleasant illusion of being a sixteenth-century traveler, warmly ensconced in a fine inn among companionable comrades.

"I tell you, kids," Ben said, playfully addressing Ray and Claire, "if you're not going to ask him, I will."

"Oh, Uncle," Claire murmured with her eyes down, then turned a little rosier. Blushing looked good on her, Gideon decided.

"All right, then, I will," Ben declared. "We have a technical question for you, Professor. Genetically speaking, just how closely related are these kids? The reason they want to know –"

"Ben," Sophie said, "I think Gideon can figure out why they want to know."

"I could make a pretty good guess," Gideon said. "What are you two anyway, cousins?"

"It's precisely that which we can't determine," Ray said with donnish perplexity. "We know we're not first cousins at any rate, but after that it gets extraordinarily confusing."

"I'll tell you what," Gideon said. "Why don't you draw up a family tree for a few generations, showing who begat who –"

"Whom," murmured Ray automatically, then winced. "Sorry, force of habit."

"– and I'll try and work out the genetic relationships from that."

This was well received, and they set to reconstructing the du Rocher genealogy, with Ben drawing it step-by-step on the back of a paper placemat. In the meantime, the first course arrived: *fruits de mer variés,* carried to the table on three broad metal platters, arranged as identically and as prettily as a set of postcards. Three big crayfish and four prawns alternating in a circle in the center, a neat mound of small, salty sea snails to be poked out of their shells with pins that came embedded in a cork, and a pile of perhaps a hundred tiny gray shrimp that Claire showed them how to eat. One held the head between thumb and forefinger, then briskly snapped off the tail with the other hand, revealing a nubbin of pale meat that had almost no flavor but nevertheless bathed the palate in a faint, luscious essence of the ocean itself.

It was slow eating, what with pins and

fingers, so that John and Gideon were able to entertain themselves contentedly while the others haggled good-humoredly over the more obscure corners of the family's history. Then, as two black kettles of *moules marinière* were put on the table, the neatly printed chart was handed to Gideon, who got out a pen of his own and started to work while he ate.

By the time the mussels had been reduced to shining, blue-black heaps of empty shells, and the last of the shallot-flavored broth soaked up with sliced baguettes, he announced his findings. "You're fifth cousins."

"What does that mean for...for children?" Claire asked, then looked down and blushed again.

Gideon smiled at her. It was nice to know there were still women like Claire left. He liked the idea of Claire and Ray as a team; there weren't too many Ray Schaefers around either.

"It means," he said, "that you two are separated by eleven degrees of consanguinity –"

"Aren't you glad you asked?" John said.

"Which means that the probability of your sharing any particular gene, nasty or otherwise, is .00049. And even if you did, the chance of any of your children getting a double dose of a recessive is only a quarter of that."

Understandably enough, Claire still looked confused, and on impulse Gideon reached out to put his hand on the back of hers. It was cool and dry. He could feel her fragile tendons through the thin skin. "For all practical purposes," he said, "you aren't related at all. There isn't anything to worry about."

Her brow finally relaxed. "Thank you, Professor Oliver," she said with a smile and took her hand back.

"Gideon." He noticed that her hand slipped under the table and Ray's moved stealthily towards it. One more glass of wine and he'd probably have said: "Bless you, my children."

The main course of leg of lamb – famous, Claire told them, for its delicate, spicy flavor that came from having been raised in the nearby coastal salt pastures – and white beans and fried potatoes was consumed in an atmosphere of increasing camaraderie that was enhanced by the fresh bottle of Médoc. Once Ben began to ask about the murder investigation, but Claire's sudden, visible shrinking (or more likely a crisp kick in the shins from Sophie) quieted him. Mostly, they talked about the history and architecture of the Mont, about which Claire was shyly knowledgeable.

"I know what," Ray said, flushed with wine and enthusiasm, and looking very boyish with his freckles and his bowtie. "Let's walk out into the bay and have a look at the Mont from there. Assuming," he added quickly, "that the tide is still out, of course."

Sophie put down her coffee. "Are you out of your mind, Raymond?"

"Why?" he responded with a startled blink. "Oh, I see. But what happened to Guillaume was a freak accident; everyone knows that. It's just that I've always wanted to walk out into Mont St. Michel Bay and see the abbey soaring behind me in the mist, like a prow of a ship, the way Henry Adams described it."

"Oh, I think it's a wonderful idea, Raymond," Claire said warmly.

"But isn't it dangerous?" asked Sophie. "After all –"

"No, no, Aunt Sophie, when I was a little girl in Avranches my friend and I used to play in the sands all day. If you simply pay attention to the tide, and know what the quicksands look like, and keep an eye out for the mist, and

278

don't go off by yourself, it's perfectly safe."

"Those are a great many qualifications," Sophie said severely.

"No," Ben laughed, "I think Claire's right. It's no secret Guillaume was getting a little, well, forgetful, and the fact is, he never should have been out there alone. Not that I know who was going to stop him." He drained his coffee with a smile. "But in any case, I'm afraid it's all moot, kids. Sorry to be a spoilsport, but I'm afraid we ought to be driving back. Sophie's coming down with a cold, and I want her to put her feet up and have a good long nap this afternoon."

"I have an idea," Gideon said. "Why don't you two go ahead and take Guillaume's car back? We can drop off Claire and Ray later on. To tell you the truth, I'd enjoy wandering around the bay myself, especially with a guide who knows something about it."

Beside him, John stirred restlessly. Gideon half-expected a thud against his own shin, but none came; merely a grumbled "I thought you wanted to tour the abbey," just to let Gideon know he wasn't getting by with anything.

"That's a wonderful idea, Gideon," Ray said. "Claire, how can we find out about the tide?"

279

"There's a tourist office in the Old Guard Room near the entrance down below. They have tidetables there."

"You don't have to go all the way down there," Ben said. "I've got one here somewhere..." He tapped the pockets of his jacket and trousers unsuccessfully, and finally located it in a coat he'd left on the rack near the door. He came back to the table thumbing through a small booklet. *"Annuaire des Marées,"* Gideon read on the blue cover, *"des Baies de Saint-Malo et Mont Saint-Michel. 1987."*

"Let's see," Ben said. "March, um, twenty-third, right?" He ran his finger carefully along a line. "Right, here it is. High tide was at 10:21 this morning, and low tide isn't until...5:15." He closed the booklet and looked at his watch. "You're in good shape. It's only a little after two, so you have three hours before it even begins to rise."

"More than that," Claire said. "It will be – What do you call it, dead water? – for at least an hour after low tide." She smiled at Sophie. "But I promise we won't stay out anywhere near so long."

"Good," Sophie said querulously. "But I still think it's a rotten idea."

280

To go down they had to go up. The path to the sands began at the Abbey Gardens on a shelf near the top of the rock, and there they stood for a few minutes looking out over the misty enormity of the Bay of Saint-Michael-in-Peril-from-the-Sea. The low rain clouds that had been hovering over the Mont had moved westward so that to their left the wooded coastline was shrouded in fog. To their right they could see a wide expanse of what looked like desert scrub brush – the famous salt pastures, Claire explained, originally planted centuries ago in futile effort to stabilize the sands – and beyond them the distant low roofs of Avranches.

In front of them was the bay itself, featureless except for a few narrow streams that wandered through it in great, lazy curves. Everything was veiled in a thin mist shot through with watery, pink-tinged sunlight, so that sand and sky blended into a bland, disorienting world of pale, diffused mauve. No, not quite blended. There, on the horizon, ten miles off or more, Gideon could just make out the gray, gleaming ribbon that was the receding tide. He watched it for a while, trying to tell if he could see it change – it was, after all, the fastest-moving tide in Europe – but it remained the same: a flat pewter strip separating a smooth and formless earth from a smooth and formless sky.

"What do you call that dog," John asked dreamily, "with the gray fur? Big dog, short hair –"

"A Weimaraner?"

"Right. That's what this sand reminds me of; what a Weimaraner must look like to a flea coming in for a landing."

Gideon laughed. "Amazing. I've never known you to be moved to poetic fancy before."

"No kidding, Doc, is that what that was?"

"You're in good company, John," Ray said. "You'll be happy to know that du Guesclin himself used the same metaphor in – 1390, I believe it was. Well, not quite the same, but close enough."

"That would have been difficult," Claire said. "Du Guesclin died in 1380."

Her eyes darted hesitantly at each of the men. She wasn't used to making jokes, Gideon could see, and she was trying to gauge whether she'd gone too far.

Ray's burst of laughter set her at ease. "Is this," he said with mock austerity, "what I have to look forward to? A lifetime of caviling fault-finding over trivial arcana?"

"Yes!" she said, bubbling over with too

much intensity, like a child learning to play. "Oh, yes!" Then she giggled; a girlish, appealing tinkle of pleasure that made her look almost pretty. "Whatever it means – what you said." She was certainly coming out of her shell.

Ray squeezed her hand, looking flustered and pleased. "Perhaps we ought to go down now," he said primly. "We want to be sure to be back within three hours."

At the base of the Mont they had to clamber over algae-slimed granite boulders, then slog through fifty feet of black mud. Claire, wearing tennis shoes she'd carried with her for·walking, led the way, moving with confidence. When they reached the sand she said: "Before we go any further, I think it would be good for you to know what quicksand looks like. Would you like me to show you?"

She went to the top of a hummock – the tidal plain, seemingly so featureless and smooth from above, was actually full of furrows, humps, and depressions – and looked around her, leaning into the misty glare and shielding her eyes with her hand like a Gilbert and Sullivan sailor. "There!" she said. "Come!"

They went to a roughly circular patch of sand perhaps ten feet in diameter. Unlike

the flat-toned, uneven surface everywhere
else it was glossy and smooth, brown rather
than mauve. And not in the least dangerous-
looking.

She pointed to smaller patches nearby.
"As you see, there's a fair amount of it. In
the summer, when the tourists come, the
sands are more stable, thank God. But in
winter you must watch where you go.
Gideon, is something wrong?"

"Claire, if it's this obvious, how could
Guillaume not have seen it?"

"Yes, that's a good question," Ray said.

"But how could he see it?" Claire asked.
"Under even an inch of water it's invisible.
The tide was rising, and he must have
stepped into it through the water –" She
frowned curiously at him. "Isn't that what
happened?"

"I suppose it is," Gideon said, and he
supposed it was. Wherever he looked there
was a logical explanation for the accidental
drowning of the man he'd known as
Guillaume. Reasonable explanations all;
doubted by no one, even John. And still . . .

They walked out into the bay for about
twenty minutes, never looking back. (This
was Ray's suggestion for heightening the
dramatic impact when they finally did turn.)
When they came to a sand dune six or seven

feet high they climbed it and found a craterlike top in which they could all sprawl comfortably, leaning against the sides of the hollow, looking back at the Mont.

From there the abbey was indeed like the prow of a tremendous ship bearing down on them over a sea of sand. For a while they lay back in the pallid sunshine, peacefully taking it in, wrapped in their own thoughts. Then, prompted by questions from Ray, Claire began to tell them the history of the rock from the time when it was not Mont St. Michel but Mont Tombe, and it reared up not from the floor of the sea but from the green forest known as Scissy. Then the terrible tide of A.D. 709 had annihilated the population and transformed the landscape, so that when the archangel Michael made his appearance there a little later, it was on today's lonely monolith, almost a mile from the shore.

Before long Gideon heard a long, contented sigh from John, followed by the immediate commencement of slowed-down, rhythmic breathing. If John were ever to suffer from insomnia (a laughable premise) he wouldn't have to resort to pills; all he'd need to do was sit himself down at anything resembling a lecture. But this time Gideon sympathized. Claire's voice was melodic and soft, and the sand beneath them radiated the warmth it had somehow managed to soak up from the wispy sunshine.

He stretched out his legs and crossed them at the ankles, luxuriating in Claire's lulling story and in the spired abbey floating above them. He would bring Julie here someday, to this very spot, to see this with him. First they would lunch at the Mouton Blanc; that was essential. It wouldn't be the same without that lovely lamb sending out its own warmth from within.

He didn't realize he was dozing until his eyelids jumped suddenly open, leaving him tense and alert. He couldn't have been drifting for long. Claire was still in the tenth century. John was still asleep.

"Listen!" he said urgently. What for, he wasn't sure. Only that there was something ...

Claire stopped in the middle of a word. John awakened instantly. All of them sat straining to hear for a moment, then leaped to their feet and looked around them.

"It's not possible!" Ray cried. The others simply stared, struck dumb.

The raised hollow in which they'd been sitting had made it impossible to see the floor of the bay or even the lower fortifications of the abbey. Now they saw that their hump of sand had become a miniature mont St. Michel, a six-foot-high island surrounded by a great tissue-thin sheet of water broken by dry patches wherever the land rose a little. Behind them the sheet thickened and extended to the horizon. In front, they could see the advancing edge of it about a thousand yards ahead, creeping unevenly towards the Mont like a film of quicksilver.

"The tide!" Claire said, still staring. "How can it be?" She looked at her watch. "It's only 3:40."

"Can – can a tidetable *lie?*" Ray murmured.

"No, no," Claire said. "I don't think so. I've never heard of such a thing."

Gideon and John exchanged a brief glance. Maybe tidetables couldn't lie, but Ben Butts sure as hell could. Gideon clenched his teeth; dammit, he had felt a faint stirring of – what? Wariness? Suspicion? – when Ben had read from the tidetable, but he had dismissed it as so much paranoia. And he hadn't been able to think of a civil way of asking to see the table for himself.

But there was no time to pursue the thought now. And unless they got out of there in a hurry, there wouldn't ever be time to pursue anything else. Even in the few seconds they had been watching, the water level around the dune had risen smoothly, like liquid seeping into a pool from the bottom, and some of the dry areas had already been swallowed up. The sound that had awakened Gideon, he realized, was the buzzing hum of millions of bubbles bursting on the sand as the water percolated through it. And now there was a louder sound, farther off but more ominous; a steady booming, like a colossal waterfall deep inside a cavern. Even as they turned automatically towards it, a cold wind full of the rank, wet odor of sea bottom tugged at their hair and slapped against their faces.

"That's the main body of the tide," Claire said without expression. "It will be here in a few minutes. We'll have to run for the Mont."

"But how will we see the quicksand?" Ray asked, sounding more curious than frightened. "Won't we step into it?"

"If we do, it won't hurt us so long as we keep our heads and stay together. It won't suck you under the way it does in the movies, but it grabs at you and holds you for the tide. But if you don't struggle, if you throw yourself flat when you feel yourself caught, someone else can pull you out." She made an effort to smile. "Most of the time. I think now we'd better try to get back."

"Forget that 'try' business," John said. "Let's just do it."

They scrambled down the dune and sloshed forward at a steady jog through calm, ankle-deep water, trying to catch up with the advancing rim of the tide and get to dry sand, but by the time they go to where the rim had been, it had rolled another five hundred feet forward, and the water was up to their calves. Behind them, the roaring was wilder, the wind stronger, the sky a scowling, turbid gray. John and Gideon were breathing hard. Claire and Ray panting. Their shoes, filled with water, were like weights, but impossible to do without an account of the pebbles and shells. The lamb in Gideon's stomach was no longer so delightful.

All the same, things were better than they might have been. No one had stepped in quicksand, and they were already over halfway to the Mont. Unless the speed of the tide increased, they were likely to make it all the way, encountering nothing worse than a soaking.

They pushed on, and in five more minutes they had reached the area of sloping sands that leads up to the base of the Mont. Exhilarated and laughing, they made a show of stepping over the crawling, inch-high verge of water onto dry land. On the North

Tower a few watchers were shouting and waving. John grinned and clasped his hands over his head, boxer-style, which seemed to confuse them.

"Now that," Raymond said as they moved on up the slope in shoes that squished water at each step, "is what I call adventure. Outracing the tide of Mont St. Michel! Just like Vercel! I never imagined it would happen to me." He grinned happily, clear-eyed and breathless. "Not that I'm sorry it's over."

19

It was a long way from over. Instead of continuing to slope smoothly upward the sandy floor dipped, and in a few more moments they found themselves on the edge of a six-foot-high bank, looking down into a shallow, brown, fast-moving stream. They were no more than a hundred yards from the rocky base of the Mont.

"Where the hell did that come from?" John said, his brows pulled together. "We didn't cross that when we came out."

"It was dry before," Claire said bleakly.

"This isn't a river, it's the tide – the main body. It flows in over the lowest ground first, then spreads. There are new channels every day. We'd better get across quickly."

Ray seemed puzzled by her gravity. "It doesn't really look too difficult. It can't be more than a dozen feet wide, and I think it's only about two feet d –"

He was cut off by a new sound, different from the cataract-roar behind them; a strange, sibilant grumble that was coming unmistakably and rapidly closer. They looked anxiously towards it, and in a few seconds a thick surge of dark water, almost as high as the banks of the stream, rolled heavily down it at their feet, pushing an edging of dirty yellow foam and bits of driftwood and plastic before it. When it had passed, hissing, the water in the stream rocked back and forth and then subsided restlessly, like water in a bathtub. But it didn't subside all the way.

"It's gone up almost a foot," Gideon said grimly, telling them what he knew they knew. It was also flowing faster, with little swells and eddies where there had been none before.

"We *are* going to get wet, aren't we?" a subdued but undaunted Ray murmured.

"Well, the first thing we need is a sensible tactical plan –"

But John, as Gideon well knew, was not big on tactical plans. "We'll make a chain," he said tersely. "I go in first. Then Claire gives me her hand, then you grab hers, Doc, then Ray grabs yours." He moved to the edge of the bank.

"John, wait –" Claire said.

But he was already sliding feet-first into the stream, riding down the crumbling bank on the seat of his pants. "Well, it's not too cold, anyway." He rocked slightly as his feet hit bottom. The water level was up to his hips. "But watch out; the current's stronger than it looks." He held a hand up to them. "Let's go. Doc, can you sort of pass Claire down to me?"

In not much more than a minute they had worked their way across without mishap. John, who tended to see himself as captain of the ship at times like this, stayed in the water until he had handed everyone out.

Then, as Gideon knelt to give him a hand up, there was another hissing, grumbling prelude, and another dark tidal surge, much larger this time, like a ship's wake, boiled angrily down the stream. It slammed into John as he tried to clamber up, ripping his hand out of Gideon's and carrying him on

292

its crest for twenty feet, like so much Styrofoam, before flinging him carelessly aside, leaving him to draw himself to a stop against the opposite bank, the one from which they had come.

"I'm fine, I'm fine!" he shouted, streaming and spluttering, but he flopped and stumbled before he could right himself. "Boy, the flow's getting stronger by the second."

And higher, Gideon noticed. The water now swirled above John's waist, billowing out his ski jacket. The next surge would have it up to his armpits. "Come on, John, it's rising. Do you need help?"

"Nah, I'm okay. I'm –"

He froze, open-mouthed, with an expression that Gideon, a native Californian, had always associated with the first startling tremor of an earthquake: a puzzled, listening sort of expression, as if you couldn't quite make yourself believe that the dependable old earth had actually lurched beneath you. No matter how many earthquakes you'd been through, that first incredulous reaction was the same.

Only there hadn't been an earthquake.

"*Quicksand?*" he asked urgently.

"I think so," John said. "My foot's – I can't –"

293

"Oh, my God," Claire said. "John, don't try to move!"

He managed a laugh. "Who can move?" But he pulled against the bank anyway, to no avail. The edges crumbled under his fingers and slid in tiny avalanches into the stream. He shook his head and looked up at them. "What do we do now, folks?"

"We get you out," Gideon said. "How deep are you caught?"

"I don't know." He bent, holding his face above the surface while he explored below with his hand. A stray wavelet lapped at his mouth and made him cough. No, not a stray wavelet. The water level had climbed another inch. Gideon fidgeted uneasily. He had no doubts about being able to rescue his friend, but John Lau helpless and dependent was an unnatural and disturbing phenomenon.

"Just above the ankles," John called above the rapid gurgle of the stream and the deeper roar in the background. He wobbled in the current's pull and tried to steady himself by propping one arm against the bank. There were more avalanches of sand.

"That's not too bad," Claire said to Gideon. "I think we can pull him out."

"We need something he can grab hold of," Ray said, distracted enough to let the terminal preposition stand.

294

Claire nodded. She was the only one in a long coat and she quickly stripped it off and handed it to Gideon. She shivered as a burst of raw, wet wind plastered her silky dress to her thin frame. Quickly Ray peeled off his mackintosh and put it over her shoulders.

Gideon took Claire's coat but shook his head. "No way. It won't reach from the bank," he said quietly. "I'm going in and pull him out."

"But the quicksand –" Claire began.

"Maybe it's only over there where John is. You and Ray hang on to one end of the coat and I'll go in holding on to the other. It's only a few steps to him. If I run into quicksand you can pull me back and we'll try something else."

Like what, he wondered darkly as he lowered himself down the bank, holding on to a sleeve of the coat with one hand. Let's just hope Ray had a nice, neat alternative tactical plan all worked out. Above him, the two of them hung on to the coat with teeth-gritting determination, their slight bodies braced as if they had a tank on the other end.

It was a good thing they did. He had prepared himself for a stiffer current than before, but it caught him by surprise all the same. It was no longer the hard, pummeling

295

push they'd waded through a few minutes earlier, but an intense suction that clutched at his heavy, sodden clothes and yanked him to his right like a bug caught by a vacuum cleaner. He lost his footing before he ever found it, and would have tumbled downstream if not for Claire's and Ray's dug-in heels and resolute grip on their end of the coat. With his legs drifting like streamers in the current, he held doggedly to the sleeve until he righted himself, turning sideways to the flow to offer as little resistance as possible. The sand under his feet seemed solid enough.

"Sort of grabs you, doesn't it?" John said, barely audible over the increasing tumult of the water.

"No problem," said Gideon. "Everything's under control. You ready to be rescued?" He glanced warily to his left. No surges on the way.

"I don't know about this," John said. "This is going to be a hell of a blow to my ego."

"Gideon!" Claire called. "If your feet are all right, don't take any chances – try to reach him without moving them!"

That made sense. All they needed was for both of them to be stuck in the quicksand. Keeping his feet planted and one hand twisted firmly around the coat sleeve, Gideon reached out his other hand and leaned across the stream, trembling with the strain of staying upright in the powerful and unrelenting drag of the current. But even with his arm extended to its utmost, so that he was grunting with the effort, his straining fingertips were a foot short of John's.

On the bank, Ray was going through the contortions of getting out of his tweed jacket without releasing his grip on Claire's coat. "Gideon, if I give you my jacket, you can let John grab hold of it. If I can just..."

But Gideon doubted that the coat-to-Gideon to-jacket-to-John arrangement would provide enough leverage to pull John's 200-pound body out of the sand. And he wasn't sure the struggling Ray could extricate himself in time anyway. Even in the minute or so that he had been in the stream there had been a frightening rise in the level. It was up to his ribcage now, and very soon it would be impossible to stay on his feet. Already it was almost at John's armpits, so that he was trying to keep himself upright by paddling his arms like a man treading water.

No, there was no time to wait. What he should have done, he realized now, was to ford the stream where they'd crossed it before and knew it was free of quicksand, and then pull John out from the bank on the far side. But it was too late for that now. He was going to have to take a chance with the quicksand.

Carefully, he moved towards John, "skating" over the surface as Claire had told them to do if they found themselves near it. He inched his left foot gingerly forward, feeling for the quicksand (what did it feel like?), listening tensely for the next surge. His outstretched fingers were within ten inches of John's ... six inches ... By God, he was going to make it. Two inches ...

John strained towards him. "Just ... a little ..."

"*Unnh ...*" Gideon slid his foot forward another couple of inches.

At the precise moment their fingertips touched, he stepped into it, and he understood the expression John had had on his face. It felt as if he'd put his left foot into a swaying rowboat, or taken a step on an unsteady trampoline, or an old-fashioned waterbed. Or a huge, wobbly bowl of gelatin that would capsize if he put any weight on it. It was nothing like what he expected, and it was weird, all right.

He teetered, off balance, and leaned backwards onto the leg that was on firm sand. As he did things got even worse.

Another surge, a curling, crashing breaker this time, rumbled down the channel towards them, and Claire and Ray jerked ferociously on the coat, dragging him up the bank and out of its way.

"John!" he shouted futilely, scrambling to his feet, safe himself but still able to feel the touch of his friend's fingers on his own. They had been so agonizingly close . . . There was nothing he could do but watch, powerless and shaken, as the great swell of water swept by them, burying John for terrible, slow seconds.

"Look, he's all right! He's alive!" Ray blurted out when John's head emerged at last from the settling water.

With his eyes tightly closed, his black hair matted and wet, and his cheeks puffed out from holding his breath, his head looked to Gideon like something that had been stuck on a pike on London Bridge, but after a moment he proved Ray right, sucking in a huge breath and opening his eyes.

"I think it's time for plan B," he called weakly across the stream. The water, rising more and more swiftly, was lapping at his chin. He glanced apprehensively to his right, looking for the next surge.

And Gideon felt the first sick stab of real fear. What the hell was he going to do? How was he going to get John out before the next wave did him in? Goddamn him for being dumb enough to step in the crap just when they were almost home!

Panting with frustration, practically hopping from foot to foot, he looked wildly around for a stick, a pole, an idea, but of course there was nothing. Ray and Claire stood slumped together, with no suggestions, still pointlessly hanging on to the dripping black coat. John, God damn him, just sat there uselessly, like a bump on a log, up to his neck, with nothing to say. One more surge –

At the sibilant, rumbling murmer all of them looked sharply up to see the dull, brownish-gray breaker, nudging its scud of flotsam and yellow foam before it, roll smoothly and evilly down the channel towards them, so high this time that it spilled over the sides.

And Gideon had an idea. He ran quickly upstream along the bank, towards the oncoming breaker, only managing to get in four or five strides before pulling level with it. Then, pushing off against the edge of the bank, he launched himself into it in a shallow dive angled back downstream, in John's direction. Out of the corner of his eye he saw

Claire and Ray staring open-mouthed at him.

What he had in mind was to grab John – to more or less tackle him underwater – as the powerful wave swept Gideon downstream, and use the combined impetus of the surge and his own weight to pluck John out of the sand. Not much of an idea in the first place, and half-formed at best, but it was all he could think of, and under the circumstances it wasn't bad.

Or it wouldn't have been, except for two things. First, his hurried dive landed him not in the billowing crown of the swell but just in front of it, under the heavy, overhanging curl. Instead of being buoyed forward in John's direction, he was pounded by the crashing curtain of water and forced downward, sprawling and contorted, to bump hard against the gritty bottom and get most of the wind knocked out of him. Then, before he could raise his head to the surface and snatch a breath, the fat part of the swell sent him somersaulting forward, muddled and strangling, close to panicking because John too was under water by now, with his legs gripped fast in the quicksand, and Gideon couldn't see where he was. There would be only one chance to grab for him, and if he missed, then –

He tried to force open his eyes but the lancing pain of the salt water pinched them shut. Bursting with the effort to hold his breath, unable to tell up from down, he flailed his arms and even his legs ferociously, desperately hoping to catch hold of John as he swept by. And miraculously, he tumbled squarely into him.

It was at this point that the second thing went wrong. When the breaker had borne down on him, John had instinctively twisted his face away from it and hadn't seen Gideon dive in. So when some hideous creature dragged from the deep by the tide clutched at him from behind with its thrashing tentacles, he naturally swung his fist blindly into the mass of it as hard as he could.

The punch caught Gideon just under the diaphragm and drove the stopped-up air out of his mouth in an explosion of bubbles. Convulsively, he tightened his grip, only to be hit again, this time in the chest, and then, clumsily and with diminishing force, in the side of the neck. With his head exploding from the need for oxygen, he involuntarily sucked in a throatful of seawater, vomiting it up at once with the last residue of breath in his lungs. He *had* to come up for air, if he could figure out which way up was, but if he let go of John . . .

The lazily rotating pinpoints of light told him that he was losing consciousness, could no longer hold on against the overpowering pull of the tidal surge. He began to lose touch with where he was, what he was doing. The excruciating fire in his chest receded to some more distant dimension. His mind sagged and drifted, and he must have begun to suck in a breath because salt water suddenly burned in his nose. He stopped himself from taking it into his lungs but this time he couldn't expel it; it pooled at the back of his throat like an icy jelly. He was dimly aware that his legs had been yanked behind him by the full force of the surge, so that he was stretched out horizontally below the surface of the water, like a flag in a windstorm, hanging on with rigid and unfeeling hands to the slick, spongy material of John's collar.

It was time to let go, to give in to the tide and be swept away, time to leave John to die in peace, but still he held on, unable to order his stony fingers to unclench. Vaguely he realized that John was still struggling weakly, pulling at Gideon's wrist. Angered, Gideon shook the collar feebly. Why couldn't the stupid bastard let *him* die in peace? John struggled harder, and Gideon, foggily enraged, shook him harder in return as a new tidal surge pulled powerfully at them.

There was the sensation of a stopper popping from a bottle, and then he was tumbling again, his hands still knotted in John's collar, and John was tumbling and bouncing along with him. Dreamily, not understanding what was happening, he understood nevertheless that he had done what he had tried to do. When he opened his mouth to exult, the waiting sea-water rushed in, and the swirling, mushrooming blackness followed after it, pouring down his throat and expanding to fill his ballooning insides.

"I think he's all right," Claire's worried voice said above him.

"Of course I'm all right," Gideon said irritatedly. Or was he? He was on his back in two or three inches of water, with his head raised and his cheek lying against cold, wet cloth. Claire's dress, he realized. His head was on her lap. What was going on? Were they still in the bay? Had he had an accident? Fallen? Abruptly he remembered and pushed himself to his elbows.

"John –"

"Right here," John said. "I'm okay." He was kneeling at Gideon's side. "Thanks for coming in to get me, Doc," he said awkwardly. "Sorry about belting you."

"Think nothing of it," Gideon said woozily. "Anytime."

"How're you feeling?"

"Fine." And he was, more or less. Aching throat, queasiness, mild nausea, muscles as weak as a baby's and still quivering, but he didn't seem to be hurt. "How long was I out?"

"No more than a couple of minutes. I'm not sure if you were ever completely out."

It had felt like a week. "How did I get up here? Did you pull me out?"

John shook his head. "Couldn't. We washed up on a rise in a couple of feet of water. I tried to drag you out, but I didn't have the strength. I couldn't even pull myself out. All I could do was get your head out of the water. We would have just lay there and bought it on the next surge if Ray hadn't dragged us out. Just in time too."

"*Ray* pulled us out?"

"Now, really," Ray's mild voice remarked from Gideon's other side. "Is a tone of such marked incredulity necessary?"

Gideon and John were both tottery but able to walk unsupported, and the four of them reached the base of the Mont at last, hauled themselves off the tidal plain, and mounted the stone steps to the gardens in a weary, none-too-steady file. Looking straight ahead, they walked with dignity (which wasn't easy; John had lost his shoes and socks, Gideon one of his shoes) past the sullen and staring group of people who craned their necks to see them from the North Tower.

"Why do you suppose they're looking at us that way?" Ray asked, sounding giddy. "Are they annoyed with us for being lackbrained enough to walk merrily out into an incoming tide, or because we spoiled their afternoon by not getting drowned after all?"

In their shaky condition it seemed hilarious, and they made their way down the Grand Rue snorting and choking with laughter. But by time they got to the car a predictable reaction had set in; they were depressed and their teeth had begun to chatter with cold. Their clothes, still dripping, clung freezingly to them. Gideon stopped at the first hotel they came to, a brown, grimy old place near the railroad station on the Rue Couesnon in Pontorson, a few blocks from the causeway.

The landlady, Madame Gluges, was not wildly hospitable. For exactly what purpose, she demanded in plain-speaking French, did they wish a room? Having put this question to them before committing herself as to whether or not space was available, she folded her stocky, sweatered arms and eyed them suspiciously, waiting for them to defend themselves.

Her guardedness was understandable; the foursome did not evoke confidence: three wet, bedraggled foreigners – two of them hulking, dangerous-looking devils – and a frowzy Frenchwoman, all of them water-logged and luggageless. The brawny Oriental was actually barefoot, as if he'd come straight from the jungle, the other big one was wearing just one red and gray jogging shoe, and all of them had an overexcited, wild-eyed look. Drugs? Whiskey? Who knew what their story was? Fugitives from the police? Escaped convicts who had just swum ashore? Hardly a sight to warm the heart of a provincial hotel proprietress used to a quiet clientele of respectable (or at least solitary) traveling business representatives.

Ray didn't help matters by promising they would be on their way by six, inasmuch as they only needed the room for an hour, but Claire quickly explained that they had been caught in the bay and wished merely to stay long enough to take hot showers and, if possible, to dry their clothes.

Very well, madame said, thawing a little

at Claire's soft manner, but it would not be possible for all of them to share a single room. The men in one, the woman in the other. On different floors. Only when this unequivocal condition was humbly accepted did she soften. She would charge them for only one room, not two, and if they would leave their clothes outside their doors, she would have them taken to the basement and put in the linen dryer.

With propriety thus guaranteed, Madame Gluges relented still further. While they were getting out of their wet clothes she knocked on their doors, bringing to each room an insulated pitcher of black coffee laced with cognac – and incidentally assuring herself that Claire was where she was supposed to be. Nevertheless, it was a kindess and gratefully received, so that by the time they had handed over their clothes and donned blankets or bedspreads, their hearts and bodies were beginning to rewarm.

There was one shower per floor, and while Ray, gorgeously draped in a royal blue chenille bedspread, stalked like an Indian chief through the dim hallways in search of it, Gideon and John, a couple of braves in plain gray blankets from the closet, sat in the room, nursed their bracing coffees, and talked.

"What do you think, John?" It was hardly necessary to say about what.

"I think Ray was right; tidetables don't lie."

"That's what I think. So why should Ben Butts want to do us in?"

"I don't think he did, Doc. I think he wanted to do *you* in, and the rest of us just lucked out by being along."

"*Me?*" Gideon put his cup sharply down on the low table. "*Why?*" Before the words were out of his mouth he nodded at John. "Never mind, dumb question. I wonder why I have such a hard time getting used to the fact that someone's trying to kill me." He picked up the cup again and took a fortifying swallow, then held it under his nose and savored the thick, sweet, pungent aroma of brandy.

"Ben," he mused. "Why Ben? What would he have against Claude? What would he have against Guillaume? Why kill them?"

"Guillaume?"

"The fake Guillaume, I mean; Mr. X. I don't know what else to call him."

John poured the last of the coffee into their cups. "You don't ever quit, do you?" he said, laughing. "You're going to prove the poor guy was murdered whether he was or not."

"John, are you serious? If we didn't learn anything else out there, at least we know how it was done now. Ben came damn near drowning all of us –" He downed the last warming slug of coffee. "– vital and nimble-witted though we are. Is it really so hard to believe he did the same thing to 'Guillaume'? Where do you suppose we'd be right now if *we* were sick, and old, and lame?"

John nodded slowly. Wrapped in a blanket, with his arms folded on his chest and his dark, flat, high-cheekboned face thoughtful, he really did look like a nineteenth-century Plains warrior sitting for his portrait by Catlin, remote and unfathomable.

"Doc, you got a point," he said fathomably.

"I just thought of another point. Ben's a corporate lawyer for Southwest Electroplating."

John's look suggested that if anybody was being unfathomable, it wasn't him.

"Electroplating's the same thing as silver-plating, isn't it?" Gideon said. "Didn't you tell me cyanide is used in silver-plating? Surely Ben wouldn't have had any trouble making off with a little cyanide from his own firm without anybody knowing it."

"Yeah," John said, unconvinced, "only cyanide's not that hard for anyone to get. But

310

I guess it's something to think about." He shook his head. "I don't know, Doc. It's hard to see Ben as the one behind it all. Does it feel right to you?"

No, Gideon admitted with a sigh, it didn't. And the more he thought about it, the less right it felt. For one thing, he liked Ben too much to willingly accept him as a killer, but let that pass. There were too many other things that didn't add up, too many downright absurdities. Surely Ben Butts was smart enough to think up a less whimsical plan than this for murder. How could he possibly know Gideon would show up at Mont St. Michel that particular day, and just in time to be hustled out into the incoming tide? And if he did somehow know, was he really the kind of monster who would sacrifice the others too? Say he was; how could he gamble they'd all be killed? Because if they weren't, embarrassing questions would arise, such as the questions he and John were now asking. And how could Ben know that they would want to walk in the bay, anyway? What had he been doing, carrying around a tidetable on the slim chance that he'd have an opportunity to play his droll little trick on them? It just wasn't credible.

On the other hand, if not for that purpose,

then why *did* he have a tidetable with him? He certainly hadn't planned to go out into the bay himself. And on the other hand, there was the one overwhelming, inarguable fact that overrode everything else: Ben had peered amicably into that tidetable of his and calmly given them misinformation that was not merely a little bit off – the sort of error you'd make if you happened to read the wrong line in a tidetable – but hugely and serendipitously off. The sort of error you'd make if you were trying to drown a few of your friends.

"I suppose," John said, "that what we *ought* to do is call Joly and tell him about this." He paused and lifted his eyebrows pensively. It wasn't his first choice.

It wasn't Gideon's either. "I don't know about you, John, but I'm tired of bugging Joly with every little thing. Why don't we just go and have a little talk with Ben ourselves?"

"You're on." John grinned and hugged the slipping blanket closer around his shoulders. "I can hardly wait to see what that mother says when we walk in the door."

312

20

What Ben said was, "Hee, hee, hee."

On the surface this was not unreasonable. They had stopped at a Monoprix department store near Dinan to buy sweatshirts (their coats hadn't dried) and sneakers to replace their lost or sopping shoes. The French are not particularly large people, especially in Brittany, and clothing in sizes to fit John and Gideon was not easy to come by. As a result, the two men emerged from the store in identical lurid violet sweatshirts, each with a plump and smiling *escargot* on the chest. On their feet they wore loose, slipperlike canvas shoes of a particularly repulsive yellowish-green, with elastic side bands instead of laces; the sort of thing Quasimodo might have worn to good effect.

Gideon has also bought a tide schedule, the cover of which was identical to Ben's. While Ray and Claire shopped he had taken a few minutes to go through it with John. They were not surprised by what they found. The afternoon low tide for March 23 was not shown at 5:15, as Ben had said, or anywhere near it. It was more than five hours later, at 11:33 P.M. But *high* tide was clearly shown as 4:43 P.M. – 16:43, in the French system – when Ben had had every reason to think they'd still be in the bay. Gideon whistled softly at the height: 13.05 meters, with the previous low at 0.90 meters. A change of nearly fifty feet in a single tidal cycle! He breathed out a long sigh. They really had been lucky.

Every month was on a different page, one day per line. He scanned the entire page for march, seeking without much hope for some source of honest error on Ben's part. But there weren't any 5:15 low tides, A.M. or P.M. He thumbed through the rest of the booklet to see if there was a low tide at 5:15 on the twenty-third of *any* month, just in case Ben had gotten the right line but the wrong page. There wasn't. There was no tide at precisely 5:15, morning or afternoon, high or low, on any day of the year.

It was impossible to get around it, then; whether it felt right or not, Ben Butts, in his smiling and easygoing way, had deliberately sent them out into a Mont St. Michel flood tide that even at that moment had already been rolling steadily towards them.

All of which made his whicker of laughter when they walked into the salon thoroughly surprising. He had been alone, apparently the first one down to await the call for pre-dinner cocktails, and he had been seated in one of the wingbacked chairs in front of the fire, his back to the door, seemingly absorbed in the sports section of the *International Herald Tribune*. On John's firm suggestions, Ray and Claire had gone up to their rooms to change, having stoutly maintained their belief in his innocence during the drive.

"Hello, Ben," Gideon had said quietly from behind him, watching carefully for a giveaway sign when he turned – the sudden pallor of astonishment, perhaps, or the deep flush of rage. Instead, that high-pitched and convincing neigh of pleasure.

"That's great!" he cried, taking in their violet sweatshirts and green shoes. "All you need are matching beanies. What are you going to do for your first number?"

It was hardly the snarl of a confounded murderer. Gideon's doubts began to mount again.

As they regarded him silently, Ben's grin rigidified. "All right, I give up. What are we playing?"

"Ben, you still got that tidetable?" John asked, smiling.

"Sure, of course I do." He folded the newspaper neatly, stood up, and began

315

patting his pockets. "At least I think I do. Ah." He produced it from the left hip pocket of his mohair jacket. John took it and handed it to Gideon.

"What's going on?" Ben asked uncomfortably. "Why do I have the feeling everybody's mad at me? Did I read the table wrong or something?" Abruptly, his face fell. "You're kidding. I couldn't have."

"Let's just see," Gideon said. He turned quickly to the page for March, found the line for the current day, and moved his finger to the column headed *basses mers* – low tides. He stared, blinked, and stared again. Then he looked up at the others, thoroughly confused.

"According to this, low tide was at 5:15," he murmured.

"Well, of course," Ben said. "That's what I said, isn't it?"

Gideon took out the booklet he had bought at Monoprix and compared it to Ben's. The covers were the same, all right, and at first glance so were the contents. Sixty-four pages in all, mostly boating data and advertisements, and bound with a single hefty staple through the middle. The tidal information for March was on page 32, which was the left center page in each book, and the dates and days of the week in the two booklets matched. March 1 was shown as a Sunday, and so on. But the contents of the columns – the times and heights of the tides – were entirely different. As were the data, Gideon quickly ascertained, for the months on pages 31, 33, and 34, which were the other pages printed on the same folded sheet. The other pages seemed to be in the same in each booklet.

"Ben, where did you get this thing?"

"From the car. It was in the door pocket. I wanted to see if we'd have a chance to watch a flood tide come in."

"The car? What car?"

"I told you; the one we picked up at Mont St. Michel. Guillaume's car. The Citroën. How about telling me what's going on?"

"Nothing, Ben," John said. "Just looking up some things."

"Don't give me that, John. I may not be the brightest person in the world, but I sure know the difference between chicken shit and chicken salad." He laughed softly. "So my Aunt Gussie was wont to say."

They left him staring bemusedly after them and walked out into the hallway.

Gideon looked at John. "Well, I guess that answers that."

"What answers what? What's the question?"

"The question is: Why did Guillaume go out into the bay without checking a tidetable? And the answer is that he didn't. He had this little gem right in the car with him; a perfectly nice little schedule, except for the small matter of a few pages in the middle. Which day did he die, do you remember? Last Sunday?"

"Monday. That would have been, uh –"

"The sixteenth." Gideon found the relevant row. "He went out in the morning, and with this to guide him, he wouldn't have been expecting a high tide until early evening. Whereas, actually..." He closed the bogus tidetable and opened the one from Monoprix. "...it crested at five minutes after ten. *A.M.* A nasty little surprise. The same sort of thing happened to us, you may recall."

John nodded grimly. "Okay, Doc, you win. I'm a believer. He was set up. So what do you think, Ben –"

"Not necessarily Ben. Any one of them could have doctored the thing for 'Guillaume's' benefit, and then Ben could have done just what he said he did: innocently picked up the table when he saw it in the car. I hope so."

"Me too." He shook his head. "Look, doesn't it seem a little odd that a murderer

318

would leave evidence like this just sitting around in the car for a week?"

"Not really. Whoever did it probably never dreamed that anyone would get suspicious about Guillaume's death. I practically had to get us all drowned to convince *you*."

"That's what I like about you. You never rub it in." He took the open booklets from Gideon and looked hard at them. "What did you mean, 'doctored'? You're talking about a major production here. Look at the paper and the printing on the phony pages. They're exactly the same as the real ones. That took work. It would have had to be set up way ahead of time, and whoever did it would have had to have a real tide schedule on hand, which means –"

Gideon was shaking his head. "No, I think it was simpler than that. If I could get into Guillaume's files, I think I could show you."

"Guillaume's files? They must be right here in his study, where Joly's been doing most of his interviewing." He walked a few steps to a closed door and turned the handle. The door opened. "What's stopping us?"

Gideon hesitated. "Don't you feel a little awkward about snooping around other people's homes without being invited?"

"Are you kidding me?"

"Well, I do."

"Doc," John said with a sigh, "you got to get over these overfastidious sensitivities. That is, if you ever hope to operate anything like an honest-to-God detective."

"That's the last thing I hope to do," Gideon muttered, but in he went behind John. They left the door ajar as a salve to his conscience (it wasn't really snooping if they did it openly) and flicked on the light.

The study was very different from the other rooms Gideon has seen, its contents reflecting the wintry personality of its dead user: functional, gray metal desk with nothing on it but a marble pen set with the two pens neatly inserted in their holders; two three-drawer file cabinets of matching blue steel (a grudging concession to cosmetic considerations?); a tripartite glass-fronted display case filled with tiny seashells meticulously arranged in long, dull, rows. Everything labeled, efficient, and ruthlessly neat, a private sanctuary of austerity in the lush manoir.

Gideon went to the right-hand file cabinet, to the drawer labeled "M-P." There, in a hanging folder under *"Marées,"* he quickly found what he expected to find: Guillaume's tide schedules, a set of blue booklets all

320

looking just like the ones he had already seen, except for the years. There were eleven in all, arranged in order (naturally) from 1976 to 1986. The table for 1987 was not in its place. Presumably, that was the one he'd gotten from Ben, which he now put on the desk alongside the one he'd bought at the store.

He sat down and began going through the stack, starting with 1976, opening each one to the page for January, glancing briefly at it, and moving on to the next booklet.

"So what are we looking for?" John asked, leaning over his shoulder.

"We're looking for a year where the dates –" But he had already found it. "Here," he said, "Nineteen eighty-one. Look." He pointed to the entry under *Jours* for January 1. " 'J'," he said, "for *jeudi*. Thursday."

"Yeah," John said. "So?"

"So in 1981 January started on a Thursday, just the way it did this year, which means –" He flipped a few pages. "– that the days for March also must correspond.

"Unless 1981 was a leap year."

"It wasn't."

"I bet anything there's some point to this," John said.

"You better believe it. Look at the afternoon high tide for March 23, 1981." He put his finger on the place.

"Sixteen-forty-three," John said, still not comprehending. "Huh. The same time as it was today. That's funny."

"It's more than funny. If we match the rest of the times with the ones on the schedule from Monoprix, I think they'll match too. But only on pages 31 to 34." He opened the Monoprix booklet to compare, and sighed with satisfaction. "See?"

Even the three-line advertisement at the bottom of page 32 matched. *"Le Galle Frères, Opticiens,"* it proclaimed. *"L'ami de vos yeux."* But the advertisement on page 32 of the one Ben had found in the car was for aluminium boats.

"Doc," John said, frowning over the booklets, "I still don't –"

"John, look at the individual pages. Do you see any indication of the year? There isn't any. Just *"Mars,"* or *"Avril,"* or whatever. They're printed up in exactly the same format every year, and the only place you can find the date is on the cover. Just like the schedules we use to go clamming at Sequim Bay. It'd be the easiest thing in the world –"

"– to open up the staple and switch pages from one year to another!" John smacked the table. "Damn! As long as you used a year where the dates fell on the same days of the week you could get away with it!"

"At last, the light."

"Not bad," John said appreciatively. "Somebody hears the old guy say he's going tidepooling the next morning, sneaks in here during the night, switches a few pages from 1981 to 1987 –"

"And vice-versa, so there aren't any missing pages in the 1981 schedule, just in case Guillaume happens to look."

John nodded slowly. "And goodbye, Guillaume."

"Right. Only of course it wasn't really Guillaume."

"Oh, yeah." John tapped his temple with a forefinger. "It's hard to keep these little details straight. Sometimes I start wondering who *I* am. Hey, we better cut Joly in on this right now, don't you think? Most of these people aren't going to be around after tomorrow."

Gideon used the telephone in the study to contact the inspector, reaching him at home. Joly listened without interruption to his account of the altered tidetables. He was impressed enough to dispense with his usual mordant observations on Gideon's continuing contributions to the case, but not so much that he admitted to having been wrong about "Guillaume's" murder.

"I thought I asked you to exercise reasonable prudence," was his comment. "I should have thought that would include keeping your distance from Rochebonne."

"I did, Lucien, but, uh, events intervened."

"I'm not sure I like the sound of that. Are there any other developments you should be telling me about?"

"Nothing important." It seemed a poor time to mention that the four of them had almost staged their own re-creation of the drowning in the bay.

"Well," Joly said, "I think it would be best if I came there, and you might as well wait for me now, if you don't mind. Is John there? Stay close to him. I don't want anything happening to you."

"Right, right," Gideon grumbled.

"And keep the falsified schedules for me. Better yet, give them to John to keep."

"Lucien, it might surprise you, but I'm perfectly capable –"

"And do try not to handle them. There may very well be fingerprints."

"Oh," Gideon said. "Sure." He looked down at the two schedules spread flat on the desk by the pressure of all five fingers of his left hand. "Glad you mentioned it."

While he was putting the other schedules back into the cabinet, Mathilde loomed in the doorway, dowdily imposing in navy blue sweater, pearls, and dark, boxy, pleated skirt.

"Is there something I can help you with, Dr. Oliver?"

"Oh...uh, no," Gideon said, caught with his hands in the till, so to speak. He closed the file drawer sheepishly. "I was just, uh..."

"Yes," she said frostily. "I understand you were kind enough to drive Raymond back. You'll stay for dinner, I hope? You too, Mr. Lau?"

"Well –"

"Great," John said from his innocent perch on the corner of the desk. "We'd love it."

She looked frigidly at the friendly purple snails smiling from their breasts, at the giant green slipper-shoes on their feet. "You wouldn't happen to have any...ah, less *fantasque* clothing with you, I suppose? Well, no matter. Please join us upstairs for apéritifs when you've finished here –" She smiled thinly. "– with whatever you're doing."

"Whew," John said when she'd left. "I

bet it feels like hell to get caught snooping around somebody's house without permission."

"It does," Gideon said. "Sometimes I wonder how I let myself–" An echo from their earlier conversation drifted unexpectedly through his mind. "John, what you said before about wondering who you were sometimes–" He clapped his hands together. "It's a long shot, but, my God, why didn't I think of it before?"

"I can't imagine," John said blandly.

"Shut the door, will you? We need to make another call."

"Dr. Loti, do you remember telling me that when Guillaume du Rocher was found in the rubble in St. Malo he was hallucinating?"

"Yes, certainly." The doctor had been roused from his evening meal; he was still chewing.

"And that he didn't know who he was?"

"Yes, that's right."

"Well, can you remember whether he had simple amnesia, so that he had no idea who he was? Or did he imagine he was somebody else?"

"Oh," Dr. Loti said, "I remember very well."

"And?"

"He imagined he was someone else. He claimed it for two days." Continuing to display an unexpected flair for suspence, Dr. Loti continued his leisurely mastication.

"And that was...?"

"He believed he was his cousin Alain."

Bingo. A whole set of puzzle pieces clattered into place.

"Perhaps you've heard of him?" Dr. Loti prompted, possibly disappointed in the lack of an overt response.

"I sure have," Gideon breathed. To John he made a raised-fist gesture of success that elicited a mystified frown.

"It was quite a strong delusion," Dr. Loti continued and chuckled at the memory. "He very nearly had *me* convinced, even though I knew full well that poor Alain du Rocher had been executed by the Germans some years before. And then one morning, suddenly, his memory returned. He was himself, Guillaume du Rocher, just like that."

Just like that. Alain du Rocher, Resistance hero of beloved memory, mourned as dead at the hands of the SS these forty-five years. Only now – just like that – it seemed he had been alive the whole time, until a week ago, living high off the hog as Guillaume du Rocher, lord of the manor...while

Guillaume himself lay moldering to dust and bones in the gloomy cellar. Gideon nodded with something like gratification. Not so much because he'd anticipated this (he had, but it hadn't been much more than a shot in the dark), but because it seemed to satisfy a certain daffy symmetry in the increasingly bizarre twists and contortions in the House of du Rocher.

"Yes, yes, I remember it very well," Dr. Loti said in a settling-down-in-his-chair tone, clearly more inclined to reminisce than to return to his dinner. "An extremely interesting case . . ."

Gideon headed him off. "It certainly is. You've been very helpful, Doctor. Thanks very much."

"Alain!" John exploded. "How the hell could it be Alain?"

Gideon, foreseeing this reaction, had taken him outside before telling him what he'd learned. "You're nuts, you know that?" John raved to the black sky while they strode over the courtyard. "You're always doing this! You – Ouch!"

He had stubbed his toe on one of the beams for the kitchen garden's new retaining wall. "Damn it, why don't they have any lights out here?" he grumbled, and bent to

328

rub his toe through the thin canvas shoe. "Look, how could Alain be alive all these years? The Nazis killed him in 1942; there were witnesses. The SS –"

"– marched him into the *mairie* early one morning, and he was never seen again. That's not necessarily the same thing as being killed."

"Okay, so what happened to him, then?" John demanded, straightening up. "How did he get away? Where was he between 1942 and 1944?"

"Who knows? He could have been anywhere."

John snorted and made one of his spasmodic gestures of impatience. "All right, tell me, what's the theory supposed to be? That while he was in the hospital he suddenly comes up with this plan to kill the real Guillaume and take over his property?"

"I don't think so," Gideon said. "I'm pretty sure Guillaume was already dead. Remember, he hadn't been seen in years either. He disappeared in 1942 too."

"Jesus," John said, starting them walking again, "this Goddamn case is crawling with disappearing people."

"In fact," Gideon said, thinking aloud, "he disappeared within a day or two of the time Alain did – supposedly to join the

329

Resistance. Only now it looks as if it was Alain who took off somewhere, while Guillaume didn't make it out of his own cellar. And when Alain came back after the Liberation, he decided that he could live a fuller, more productive, more meaningful life as his missing, rolling-in-money cousin than as himself.

"I suppose," he added ruminatively, "this sounds a little fanciful to you."

"A little? Sheesh." They walked without speaking for a few yards. "So what do you think – that Alain killed the real Guillaume – back in 1942, I mean – buried him in the cellar, and just let everybody think he was off running around with the Resistance?"

"No, I don't see how we could go that far yet. Possibly –"

"Because," John said, with a subtle change in his voice, "he would have had to kill him, wouldn't he? Or at least he'd have had to *know* Guillaume was already dead when everybody else thought he was off fighting the Germans. Otherwise, how could he be sure he wouldn't come back someday?"

As usual, John had quickly altered course after his first excitable response to an unexpected new hypothesis and settled down to constructive thinking.

"That," Gideon conceded, "is a point."

They had come to the tall stone pillars of the gateway and stood looking out into the darkness. The plane trees lining the road were dimly visible, a dense, pitchy black against the gauzy black of the sky. Gideon shivered as the night cold worked its way through his clothes, and they turned and began to walk back to the manoir.

When they came to the pile of lumber that John had stumbled over, Gideon stopped. Something stirred at the edges of his memory. "You know," he said, "it's funny..." But whatever it was evaded him, like a speck in the vision that scoots away when you try to focus on it.

"What's funny?" John asked, then laughed. "Never mind. I don't think I want to know. I can only stand so much at a time. Hey, who else do you think knows this so-called Guillaume was really Alain? Assuming that he was."

"My guess is that none of them do. Why tell them? The only ones who'd even remember the real Guillaume are Mathilde, René, and Sophie, and they were all teenagers or under in 1942. When Alain showed up two years later and claimed he was Guillaume, who could argue with him? He was the right age, he knew the ropes, he looked a lot like Guillaume to begin with,

331

and he was such a patched-up mess that no one could possibly tell the difference – even Mathilde. Even though she'd been engaged to him, she was only a kid when he left, and it wouldn't be too hard for him to keep his distance." He nodded approvingly at his own logic. "No, I'd bet no one's ever caught on to him in all these years."

"Yeah?" said John, who had listened without comment to this lengthy exposition. "Well, you'd lose."

Gideon paused with his fingers on the handle of the oak door. "Why?"

"Because somebody was so afraid you'd find out who that skeleton really was they tried to blow your head off. Or did you forget again?"

Gideon frowned, then laughed. "I forgot. Again."

Pre-dinner cocktails were being served in the Louis XV Room, an upstairs sitting room full of musty, handsome eighteenth-century clutter: lush overstuffed bergères, crystal pendant chandeliers, ormolu clocks, busy Beauvais tapestries after Boucher and Fragonard. Its delicate parquet floors and ornate, gilded wall moldings proclaimed it the centerpiece of Rochebonne but for more than four decades it had been little-used, being too sumptuous and grandiose for its dour owner. But it suited Mathilde just fine, and she was determined to return it to its onetime place of glory.

The knowledge that this was the last evening they would all be together seemed to add a sparkle, almost a conviviality, to the cocktail hour, so that for once they had abandoned their customary groupings to recombine in new permutations.

At the side of the cherrywood-fronted fireplace a dapper and liberally cologned René, drink in hand, was playing *le seigneur du manoir* to a twittery, vibrant Leona Fougeray. Leona, at her striking, brittle best in an neon orange jumpsuit cinched by a patent leather belt, laughed frequently, throwing back her head so that the reflections from the chandelier made her black Italian eyes shimmer.

A few feet away, seated somewhat stiffly in three kingly armchairs of crushed red velvet and gilded wood, Mathilde, Claire, and Sophie chatted quietly, Mathilde frequently raising her eyes to glare without effect at her pink and animated husband. And standing on the other side of the room Ray, Ben, and Jules talked man-talk. Or at least Jules did. With his rump propped against an inlaid gaming table, a martini in one hand and a quickly changing succession of canapés in the other, he prattled to his abstracted and unresponsive audience.

Gliding among them all with a tray of drinks was the granite-faced Marcel, while Beatrice hung about the entrance to a small pantry in her tentlike brown dress, lumbering grumpily out from time to time with fresh hors d'oeuvres.

When Gideon and John entered, Ray separated himself and came worriedly to them.

"Did you talk to Ben?" he asked in a low voice. "You don't still think . . . ?"

"He didn't lie about what was in the schedule," Gideon reassured him. "Someone altered the thing."

"Thank heavens." He took a relieved swig of Chablis, then did a double-take. "Altered? You mean . . . *altered?*"

"Probably not to get us," John said, looking casually around to make sure no one else was within hearing range. "Someone used it to kill Guillaume."

Ray's eyes opened wider. "Kill Guillaume?"

"Right. Oh, by the way, Guillaume was Alain."

Gideon thought that John, who had been on the receiving end of something similar a

334

few minutes before, could be forgiven for this. Ray responded with surprising aplomb, swallowing his mouthful of wine without quite choking on it. "Tell me," he said when it was safely down, "have I been leading a particularly sheltered existence? Is this what life is like for other people?"

"Only when the Skeleton Detective's around," John said.

Ray looked slowly about him. The others were still involved in their conversations or their tasks, but casting uneasy or even hostile looks toward Gideon and John. Almost, it seemed to Gideon, as if they were huddling for mutual support against the newcomers, as if everything were really just fine at the Manoir de Rochebonne – or would be, if not for the intrusion of these two unwelcome meddlers. Well, he thought, in a way they were right.

"It's so difficult to believe," Ray said softly. "One of these people is actually a murdered. But *who?* No, whom. No, who. I'm afraid this is really getting to me."

"Monsieur?" Marcel extended the tray of drinks.

Merci." As Gideon took one of the slender, fluted tumblers of vermouth the telephone rang. Marcel turned, but Mathilde, closer, picked it up. She listened, murmured something, and extended it uncordially to Gideon, her face wooden. "For you."

It was Dr. Loti.

"Yes, hello again, it's me. I think perhaps we might have been disconnected earlier," he said hopefully.

"Yes, I think we were," Gideon said, repenting for having virtually hung up on the elderly physician before.

"Ah. Well. I didn't finish what I was telling you. You'll be quite interested. You see, Guillaume didn't really regain his memory 'just like that.' That was a figure of speech. It was Mathilde du Rocher who did it all."

"Mathilde?" Gideon exclaimed inadvertently and glanced at her. She had remained standing a few feet away, edgy and suspicious, watching him, straining every nerve to hear, not bothering to pretend otherwise. An eyebrow flicked at the sound of her name.

He turned away from her and cradled the receiver against his shoulder. "What do you mean?"

"Exactly what I said, young man. Without Mathilde, Guillaume would have died. Certainly he would never have recovered his identity. Ah, Mathilde – Mathilde Sylvestre, as she was then; a strapping, buxom girl with skin like rose petals. She had just become engaged to René, and she had volunteered as a nurse at the hospital. She sat with the mutilated hulk that was Guillaume for two whole days and most of two nights, talking to him, crooning to him, keeping his interest focused on this world instead of the next." Dr. Loti heaved a gusty sigh.

"And?"

"And? His memory came back. It never would have happened without her; I'm convinced of it. And from that moment he began to recover. You could see it in him, in the renewed fire in that single fierce eye gleaming through the bandages. He had decided," Dr. Loti pronounced with sentimental relish, "to *live*."

"I see," Gideon said slowly.

He had decided to live, all right – with Mathilde's earnest help and counsel – but not his own life. More pieces of the puzzle: As a girl Mathilde had been engaged to Alain; Gideon already knew that. Now it seemed that she had still been in love with him when he returned. For whatever their reasons – his terrible injuries, her engagement to René – they had decided not to take up where they had left off. But they had put their heads together long enough to hatch a

337

plot that put Guillaume's wealth in Alain's hands instead of Claude's for forty long years ... and finally, a week ago, into Mathilde's.

"These are not the sentimental imaginings of an old man," Dr. Loti cautioned him. "I tell you as a responsible physician: If not for Mathilde, Guillaume du Rocher would never have returned to this life."

"I believe you," Gideon said. "Sincerely."

21

When Gideon hung up Mathilde was still watching him intently. This time he returned her gaze, mulling over what he'd heard. There could be no question about her being involved in Alain's deception; very probably she had authored it. How much else was she involved in?

"And what did Dr. Loti want with you?" she demanded before he had removed his hand from the telephone.

He hadn't meant to engage her. Better to let Joly handle it. But when he floundered, searching for a reply, she prodded him.

"It was about Guillaume, wasn't it?" Her

338

fluty voice sliced through the chitchat. Conversations were suspended; heads turned in their direction.

"Yes, it was." Obviously, there wasn't much point in denying it.

"What did he tell you?"

"I think it'd be better if we talked somewhere more private, Mathilde."

Gideon heard René's imploring whisper behind him. "What is it? What the devil is he talking about? What's the –?"

"Sh!" someone said imperiously, and the *seigneur du manoir* subsided.

"I am not afraid to talk in my own house, in front of my own family," Mathilde said firmly. She stood with her stocky legs planted, her deep, square prow of a bosom thrust aggressively forward. "I believe I have every right to know what you discussed."

Well, Joly wasn't going to like it, but Mathilde was clearly determined to have it out right then, and Gideon wasn't in the mood to play games putting her off. It had been a long day.

"Mathilde," he said, "I know Guillaume du Rocher was killed in 1942. And I know Alain *wasn't* killed in 1942, but was alive until a week ago, playing Guillaume's part."

There was a collective gasp and a few exclamations of consternation. René laughed disbelievingly. Then, abruptly, utter quiet, thick with expectancy and confusion. Stunned faces stared at Gideon. A lazy, disinterested tick of the golden clock on the mantel looped through the silence.

"And I know you know it too," he concluded flatly.

Under a layer of powder Mathilde's face reddened momentarily. Then, like someone putting down at last a burden she'd carried too long, she exhaled a long breath. "Yes," she said, her voice perfectly steady. "You're quite right."

Now there was an explosion of questions and ejaculations. People shouted at each other, at Mathilde, at Gideon. Mathilde waited for the noise to die down. "I think I should like to sit," she announced, and set herself bolt-upright on one of the crushed velvet chairs, hands clasped one on the other in her lap.

"And a glass of vermouth, I think." She drank briefly from the fluted tumbler that Marcel brought to her and opened her mouth to speak.

"Mother," Jules said, "you really don't have to –"

"Oh, be quiet, Jules. What's the difference now? It's out. I knew he'd find out." Jules shrugged and withdrew, and Mathilde continued, not speaking to anyone in particular. "What Dr. Oliver says is true. Guillaume has been dead for forty-five years. The man who died last week was Alain du Rocher."

"Impossible!" Sophie said. "You think I wouldn't know Alain? My own brother?"

"Well, you didn't," Mathilde said proudly. "It was Alain here in the manoir all these years, and none of you guessed." She looked disdainfully from face to face, challenging them, then took a measured sip of vermouth. "Alain was not executed by the Nazis. They let him go."

"But – but –" Ray stammered.

Ben was more terse. "Why?"

Mathilde's hand went to the strand of pearls that lay against her black sweater. "Well, I'm not really –"

"They let him go for informing on the others, didn't they?" Gideon asked.

There was a shocked hubbub of denial, but Mathilde closed her eyes for a moment, then opened them and nodded. "Yes," she said, looking straight ahead. "They tortured him with electrical prods." She looked sharply up at him. "How could you possibly know that?"

He hadn't known; he'd guessed. Joly had told him that Alain had been picked up at dawn, the others five or six hours later. He'd wondered about it at the time, and now he'd simply put two and two together. He didn't answer Mathilde's question. The more she thought he already knew, the more she'd tell.

"We all thought they'd kill him," she went on without emotion, "but he came here to the manoir the next night, a little before eleven. I'd been here for two days. We were all trying to comfort each other the best we could, waiting to hear something definite. Guillaume, René, me. You too, Sophie."

"Yes, I remember," Sophie said softly.

"Guillaume and I were the only ones still awake. When he opened the door and saw Alain standing there he was furious."

"Furious?" Ray asked. "Why should he be furious?"

"He grasped what had happened right away. He made Alain admit it. To him, Alain was a traitor, a coward. Don't forget, Guillaume had already killed that SS pig a few hours before, in revenge for his death. His supposed death." She glanced up irritably at the ring of rapt faces. "Will you all sit down, for heaven's sake? I feel like a - I don't know what. And don't look so ludicrously glum. This happened forty-five years ago."

They dropped obediently into chairs, pulling them around to face her. Gideon leaned against one end of a marble-topped side table, John against the other. Only Marcel and Beatrice, next to invisible, remained standing at the edge of the room.

"I had to pull Guillaume from Alain's throat," Mathilde said. "I was so shocked and happy to see him alive I barely knew what I was doing. He was terribly weak from what they'd done to him. I took him to the kitchen to see if there was some brandy and something to eat. He tried to explain to Guillaume that he'd tried with all his strength to hold out, but Guillaume was beside himself, screaming with rage."

"No," Sophie said, almost to herself, "how could that be? I was here. If there was shouting in the kitchen I would have heard it from my room."

"No, my dear, you're forgetting. You were hysterical. Guillaume made you take a sleeping pill at dinnertime. You were only ten, you know."

"Was I only ten? Yes, that's right," Sophie said slowly, remembering. "But René?" She looked at him. "You didn't hear?"

"I can sleep through anything," he said. "I always could."

"Go on, Mathilde," Ben said.

Mathilde sipped minutely at the vermouth. "Guillaume came into the kitchen after us. He threw Alain against the wall, he knocked him down, he – I truly believe he would have killed him if Alain hadn't ..." For the first time she faltered.

"... stabbed him with one of the kitchen knives," Gideon said.

"Oh, no," Claire said, her fingers at her mouth. There were more gasps.

"Yes," Mathilde said. "Guillaume had raised a fist over his head like some patriarch in the Bible – he was using it like a club – and Alain, to save himself, snatched up a huge knife from the counter and stabbed him. Once only, before I could move." Her lids flickered momentarily. "Guillaume looked so terribly surprised."

Gideon caught John's eye and nodded. It jibed perfectly with what they'd learned from the skeleton: the upraised arm, the heavy kitchen knife, the single thrust.

"And that's the story," Mathilde said with a shrug. "Guillaume was dead, and Alain ran off, half out of his mind with remorse. I had no idea what to do. I told everyone Guillaume had gone to join the Resistance. I didn't mention Alain at all.

344

"You said Alain ran off?" Sophie said dazedly. "Where?"

"He *did* join the Resistance; in the north. He was very brave," Mathilde said defiantly. "He wasn't a coward, and he was no traitor." She had finished the vermouth and Marcel stepped forward with another. Mathilde shook her head and handed him the empty glass. "The next time I saw him he was in the hospital in Saint Servan. I walked into a room and there in the bed, all – all *crumpled*, like a –"

And suddenly the whole starchy edifice came tumbling down. Her lips trembled, her fingers jerked at the pearls, and a single, hoarse, manlike sob was wrenched painfully out of her.

And no wonder, Gideon thought. What must it have been like when it dawned on that nineteen-year-old girl with skin like rose petals that the maimed, twisted horror lying in a crushed heap on the bed was her handsome, athletic lover?

René stood up, his arms outstretched. "My dear Mathilde –"

She sent him back into his chair with a peremptory wave. From somewhere she produced a little handkerchief and dabbed at her nose. The red splotches that had sprung out on her cheeks were already almost

345

gone. The entire emotional outburst had consisted of the one tearless sob.

"Alain had no idea that Guillaume's death was still a secret," she said, the handkerchief disappearing into wherever it had come from. "We decided the best thing was for him to pretend to be Guillaume. He didn't think he could carry it off, but I knew he could. They were so similar in physique to begin with, and with his body so broken, who could say for sure that he wasn't Guillaume?" She stared coolly around her, completely in control of herself again. "And of course he did carry it off. For forty-five years."

"But *why?*" Ray asked. "Everyone believed Guillaume was off fighting. Couldn't you have let it go at that and just let people assume he'd been killed somewhere?"

"Yes," Ben said. "Why the pretense?"

"Well." Mathilde fingered her pearls and pursed her lips. It was a critical question, and Gideon could feel a fabrication in the making.

So did John. He made his first contribution, and it showed that he was doing fine. "Because you knew that under Guillaume's old will Claude Fougeray would inherit everything."

Leona Fougeray, whose grasp of English
346

was not as good as some of the others', sat up at her husband's name and shot a series of staccato questions at her daughter in French.

Mathilde waited until Claire's brief, embarrassed explanations were done, then answered John. "Yes, you're quite right. It was Alain's idea, actually."

Leona snorted her disbelief.

"No, really, it was. It was important to him that the domaine stay with the du Rochers. The thought that it might go to Claude was horrible to him. I agreed with him." She looked at Claire. "I'm sorry, my dear. I'm sure you understand."

Claire didn't look as if she understood, but Leona did. "Sure you agreed," she said in her Italian-accented French, her voice rising shrilly. "You knew everything would come to you one day!"

"That," Mathilde scoffed unconvincingly, "is patently ridiculous." In the thoughtful, evaluative quiet that followed this, René leaned towards Jules, who sat alone on a plump little sofa beginning on his third martini, served to him with three stuffed olives on a toothpick, as he had trained Marcel to do.

"Did you know all this?" René asked him.

Jules seemed about to deny it, then lifted his shoulder in a nonchalant shrug. "Yes, I knew."

I didn't know it," René said without rancor.

Jules looked pityingly at him and sucked the first of the olives from the toothpick.

"Let's go back a little, Mathilde," Ben said. "You buried Guillaume in the cellar? That's his skeleton they found?"

"Yes, of course," Mathilde said crossly. "How many skeletons do you suppose are down there?"

Ray stared at her, his face gray. "But it was – it was *dismembered!*"

"Yes," Mathilde said after a pause. "That's right. Marcel, I would like another vermouth after all." When it was brought she swallowed some, drew herself more erect, and set her gaze on the middle distance. "We didn't know what to do with him," she said expressionlessly, as if reading from a script in a language she didn't understand. "With the body. We couldn't believe it had really happened. We put him in the big stone sink in the kitchen and I helped Alain to – to begin dismembering him. Do you know the cleaver is still there? I was looking at it a few days ago."

The hand that lifted the glass to her
348

mouth wavered slightly; not enough to spill the vermouth. "Beatrice used it for the *carbonnade flamande,* I believe."

"Oh, sweet Jesus Christ," Ben breathed, the only sound in an otherwise electrified silence.

"We were going to burn him, you see, and we knew he wouldn't all burn at once," Mathilde went grimly on, determined to finish. "We made a fire in the kitchen fireplace. But when we –" A tic jerked in the flesh below her eye and was brought firmly under control. "– placed a hand in the fire, there was a terrible smell, and it would hardly burn, and it – it *sizzled,* you see."

"Mathilde, please stop," Sophie said unsteadily. "It's enough."

But Mathilde plowed ahead, eyes fixed stonily on nothing. "I said we should boil the – the pieces first to get rid of the fat, but Alain simply couldn't face it; he was at the end of his strength. So we wrapped them – the pieces – in packages we could lift, and took them down to the cellar..."

She was winding down, beginning to sag, a millimeter at a time, against the back of the chair. "And then we buried the packages under the stones," she said, winding down. "It took us until dawn. Then Alain ran off and I went home."

John had slid along the table to join Gideon while Mathilde had been talking. "Where the hell is Joly? She's ready to admit everything."

Gideon nodded doubtfully. True, the mystery of the bones in the cellar was satisfactorily wrapped up, but he wasn't so sure how much progress had been made on what had been going on this past week; Alain's belated death in the bay, Claude's poisoning, his own near-murder. But a few ideas about those were beginning to work their way to the surface too. That lumber in the courtyard had set him thinking. Had he been barking up the wrong tree? Or the wrong branch of the right tree? He looked thoughtfully around the room.

Beatrice and Marcel, their English almost non-existent, were watching Mathilde impassively. Most of the others stared at her, half-fascinated, half-horrified, the way people at a zoo peer through the glass at a monstrous snake.

"Madame..." Claire said in her gentle voice. "Aunt Mathilde...did you kill my father?" Not an easy thing to say inoffensively, but from Claire it was not so much an accusation as a timid inquiry.

It was, however, enough to straighten up Mathilde's spine. She looked condescendingly at Claire. "My dear child, what an extraordinary idea!"

"Oh, yeah?" Leona said, this time resorting to her coarse and shaky English. Gideon's well-trained ear told him she had learned it in Naples; probably the streets of Naples. "Maybe you was afraid of what he would find out – Claude." She was quite matter-of-fact now, he noticed. The idea that Mathilde might have murdered her husband didn't seem to bother her nearly as much as the thought that she might have bilked him (and by extension, her) out of the Domaine de Rochebonne. If anything, her estimation of Mathilde appeared to have increased.

"Find out?" Mathilde replied after a moment of convincingly astonished silence.

"Yeah, when he goes down there in the cellar – Maybe he sees something, finds out something..." Leona's English or her imagination failed her. "Who knows?" she finished lamely, and fell back against her chair.

Mathilde glanced around the room, then appealed to Gideon. "I have no idea what the woman's talking about."

"Did Claude go down into the cellar?" René asked mildly. "I didn't know that."

"He was *going* to go," Leona said, resorting again to French. "To watch what *he* was doing." She indicated Gideon by extending her fluorescent orange lips towards him.

Jules put down his glass with a peevish thump. "I must say, I don't see why we should have to sit here and listen to this," he said querulously, his soft, babyish cheeks streaked with sullen red. "I mean, here's this woman, a *guest* in our house, and she has the, the . . ."

Gideon had stopped listening. A few more of the last remaining odd-shaped pieces that had been rattling disconnectedly around his mind had just dropped into their slots.

". . . have to sit here and listen to this," Jules concluded sulkily, back where he'd begun.

Gideon, thoughtful, looked towards the doorway. "Marcel?"

The servant started. "Monsieur?"

"On the day Claude Fougeray died, did you tell him that he could come down to the cellar at ten o'clock to watch me at work?"

Gideon winced, feeling silly. The ponderous question had reverberated like a line out of the old Perry Mason show. The others, John included, stared uncertainly at him. So did Marcel. He spread his hands and shook his head to show he didn't understand. A quick darting of his eyes at Beatrice,

352

however, indicated that Claude's name had registered well enough.

Gideon repeated the question in French, trying to make it a little less turgid.

No, Marcel replied defensively, he hadn't told that to Monsieur Fougeray. Why should he? There was an uneasy, aggressive shifting of his wiry shoulders, another darty glance at Beatrice. He did not like being questioned about Claude Fougeray.

But Gideon had other game in mind. "Jules, didn't you tell Marcel to give that information to Claude?"

There was a pause while Jules vacuumed up the last of the olives with his lips. "What information?"

"The night before Claude died," Gideon said patiently, "Joly asked you to tell Claude to come down to the cellar the next morning. You said you'd tell Marcel to pass it on."

With his tongue Jules tucked the olive into one cheek, presumably for future attention. "I did tell him."

"He doesn't seem to remember."

Jules glanced pettishly at Gideon. "Maybe I didn't have a chance to mention it. There wasn't much point after Claude died, and he *did* die awfully early the next morning – *ridiculously* early, if I may say so." He crossed one leg over the other, looked pleased with this grotesque attempt at humor.

"Yes," Gideon said, deciding that if there was ever a moment for a denouement, this was it. "You killed him."

The reactions were varied. Predictably, Claire gasped and Ray looked dumbfounded.

Leona examined Jules with frank new interest.

Mathilde slowly opened her mouth. "*Jules?*" she whispered.

"No, really?" René murmured to Sophie, sitting nearby. "Do you think that's true?"

At Gideon's side John murmured: "I love this part."

Gideon waited for Jules to speak for himself. The young man took the olive from his mouth and placed it in an ashtray, uncrossing his plump thighs to lean forward.

"That's stupid. Why would I do that?"

"Because at the reading of the will he'd said he didn't believe Guillaume had really written it. You knew he'd studied to be a doctor, and you were afraid that if he saw the skeleton he'd recognize the rickets and realise *that* was Guillaume."

Jules laughed. "So what? Why should I care? *I* didn't kill Guillaume, did I?" He

354

glanced with unmistakable meaning at his mother, then held up his empty glass to Marcel.

"You've had enough, Jules," Mathilde said icily. Jules glared at her but put down the glass.

"No, you didn't care about that," Gideon said, "but you cared one hell of a lot about the inheritance. And if anyone found out the guy who wrote that will wasn't who he said he was, that would have been the end of it. No fabulous inheritance for your parents – or for you not too far down the line. And that was something you weren't about to let happen."

"Dr. Oliver," Mathilde announced in her most imperious contralto, "I cannot have you –"

"Be quiet, Mathilde," Sophie interrupted curtly. "Let's get it sorted out once and for all, for God's sake."

Gideon could almost see the tiny gears whizzing behind Jules' little eyes. "I see your point," he said with strained reasonableness, "but why pick on me? I'm not the only one here who knew about the fraud, am I?" He permitted his gaze to rest once again on his mother. A dew of sweat had formed on his upper lip.

"What a miserable little shit," John muttered out of the side of his mouth.

Gideon agreed. Whatever discomfort he'd felt about browbeating the sluglike Jules was rapidly disappearing.

"That's right," he said. "Two people knew; you and your mother. But only one person knew Claude was going to see the bones the next day. And that's you."

"You're out of your mind. That inspector told me about it while we were all having drinks. *Anybody* could have heard."

"No, the rest had gone in to dinner. There were just you, me, and John."

Jules licked his lips, beginning to look concerned. He'd already as much as accused his mother. Was he going to accuse John now?

"I must have mentioned it to – to someone else. I'm *sure* I told Marcel. Marcel, didn't –"

"And of course that's why you tried to kill me too; to keep me from figuring out it was Guillaume down there."

More gasps. He'd forgotten that none of them knew about the letter-bomb. This was turning into quite an evening for them all.

"This is ridiculous!" Jules said with abrupt heat. The red streaks had reappeared in his downy, round cheeks. "I'm not going to sit here –"

"And Alain as well. That's why you saw to it he drowned in the bay."

Jules' slack-jawed blink of amazement was so transparently sincere that for a moment Gideon thought he might have it wrong, but he realized that what he was seeing was simply Jules' astonishment that anyone had even caught on to the fact that the murder had occurred. And it *had* been a clever thing; for that much Gideon gave him credit, if you could call it credit. It had been sheer luck, nothing else, that had uncovered it.

Jules shut his mouth so hard his puppy's teeth clicked. "I'm not going to sit here and take this – this abuse – from someone who – who wasn't even *invited* . . ."

"But why?" Sophie said. "Why kill Alain after so many years?"

Gideon answered. "Because Alain was going to admit who he really was. That's what the council was going to be about. Jules was the only one who knew, and he couldn't let it happen. Right, Jules?" He hoped he sounded confident; the further he went, the deeper into guesswork he got. Peculiar, the situations he found himself in.

"No! Wrong!" Jules was shouting now; the martinis were starting to show in his eyes,

357

his speech. His bow-shaped baby's mouth had curled into a pout. "It was to tell us he was selling this place to a hotel!"

"Selling his house to a hotel is 'a matter of singular family importance'?"

"How do I know what the old fart meant?" Jules spread his arms, beseeching the others. "He *told* me what it was about!"

"Yes, I know he did. You were the only one who knew."

He lowered his arms. "That's *right*," he said suspiciously.

"That's what started me wondering why you were lying about it, and the answer wasn't too hard to come up with." Gideon was beginning to tire, wishing that Joly would come, or that Jules would just give up and admit it.

He didn't. "*You're* lying!" he shouted.

"No, Jules," Gideon said, and wound up for what he hoped was the knockout punch. "He wasn't selling Rochebonne to a hotel chain. If he were, there wouldn't be much sense in enlarging the kitchen garden, would there?" He held his breath. He was up to his elbows in speculative inference here. It was conceivable that a deal with the chain was contingent on a bigger garden going in, or that they were paying for it, or a dozen other possibilities.

But no, he'd guessed right. Jules' forehead was suddenly glossy with sweat. The area under his eyes and around his mouth seemed to sink and turn a shiny gray.

"I," he said with a wretched, sodden try at dignity, "am leaving now." When he stood up crumbs rolled from his lap.

"No," John said pleasantly, "you're not. You're staying right there."

Jules spun angrily on him. "You can't –"

"I sure can. Consider it a citizen's arrest."

"You – you're not even a *citizen!*"

"All the same," John said, his arms folded easily on his chest, "if I were you I'd just sit back down and wait till Joly gets here."

"Joly's already here," said the familiar crisp voice from the doorway. He strode into the room and stood stiffly in front of Jules. "Monsieur du Rocher, please consider youself under the provisions of the *garde à vue* from this moment. You will be detained –"

Jules looked wildly at Mathilde. "*Maman* –"

She stared blazingly at him. "You killed Alain," she said in a voice like cracking ice. "Your own father."

This time Gideon was part of the stunned silence too. It took René to break it.

"His father?" he said, as wide-eyed as the rest of them. "Do you mean Jules isn't my son?"

Had it not been for the sorry circumstances, Gideon might almost have thought it was said with relief.

22

"Want some more coffee?" Julie asked.

"Sure," Gideon said, starting to rise.

"I'll make it." She jumped up and headed for the kitchen.

"I thought you were going to be keeping me less contented."

"I figure almost getting yourself killed entitles you to one day of being spoiled. Tomorrow things change, pal."

They were having a late breakfast in the living room. Gideon leaned back, hands behind his neck, and stretched out his legs, wallowing in the satisfaction of being back home, back with Julie. Through the big window he could look down the hill and see the Coho ferry from Victoria just rounding Ediz Hook and easing its way through the morning fog into Port Angeles Harbor. In the kitchen Julie made domestic noises and whistled happily.

"I'm a lucky man," he told her.

"You better believe it," she called back. "What's the bagel situation in there?"

"Plenty. Lox and cream cheese too."

He had arrived at a little before ten the night before. Julie had met him at Sea-Tac and for most of the long drive to Port Angeles – a slow, stately ferry across Puget Sound and then seventy miles of blackly forested highway on the Olympic Peninsula – he had told her how things had worked out at Rochebonne. When they'd reached home they'd opened a bottle of cognac he'd brought from France and their talk and attention had turned to more intimate and enjoyable things. It had been three in the morning before they'd finally drifted off to sleep, and they hadn't awakened until nine-thirty.

"Did you hear any creepy noises last night?" he called.

"I did hear some pretty strange ones now that you mention it, yes."

He laughed. "I mean *after* we fell asleep."

She came in with a tray. "No, not after," she said, smiling, and then made a face.

361

"Gideon, you're not really going to be wearing those things, are you?"

He looked down and wiggled his toes. "You don't like my shoes? Wait till you see my new sweatshirt."

"Oh, it's not that I don't like them. I think chartreuse canvas is extremely handsome, and that casual baggy look is very attractive, very with-it. I just like some of your others better."

"Well, I can't find my gray running shoes. Do you know if I took them?"

Laughing, she sat down beside him and poured coffee for them. "Do you know you never take a trip without leaving something behind? Someday you're going to come home without me, and then wander around the house muttering to yourself and wondering what it is that seems to be missing."

"When one has a perplexing case to think about," he said magisterially, "one cannot be bothered with the immediate trivialities of the moment. How about passing me a bagel?"

She did and absentmindedly nibbled on one herself. "I still think my cyanide theory was a good one."

"About it being a symbolic revenge weapon? It *was* a good one. It just didn't turn

362

out to be true, that's all; a minor problem. It happens all the time to the finest theories, take it from me."

"I suppose so . . ."

Gideon looked up from lathering cream cheese on half a bagel. "Something bothering you?"

"Kind of. Look, you said that Jules didn't buy the poison in Brittany, right? He brought it with him from Germany."

"True."

"Well, why? If he didn't decide to kill Claude until after the skeleton turned up, why would he buy it ahead of time and bring it with him?"

"Ah, good question. John and I had that figured wrong." He returned to the bagel, putting a couple of thin, moist layers of smoked salmon on the cheese and topping it with the other half. "He brought the cyanide with him to kill Alain."

She shook her head. "Huh?"

"He was going to poison Alain, but when the chance came up to do him a lot more subtly by way of the tide schedule, he jumped at it. That left him with some perfectly good cyanide to put to use when poor Claude blustered into his way."

"Charming. A wonderful family, all in all.

363

Do you want to eat in peace, or can I ask some more questions?"

"Ask," he said, chewing.

"Was Mathilde having an affair with Alain during those years he was pretending to be Guillaume? Were they still in love?"

"I don't think so. I know she wasn't any closer to him that the rest of them for the last twenty years or so, anyway."

"But what about Jules? You think they might have had a single fling for old times' sake, and he was the result?"

"Could be. That'd be enough to make them knock it off right there."

She laughed. "One more question, and that's all. What made Alain suddenly want to confess after forty-five years of pretending to be Guillaume?"

"Nobody knows for sure, but Mathilde said he'd been getting more depressed for years about living someone else's life, that he'd grumbled to her once about being buried with someone else's gravestone over him."

"I can understand that," she said with a little shudder. "So when he found he only had a year to live, that decided him?"

"Looks like it."

She sipped her coffee quietly, watching through the window as the big ferry tooted and backed slowly into its berth. "It's hard to imagine Ray Schaefer planning to get married."

"I know, but Claire was practically made for him. Vice-versa too, I think. They're planning on coming up this way in the summer. You'll like her."

"I'm sure I will." She had tipped her head to rest it against Gideon's shoulder, but now sat up suddenly. "The inheritance – Who's going to get it?"

"Well, Joly says he thinks it'll work like this: The will Guillaume made in 1941 is the last one anybody can find, so it's the one that counts. At that time he left everything to his closest relative; his father's sister. She died in 1942, a little before Guillaume, which means it should have gone to Claude, her son."

"You mean Claude was right? He really *was* the legitimate heir?"

Gideon nodded. "But now with him being dead, Joly says it'll go to Claire, with maybe something to Leona."

"Mm, so Aunt Sophie doesn't get her library."

Gideon shook his head. "Claire took her aside and told her she wants her to have it. Sophie, of course, said not on your life, but she'd love to have a picture book or two.

Claire also told the servants that they don't have to worry about their stipend."

"She does sound nice. But I wonder if this is going to make problems between her and Ray."

"You mean because she's going to be rich? Are you serious?"

"Well, yes. It's bound to make some big changes for them, and Raymond is a very sweet man, but you have to admit he tends to get a little nervous when anything upsets that nice, orderly routine of his."

Gideon tipped her head back to his shoulder and stroked her dense, black hair. "Well, you know what they say: Maybe money doesn't bring happiness, but it sure enough quiets the nerves."

She laughed and snuggled in a little closer. "*Who* says?"

"Do you mean to tell me," Gideon said, "I never told you about my Uncle Bubba Jim?"

The publishers hope that this book has given you enjoyable reading. Large Print Books are specially designed to be as easy to see and hold as possible. If you wish a complete list of our books, please ask at your local library or write directly to: John Curley & Associates, Inc. P.O. Box 37, South Yarmouth, Massachusetts, 02664.

RECON

OLD BONES.   *Sha*
ELKINS, AARON

LT   94325
M   *WM-94*

OLD BONES. 89   R E N E W
ELKINS, AARON   R E N E W
   APR 19 89

LT   94325
M   17.95

MAR 8 89   HWLND
MAR 22 89   NR 7270
APR 5 89   R E N E W
APR 19 89   R E N E W
MAY 3 89

                              BF